JCWATSON

FICTION:

Lake in Heaven

Reckless

The Flying Horse

Nobody Gets Out Alive

POETRY:

Argument for Mercy

The Journey of Lost Things

The Awakenings Journal

APPLE iBOOK:

Reversing Paradise

CURRENT WISDOM

JC WATSON

CURRENT WISDOM

COPYRIGHT JCWATSON 2005

PUBLISHED IN THE UNITED STATES

PITTSBURGH, PENNSYLVANIA
LBF BOOKS
FIRST EDITION 2005

GILROY, CALIFORNIA
VIOLETCLAIRE PRESS ❧
SECOND EDITION 2016

SAN JOSE, CALIFORNIA
VIOLETCLAIRE PRESS ❧
THIRD EDITION 2019

ISBN: 978-0-578-49731-0

BOOK DESIGN: JCWatson, William Watson

DEDICATION

For the stars that are loaned to us,
Alex, Emma, Claire, Max and Leo

ACKNOWLEDGEMENTS

A book is the product of many hands and minds, though the cover may bear one name. I must first thank my teachers who have guided me along my difficult, mysterious path. They are too numerous to name, but one stands out (Molly Giles) for declaring to my graduate fiction class that they would long remember one of my characters. True or not, it is that kind of support that keeps the writer on the path despite voices internally that call her away.

I also want to thank my readers, Mary Lee McNeal and Kathleen St.Claire for their dedicated attention to *Current Wisdom* and their insight and observation in all areas of this project.

And lastly, but firstly, to my husband, my guiding light and heart of my heart for his patience, wisdom, and unwavering devotion to this, my book, my child.

Again, traveler, you have come a long way led by that star.
But the kingdom of the wish is at the other end of the night.
May you fare well, companero: let us journey together joyfully,
Living on catastrophe, eating pure light.

Thomas McGraph
Epitaph

CURRENT WISDOM

ONE

RHINESTONES

RHINESTONES

The day Global Air in the form of a petite blond ticket agent, her odd aquamarine irises firm and bright, informed Mimi that, No, no, Harold Piccolo was neither on the flight list, nor on the plane from Heathrow, nor on the recent list of cancellations—that was the first time Mimi had felt truly alone in all her thirty-eight years, with the exception of her first day of marriage.

From her parents' house she'd floated like a dandelion, like milkweed fluff, the eye of her brain shut tight to anything past the church and the endless drive to Chicago. When it flew open she found herself, shiny band on her finger (she'd thought of racing pigeons) in a small grey apartment half underground with Harold Piccolo on the army cot couch, crying like a new widow instead of smiling like a bride.

It wasn't until Harold's accident, his bicycle a small tin pretzel, his ribs cracked in four places, pain moving into him every winter thereafter, that she actually felt mated to him. On the afternoon of their fifth wedding anniversary in Indian summer September, when she was thirty and a half and had yet to experience her first orgasm, she looked down at his slit face and black eyes and felt needed by him for the first time. This is what she imagined love to be. It's what her parents gave and her brothers and Alice and Grandma Tinker—they had given her their need. And needed, Mimi was in her element completely.

In India, Harold was to find himself, for not Mimi, not teaching high school physics, not even his flourishing amateur photography career, certainly not his family—none of these was enough to ease him round the bend into mid-life. It had begun like so many stories do, with what can only be described as a loosely connected set of circumstances. In preparation for his most unwelcome fortieth birthday, Harold had begun to study Tai chi. He and his Tai-chi master, Ting Lee, often went out after class; the teacher would describe his own journey to self-awareness, his life of what he called "alert waiting." Harold came home with stories of his teacher's treks. First, to the north woods of Wisconsin, where he had built a one-room cabin, his weeks of fasting, reading and tai chi. Most recently, was Ting's trip to India and the Himalayas— not to climb them but to see them. It seemed there was some sort of energy there, some resource Harold found difficult to articulate. The "Well Spring," he'd called it. She was more than shocked; Harold had always been a mild atheist, never a seeker of any sort. In fact, she had never seen him impassioned about anything except his father's disowning him for not joining his construction business. He described the business as "the white enslavement of family members." So, Mimi listened, then finally helped pack him up. She was confused, troubled, but mute. She smiled and waved him off. He never returned.

But today, a drizzly Monday in what was supposed to be spring (which Chicago never truly experienced, but for which, yearly, everyone hoped), she vowed to give up on Harold, on his return, on anything remotely resembling their life together. In front of the splotched bathroom mirror—not because it had been two years to the exact day that he had not returned, but her face. "At forty, a woman has the face she deserves." Some feminist had said that. Trying to help out. Trying to say something about meanness, or narcissism, or the fact that an ironclad heart smears itself across one's countenance—but instead, making everyone feel guilty about the tricks of aging, the outcome for a body five feet or so above the ground struggling with the unhappy force of gravity.

"Guilty," she went on aloud, "for aging." A nod of respect for those, whom through genetics and practical luck, gravity worked a slower, gentler pace. Mimi, at this last thought, stood back and observed, without pity, that she'd been one of those. But now, her time had come.

She had purchased one of those clock kits from a household goods catalogue, constructed it right on the mirror so that she would never be late again. She'd glued each white dot into its place——yet here she was, late, phone ringing. Her first graders would be standing outside the classroom bopping each other with their lunch pails. Oh, what had ever happened to the school lunch, anyway? She had to deal with some sort of lunchbox accident everyday. Mimi was glad they were now making the soft pack kind.

She flew in her Metro too swiftly toward Lincoln School and her small sea of needy students. Babies, she reflected. Baby fat and snot and sometimes embarrassing miscalculations of their toilet needs. Mimi had become a mother after all. Not anymore.

Not anymore. Not. Not, not anymore—her mind sang as she flew through the huge mahogany doors of the school with Mr. Weekday, the toy heron upon whose neck a child hung the correct day of the week. But when she arrived at A-1, Mr. Luwendowski, the janitor, had opened the classroom and was herding the children in, temporarily confiscating any flying lunchboxes. She gave the small man a hug and with this gesture began another week—hopefully, one of her last—without incident.

*　　　*　　　*　　　*

When she and Mr. Weekday returned to her apartment (Mimi had always to come and go with him for he'd once been stolen) she had five messages. The last one would be sliding off the machine, but it would be Harold's mom, Alice, who always tried to catch her just as she returned from school. Her message, even her phrasing, was ever the same. She often thought if there had been a secret camera filming the daily playing of the tape, she could easily be blackmailed.

Camera rolls. Mimi hits the red button, first message:

"Tiny Tim's sick again! Tonsillitis. Again."

Her friend, Mary Beth.

"Guess we have to bite the bullet and yank those suckers. Martin's in Davenport selling threshers. He only knows the kids if I pin their names on them. He says he still remembers my face from high school. Mostly the eyes. If you don't come over here and save me with three-syllable words, I'll kill you."

Mimi smiles, the camera records. Mary Beth gets a nod. Number two.

Next, "Ahhemm . . . "

Mom.

"Hi, sweetheart. Daddy and I are all right. We've been to church. There was ice on the porch at seven thirty! In April! We haven't seen you in two months. I don't think I can bend to plant the impatiens. Mickey and Teddy have a new business! Daddy says his heart has stopped jumping around. Grandma Tinker fell in her bathtub and lay there two hours in the cold water . . . Oh, and we love you."

Vicious frown. Cutting frown. Possible smoke from nostrils. *Mom—X.*

"Hi, Mimi?"

Who did Jerry think he might have called? Mimi could not abide her colleague's adding a question mark to every sentence. Hadn't he heard my thoughtful, clever message? *Hi, this is Mimi Malone . . .*

"It's Gerry Mertz from Lincoln?"

Well, was it Gerry and . . . Mertz? Why the question? I had lunch with him last Friday! Did he think I might have forgotten the assistant principal's entire name? The people with brains teach. The feeble administer.

Her mouth tight and wide . . .

"I have an afternoon meeting Friday and . . . and I thought well, hell, why not just call Mimi for early drinks and dinner, say about four? I'll be at the gym now."

He needs to inform me he's an athlete.

"So call me before nine? I'm not a night person?"

Ugh. Ugh. Ugh. Gerry—X-minus.

And then,

"Mimi! Call me when you can. Richard didn't come home last night, er, this morning until five. He smelled funny. Not booze —something . . . I called Lou in Atlanta to talk about it and a female, barely able to form a complete sentence, answered. I am certain she has no body hair. He's been gone ten days! 'Heartbroken,' I believe he mentioned in his parting lines. My boss, Laura, asked me out. On a date, I think. When it rains, it pours. You never reported back on your lunch with Gerry Mertz. Are we having dinner with everybody at your apartment, Friday? And a jewelry class, right? I can make it if I'm still alive. Call me anytime.

"Ahh, Jan . . . rare real person. In trouble, always. Smile. Frown. Head shake. Check for Jan . . . always.

"Mimi, it's Mother Piccolo!"

Why do the deaf shout?

"It's three thirty, I thought you'd be home by now."

She's never caught on to the commuting concept.

"Today's the two year anniversary of Harold not coming back."

I guess she thinks I forgot.

"I've been crying most of the day. Sunday's mass is dedicated to him. Are you coming? Eleven fifteen. There's dinner after, here. Rigatonies with that turkey sausage you like. Father Ben will be here."

Thank you God, for having her say something slightly different.

She stood, bringing Mr. Weekday upright, his knob of a head close to her chest, and swayed, standing by the phone. She was weeping and recognized that she was not going to stop for a while, for Howard had not called to say that, it being his birthday, "a man gets thoughtful, a man thinks about everything. I am really all right. I am sorry. How are you? Without you, I have felt these two years that my heart has been crowbarred out and there's a big black-red hole, empty in my chest. But I'm all right now. I'm coming home."

After a time, she placed Mr. Weekday in his small rocker by the door and went into the kitchen to crack a beer. So good! She sat on the old stool Harold had made in the ninth grade and wept until she could bear her hunger no longer. She talked to the tofu as she sliced, then cubed it.

"Well, my white virgin, what are we going to do with you tonight? It's too late for tofu bulgur loaf, you know that! How about a little stir fry . . . Ahh, but I have nothing to stir or fry. Oh, maybe some spinach. Yes, some spinach." She heated the sesame oil and added the spinach and tofu, garlic and some stale cashews she found. "Oh, that's fat. Harold would hate it if I got fat! I mustn't eat it . . . but then . . . " She put down the wooden spoon, and stared at the sizzling food. "Harold is not coming home."

*   *   *   *

The sun was down, but the evening sky was still pale when Mimi soaked the dinner dishes and left for her run. The air was cool as winter. Her new running shoes were working out well, she thought, but there it was, the ping, pinging pain in her left knee. If she'd had good legs and feet—a good all-around skeleton, she could have run like the wind, for her heart and lungs never gave out. Nothing wrong with her endurance! She cut up Wing and down Starling, which was new and wide.

"Another school torn down," she mumbled, pumping past a vacant lot. Mimi was having the usual ongoing monologue with herself.

"Hasn't anybody noticed that," pant, pant—nice even pants, "every three out of four women are pregnant? It's a regular epidemic! A triumph, as somebody had said about marriage, of optimism over experience, or something like that."

She'd read that if you could talk while you jogged, you were running at the right speed. She was perfect. People stared. The Running Schizophrenic. She thought, suddenly, how she would like to do a painting titled "Running Schizophrenic." She'd paint the head, slightly aloft, colored silk ribbons connecting it to the body. Fiery points would dance from the eye sockets and the runner would be anorexically thin, with rhinestones where the nipples should have been. She'd be dressed in gigantic running shorts.

"And teeth—just loads and loads of teeth for hair."

This last part she said out loud, adding, "Because she can never rest." A small boy on a bike with training wheels, called "Huh?" as she streaked by.

TWO

SICK UNTO THE LORD

In church she sat beside Grandma Tinker and with her family in her mother's pew as she thought of it, the very first, the one in front of the pulpit. She was surprised to see her parents had brought the old lady after her recent fall, but she seemed none the worse for wear. Grandma had lived in the house beside Mimi's all the years she'd lived on Jackson, which had been most of her life. She still did. Miss Tinker was a "bachelor lady," as Mimi's mom described her. A sprinkling of far-flung nieces and nephews showed up at her cottage erratically and rarely, so Mimi's family had adopted her, which suited all of them just fine. Mimi hugged her parents and also Teddy and Mickey, who wore suspiciously new-looking jackets. She wondered if her mother had bought them. When she hugged her mother, Edie rolled her eyes and claimed in her very loud church whisper,

"That Grandma—she always bounces back."

At the entry hymn they rose and sang as Father Ben and several shiny-haired altar boys came in procession up the center aisle. Father Ben was an imposing figure in his white and gold chasuble. Striking but not handsome. It was his hair that God had chosen for beneficence. Thick, black, and wavy. After Harold's disappearance, he'd called Mimi about once a month, more often at first, and simply listened. When their schedules had allowed, they'd grabbed coffee together on Saturday afternoons, but after the first year, each recognized that these sessions had come to a natural end.

As Mimi moved through the old motions of rising and kneeling, her mind hummed just below the Creed and the Offertory. She reflected on the way Father Ben had counseled her. He hadn't been aggressive, but had gradually begun to urge her to pay more attention to her jewelry making, to do things with her women friends, to run again. And these things, she had done.

And here I am today . . . Mimi frowned into her open hands. *Choose one of the above: a widow, a scorned woman, a wife whose wifeliness is on hold. Someone will call and say they'd found him, like a POW in some back-world, backwoods detention camp—ninety pounds but alive. It happened.* This, Mimi felt she knew better than anyone, for it had occurred so often in her demon dreams. And she had read The Dead Return by Audrey Berkowitz. One woman, Liddy Cole, had been seventy-five and alone for fifteen years when her husband motored up in his ancient aqua Volvo and plunged the same old key in the lock.

"This is My body." The large white disc over Father Ben's head. Mimi imagined rays of grace coming from the wafer. *Why does a God become bread to be eaten? Why do we need his body? If He is everywhere, isn't that in and out of our bodies? How is it that we receive the body of Christ into our bodies? And to what purpose? What I need is grace and strength and finally, to know—just to know.* Mimi prayed, "God give me the serenity to accept the things I cannot change" over and over. It was all she could think of.

*　　　*　　　*　　　*

At Mom Piccolo's, after promising her mother she would plant her impatiens and take Grandma Tinker to the reservoir, Mimi escaped from Edie to a sit at the long mahogany table. Mom Piccolo had hired two women to serve the food; Mimi wasn't needed in the kitchen. Father Ben sat quickly beside her. He had chosen to wear his old cassock again, instead of the more modern black suit.

"Well, how's the fledgling business coming along, my dear? Are you making a lot of beautiful things?" He patted her hand as he sat down.

"Current Wisdom—now that's the part of my life that is going well. If God would just grant me eight or nine more hours a day . . . " She smiled a little wanly into his friendly black eyes.

"Well, do you really need to sleep?" he asked, and they laughed.

"Yes, I see what you mean. I just haven't looked hard enough for a time slot."

She told him she wanted to quit teaching, that she wanted to try for a year to make jewelry full time. And that she had taken a loan from Sparta Banking. Father Ben looked suddenly serious. He said that she was young and should give it a try but that she should get an accountant or some sort of financial advisor and not be afraid to quit her plan, not to stick to CURRENT WISDOM for longer than she should. But she laughed a little at his fatherly concern and turned the talk to art. The Piccolos had some nice pieces, originals, gracing their walls, and she was delighted to learn of his interest in painting. She mentioned "The Running Schizophrenic," detailing her mental sketch.

"Well I didn't know you painted. Actually, that's what I thought I would do before I understood I had a vocation. Hmm . . . 'The Running Schizophrenic . . . ' Teeth? For hair?"

"Well, yes—the creature, well, she's a woman—I feel she's running from something. Something that talks all the time and is . . . well, devouring her."

"Mimi . . . "

The priest, she noticed, wore a frighteningly deep furrow between his eyes.

"Perhaps . . . do you need to talk? You look, well, not to take away from your natural good looks, but, you look pale." He leaned towards her. "There's just, excuse me, I don't know how this sounds, a bit of a wild look to you—in your eyes, your whole demeanor, actually. And yet, you look, well, wrung out at the same time."

Her hand flew to her cheek and she looked down, embarrassed, then into his face, and finally fastened on a painting over the priest's shoulder: a man on a horse with a dog at his side.

"I don't know what I am doing . . . most of the time. I'm not sure, sometimes, what room I am standing in. I'm disoriented, somehow."

"What about Friday afternoon. I have confessions at seven-thirty."

"I, well, I have dinner with my bunch at six-thirty. So . . . five o'clock?"

"Five to six thirty. Good then."

*   *   *   *

Holding Mr. Weekday, hung with his Monday-through-Friday cards, her stuffed briefcase, and an abandoned Barney lunch pail, she swung open her classroom door for the maintenance crew at three-forty five and crashed headlong into Gerry Mertz. He smelled lovely. She pondered briefly how to ask him about his cologne without seeming to be interested in him.

"I thought I'd just be spontaneous and march on over here and see if you'd made plans for dinner? I didn't get a message?"

He had his gym bag hanging from his hand.

"Ohhh, Gerry, I forgot to return your call."

White lies are just little sins.

"And yes, yes, I do have plans. I . . . my girlfriends and I . . . "

He stepped closer. Mimi could feel the uneven swingings from various parts of her body.

"Mimi? Should I call? I mean, maybe, is this awkward for you?"

"I . . . " She moved her shoulders and re-gripped the heron. "Yes, I think it is. Maybe it's not time yet."

"Mimi, when the time does feel right—well, just call. I mean, I want you to call, you know?"

She realized she was looking through her bangs. "Oh, thank you, Gerry. For the open invitation. That's nice. I appreciate it."

He looked at his feet, then toward her orange sunlit classroom. "I just thought . . . well, it's been two years?"

Ugh. Ugh.

"Yes, two years last Thursday.

"Well . . . "

"Thanks."

She turned in the opposite direction though her car was parked three slots from his and she was loaded down.

Turd. Turd. Turd. Never.

*   *   *   *

It was a strangely warm afternoon. The end of April and finally, the forsythias were popping. Birds were gossiping. Mimi rolled down the windows of her Metro and sang out loud,

"I could drink a case of you, ou, ou, darlin, and I would still be on my feet. I would still be on my feet."

Where the hell was Joni Mitchell anyway? Pump out another album, honey, my soul is sick unto the Lord.

The phone was ringing as she let herself into the apartment. In honor of Friday, she gave herself permission not to answer it, and headed straight for the kitchen and the teapot.

"Chamomile—Oh, chamomile-ile, with your face sketched on it twice. You're in my blood, you're my holy wine. You taste so bitter and so sweet."

She did not have a bad voice. "I coulda been a contender," she thought. It wasn't the strength of her voice, but some way her heart was carried on it or in it. The nuns had called it expressive. They had said that she, her voice quality, was very expressive.

"I won't look at the mail, and I refuse to pick up my phone messages," she spoke to the empty apartment.

This was becoming her small tradition for Fridays; if she did not meet her friends, she closed herself off from all connections. Mimi placed Friday's stack of envelopes and flyers on top of yesterday's on the kitchen counter and went to sit down in the living room in the overstuffed chair, placing the ottoman under her weary legs. Staring at her wedding picture, huge somehow, on the wall above the sofa, she noticed the gap between her front teeth. I haven't thought of those silly teeth for a long time. I think that's why I married Harold. He thought they made me look like a country girl, he said, someone who'd always be young.

"Well, my teeth are fixed and I'm old and Harold isn't in the picture anymore. And if he's still alive I'll kill him," Mimi shouted to the empty apartment. Her hands were shaking.

She rose and went across to the picture. Now her entire body was shaking, a spasm of sorts. She plucked the frame from the wall, avoiding Harold's confused smile, but did not know what she would do with it. For the time being. She was nearly running down the hall to her bedroom. By her bed, she stooped and pulled out the summer spread she had stashed there last October. She turned the wedding picture upside down and slipped it beneath. Sweating. She was drenched, and lay face-down on the bed for several minutes. When she glanced at her watch, she found it was already five o'clock.

*   *   *   *

"Mimi." Father Ben extended his hand. "Please sit down. I ordered you a Cafe Borgia. Is that right? It always takes a little time here. How are you?"

Her heart sank as she became aware of the cacophony of jangled conversations, the intermittent shiiish of the espresso machine, the crashing of dishes, the boys from the kitchen calling to the counter persons. A phone was ringing somewhere that only she apparently heard.

"I'm better than I was Sunday. I'm grateful for the time you're giving for a check-up. I know you are always rushed."

Ben laughed at this. "Well, not quite always. And frankly, I don't feel it's a check up. I always learn a great deal from our talks."

"Oh yeah? Like what?" She startled both of them with her sudden anger. His face became abruptly serious.

"Mimi?"

She placed her hand lightly on his sleeve. "Sorry. I'm sorry. I get so tired of people being nice. There's just so much nice."

"I wasn't being nice. I was being sincere. That was sincere."

She was surprised to sense a bit of anger in his eyes as well, and noticed the corners of his mouth flexing. She had never seen him anything but mild and supportive. Something important seemed to be happening, and her brain scuttled here and there looking for a word, but she did not find one. They stared at each other briefly, a little shocked.

"Father Ben, obviously I seem to be pretty low, but you seem . . . well not . . . I mean do you . . . ?"

"I am being transferred."

Mimi tightened the grip of her fingers on her hands. She looked down and noticed that the surface of the table was the kind of plastic that was supposed to resemble green marble.

"Why?"

"It's simple and complicated. Father Patrick—you know he has Alzheimer's—needs convalescent care. So, he has to go to

Saint Vincent's. I'm the assistant pastor, but Bishop Bernard claims I'm too inexperienced to head up Mark's and yet, in effect I have been doing just that for two years already. He wants an entirely new crew. Not right away. I have to break in the new guys and then . . . they don't know right now where I'll be after that."

"But aren't you about forty? That's a lot of years. Lots of experience. How long have you been a priest? Fifteen years or so?"

"Five."

"Five?"

"Yes."

"Oh."

"I'm a very late vocation. And a convert."

"You didn't grow up a Catholic?"

"No."

"Oh . . . well . . .?"

"Jewish."

They stared at each other once again.

"I think that's part of it." His expression was strange and fierce.

"Please, Mimi, I have to ask you not to discuss this with anyone. I've never had a moment like this in the church. I've never had a moment like this at all."

She shook her head slowly, her auburn bangs swaying in slow motion. My God, he's going to cry.

"The Jewish part. Tell me why it could matter."

He let out a sigh, long and full. "The parishioners might be a bit uncomfortable with a person of so different a religious and cultural background leading the flock . . . "

"But Ben. Maybe that's paranoia. This is 1995! This is post-sixties. You, excuse me for being intrusive, you must be struggling with your vow of obedience."

"God, I am! I'm struggling with everything."

"What about the Chinese priest we had for a whole summer . . . "

"Father Chou. Yes. But he wasn't the pastor and he grew up a Catholic."

"Has anyone said words to that effect? The Jewish part."

"No. No." The priest got out his handkerchief and wiped his brow. It was furiously hot in the cafe. He dabbed quickly at the corners of his eyes.

"What's the part that gets to you most, Ben, the possible prejudice, or the lack of a vote of confidence, or the separation from Mark's?"

"They're my family."

"But we each have our own families, too."

"My parents have not spoken to me in ten years."

The cafe had been clearing out. Such a noisy place to suddenly have become so quiet. She could sense he would add no more about his family.

"What about meeting with the Bishop? But it's difficult, right? You're not supposed to have attachments . . . "

"No. No attachments. I never wanted any. That vow proved delightfully easy until now ... "

They both looked down at the fake marble.

"I will, of course, go to see the Bishop, but there isn't much I can say."

"You can look at him."

"Look at him?" He stared at her.

"You can look at him with your heart. Right there in your eyes."

THREE

DREAD

Mimi was exhausted. She had no idea where The Lighthouse was. She'd been down East Wendle twice.

"God, this Metro sits low to the ground. I can't see anything. Maybe Jan meant West Wendle. She's like that. Too much on her mind. Flaky. Always was."

She wanted to go home and think about Ben's problem. Call her Uncle Freddie at St. Lawrence. "There's always a way," she remarked to herself, searching for numbers on the buildings. "Uncle Freddie has been a priest forever. He knows so many of the big guns."

She reflected that he would perhaps have been a big gun himself, if he hadn't tippled so much.

Twenty minutes late! Finally she crossed over to West Wendle and there at 1125 was the Lighthouse Restaurant, beckoning with its blue circulating lamp for anyone to see. Anyone on West Wendle.

Even in the dim light she could see that, despite her tardiness, none of the others had yet arrived. She approached the hostess, an Elvira sort with lipstick the color of dried blood. *Why does any one want to look dead?*

"Do you have a reservation for a party of four under the name of Jan Missick?"

"Yep."

The dead don't talk much. "For six-thirty?"

"Yep."

"But . . . "

"Mrs. Missick called."

"And . . . "

"She, and the other lady . . . they'll be late."

Alone at a sort of Arthurian round table in the corner, she ordered a martini. The burgundy colored booths with the brass upholstery tacks—no surprises here. She was endlessly amazed at the limitations of imagination that pressed upon her from everywhere. She felt like breaking something; the toothpicks were giving her no satisfaction whatsoever.

Link arrived first. She wore her usual "I am serious" suit. *Her hair is too red*, thought Mimi. It was striking but not in a good way. And the thing was, Link had perfectly beautiful real red hair which, when they had been in high school, she'd worn unfurled down her back, ironed straight, and shining. *She is so thin!* They hugged, and Link sat down with a plop.

"Can you smoke in here?" Link's eyes were the color of November—that grey-green with the sun trying to peek through. She had a fresh cigarette ready to go between her fingers.

"Nnno. Just in the bar."

"Shit! It's been that kind of a day. I gotta give up this stupid habit because the only places you can smoke anymore are out in the cold or in a lousy bar. And nobody smokes in my car, not even me. So, Mimi, how are you?"

"Hungry beyond belief! Why are you guys so late?" She wished one more time that she would give up the high school lingo.

Link looked puzzled. "I don't know why Jan and Mary Beth are late. I haven't talked to them. Last I heard from Jan was that we couldn't come for the jewelry lesson at your place Friday, that we should meet here. I was on East Wendle for a while"—she rolled her eyes and smiled—"and I had an argument with my boss, which took some extra time."

Mimi could never get used to the volatility of Link's business relationships. "Anything serious?"

"Nah. She hates my writing. Hates every one of my ideas. Hates the way I dress. She stands so far away from me when she talks to me, you'd think I had leprosy. But what I write sells, so she's stuck with me. So, why'd we meet here instead of your place?" She could see that Link was only vaguely interested in her response. Something was working on her, distracting her.

"Well, frankly, the place is a total disaster. You can't even walk! Then there were all the findings and beads to be sorted and then I needed to figure out what I should teach you first and . . . Mimi took a generous gulp of her martini as the hostess showed up for Link's order.

"O.J." Link asserted, and Elvira disappeared.

"O.J?"

"Yeah."

Mimi puzzled about this change silently, then wet her fingers, dampened her bangs with them and placed them behind her ears. There, a full view of the world.

"Link?" she began.

But then there appeared Jan and Mary Beth and hugs and laughing and a few choice one-liners about Jan's directions. Mimi's question for Link was swallowed in the commotion. The corpse-like hostess appeared again with Link's orange juice and asked, staring over their heads, "Did anyone else want something?" Mary Beth wanted an O'Doul's, and Jan ordered a martini.

Mary Beth was the first to take the floor. "How long have we known each other?"

Link shot, "Thirty years! With various interruptions in continuity due to a group tendency toward the nomadic lifestyle."

They gasped in unison.

Then Mary Beth continued, her Dutch-boy haircut bouncing a little as she glanced at each of their faces.

"And how long have I been fat?" Silence and some throat-clearing.

Mimi offered that Mary Beth had after all been a cheerleader, so she mustn't have been fat then. Interrupting her, Mary Beth quickly responded, "Yes. Yes, even then. I was chunky. People called it chunky then. Which was a phrase for muscular *and* fat. Even then."

"But your parents." Jan looked too tired to be talking.

A crevice, within the last month, had dug its way between Jan's brows. *The face of the newly divorced,* thought Mimi.

"Were always heavy. And did you see that article?" Jan addressed the three of them. "Yeah, it was in *American Health* or one of those non-nutsy health magazines. There is supposed to be a gene for fat—the fat gene. Did you hear that, Mary Beth?"

A real waitress appeared with the other two drinks and menus. *None too soon.* Mimi could feel her head becoming an enormous Knox Blox.

"Yes. I heard all about it." Mary Beth had tears in her eyes. "Marty sat me down and talked to me about fat last night. He says he's worried about my health, my heart. But it isn't that . . . you know the last time we slept together?"

Uh-oh.

"But your kids have been sick." Mimi offered. Mary Beth only glared at her.

"I am talking three months."

Jan produced a prodigious pile of tissues from her purse and passed it to Mary Beth, who began gesturing with them as she spoke. "Three months. Never. Never before . . . "

"But, . . . " Link sat up straight. She was grasping, then opening her fingers on her cigarette. "If you think you've always been fat, then his attitude can't be because you're fat."

"I'm fatter."

"Since Tommy?" Mimi asked. Tommy was two and resembled a small, perfect Hummel. Mary Beth nodded and sniffed.

"Much?"

Mimi had thought Mary Beth had merely gotten careless about dressing. She never tucked in her blouse and seemed to be in Marty's old clothes a lot. Here they were out to dinner, and she had on a turtleneck and a huge plaid flannel shirt.

"Yes!" She put her face in her hands. "Yes! Fifty pounds. Fifty!"

The waitress reappeared smiling, expectant. Mimi noticed she weighed about eighty-five pounds.

"Ready?"

Link seemed annoyed that the waitress had not noticed Mary Beth and her upset.

"No." She was abrupt. "Bring us some veggies and dip please. We'll start on that." The waitress, whose name tag read "Vala," slipped away.

"And I don't eat much, really. I'm hungry all the time and sooo sick of it. So sick of the Big Ladies department. You know there is no such thing as fat-hiding clothes. No such thing. As soon as you pull one of those muumuu-style sweaters over your head you are wearing a sign: 'wide load'." Mary Beth blew her nose loudly.

Link's eyes glittered. Something. Something agitated there, Mimi could see. Her hair looked like small orange sparks flying from her head.

"Maybe you should join a support group," she said, right into Mary Beth's wet blue eyes.

Jan waved her hand in front of her face like a fan.

"Oh, that's so seventies." With a start, Mimi noticed the slight silvering at Jan's temples. "I've been reading a lot about this. My sister-in-law became a vegan and lost twenty-five pounds in two months! Who cares about meat, anyway? All those body parts and blood. Ugh. And you can stuff yourself. That's what Lena says. She's stuffed after a meal. Twenty-five pounds. No support shit and she looks like a goddess!

Link's eyes hardened. She looked across the table to Jan.

"What's wrong with support groups?"

"Oh, I imagine a lot of whining . . . I admit I am powerless over my hands and that shit. I'm sick of whining. I think those groups are just outlets for frustration. But do they really make any difference? I mean Lou went to N.A. for three years and he's still an asshole. Addicts by and large are simply big babies."

The waitress reappeared with some wan-looking carrots and pale celery but Link was pushing her chair back abruptly and forcefully—stone-faced, jaw clenched. She nearly knocked the frail "Vala" off her pins.

"Careful," Vala cried out, steadying the veggie platter, but it was too late. The dip slid to the floor and the vegetables flew everywhere, rattling lightly. Link never stopped.

*　　　*　　　*　　　*

Mimi called Link as soon as she arrived home at nine o'clock, hungry and worried. They had ordered more dip and vegetables and talked a little, but the women did not have much of an appetite after Link left. They were all stumped—Jan beating herself up. They had never seen Link so upset and weird. Mimi told Jan and Mary Beth that she would call, because Jan was certain Link would merely hang up on her. But here it was, Link would not even answer her phone.

All Mimi had in her apartment was some butter just beginning to get iffy, an overly hard-boiled egg and some very stale bread, which she toasted. She took her small plate and went into the living room, where she turned on the heater. It was a very frosty night for April. Nesting on the corduroy sofa beneath the pale white square of wall where her wedding picture had hung, she waited for the whistle in the dark.

*   *   *   *

Mimi was driving with Harold to their first apartment. Only hours before she'd had on her white gown, had been the gracious hostess. Now, in her olive green suit, the same one she'd worn on their first date, she was sitting primly, the October world —a great palette of oranges, greys and blacks—slipping by Harold's new Corvair as the ice thickened round her heart and she fought tears. The way it all had been back then, but as she'd glanced at Harold, he'd begun to melt, or rather his skin had begun to pull away from his body and an enormous furry insect to pop out. The being's clawed and hairy fingers were tearing through skin as through surgical gloves.

Awake, then, and sweating, Mimi put her hands to her ears to stop the rip/pop, rip/pop sound of the dream. She must have fallen asleep after drinking her tea. She leaped from the sofa and went into the kitchen. Standing at the sink filling the kettle, Mimi forced herself to fit into the real place and hour. She then sat at the table, her hands cupping her tea, and picked through the neglected mail, abandoning the temptation to once again analyze her recurrent nightmare. Bead catalogues, Gemology school brochures, bills, and a postcard of the Eiffel Tower. *Who's in Europe?* She hadn't realized anyone she knew had taken such a trip. When she turned it over, her hands began to tremble.

"I've seen him."

She read the sentence over and over, as though the meaning were not perfectly clear. I've seen him. I've seen him. I've seen him. She did not recognize the handwriting. It was unsigned. Mimi placed the postcard picture-side up on the table, then pressed her fingers around her cup.

"And what if he is alive?" she asked aloud. "What if he came through that door right now?"

And he must be. No one would be cruel enough to send such a message without being absolutely certain. What would be the point?

She sat. The wind struck up. The honey locust in the rear alley bent and shuttered outside the kitchen window.

"What would I feel?" she asked out loud again. "I don't know. I don't know."

What she could not say, the word that emerged from her body with its sudden stiffening, was "dread."

*   *   *   *

The phone rang three times before she heard it. Before she could get to it, the machine picked it up. Mimi did not interrupt it. It was her mother.

"Mimi? Hi, honey. It's a nice day. I was thinking about the flowers. Do you think it's too early to plant? I was going to make sauerkraut. Are you sleeping in? Well, call me. Mickey and Teddy can't do it. They're opening the car wash today. Oh, did you take Grandma Tinker out yet? She was asking."

Mimi dragged herself to the kitchen and, sure enough, the sun was bearing down full-bore. How late was it? She pushed her bangs back. Ten o'clock.

"Wow. Late." She saw the Eiffel Tower card on the table, picked it up, and turned it over once again.

"My god!" she gasped. The postmark was Boise. Boise, Idaho.

The phone rang again. This time, she ran and grabbed the receiver from its base.

"It's me."

"Link?"

"Yeah. I'm getting over my melt-down."

"Ah, I . . . " Mimi was panting.

"Mimi, are you okay? You sound out-of-breath or something."

"Link. I know something was wrong last night. We said or did something stupid, but I just had a shock and I can't think . . . I can't think." She could hear Link draw her breath sharply, and knew what she was thinking.

"I got a postcard with the Eiffel Tower on it."

"And . . . "

"Well, it's too weird, it says, 'I've seen him' and not only that . . . "

"What else?"

"Well, it's postmarked Boise, Idaho."

"Jesus! Who do you know in Boise?"

"Nobody. I know no one, no one person in Boise and to my best knowledge, which could be meaningless at this point, neither does . . . did Harold."

"Somebody's just screwing around."

"But why? Why?"

"People are crazy. You know that. And of course, you don't recognize the handwriting?"

"No, not at all, not even vaguely."

"Don't throw it away. Keep it somewhere, in case."

"In case of what?"

"I don't know. Just because people are crazy, that's all."

"Did you want to talk, Link? I mean, what happened last night? You arrived. And then you left in a cloud of dust."

"Well, could you meet me for dinner maybe?"

"Not at the Lighthouse?"

"No. Not the Lighthouse. Too many bad memories. How about Peetie's?"

"Early. I get starved by six."

"Good. Six. I'll see you then, Mimi. And put that card somewhere. Don't look at it again."

"Thanks. Okay. See you soon."

FOUR

BEAUTIFUL THINGS

42

BEAUTIFUL THINGS

When she neared her parents' home, her childhood home, she saw it as she did sometimes, small and sagging. Fading plastic geraniums in plastic pots. The weedy yard. Twenty-two Jackson Avenue. Mimi had always thought that avenues ought to be grand, like Park in New York or Michigan in the Loop. Jackson was an old bus and truck route for vehicles on their way from Chicago to St. Louis, and her parents lived smack on the main drag. The last lot when the area had sold off its farmland after World War II. It had been the last to sell because not only was it situated on a highway, but the rear yard gave way very quickly to a rough wooded ravine. All her childhood, when summer nights had come, if they'd sat out in the front of the house they'd had to shout; in the back you couldn't get more than a couple of chairs set out before someone teetered at the edge of the ravine. She ticked on her turn signal well before her parents' driveway; no one ever seemed to believe anyone would actually turn into one of the houses on Jackson. She rolled down its steep incline, and found them standing on the front porch. Now, whenever she came home, she could see her parents aging in quick stages, leaps. Her father had begun to stoop and look off. Her mother, who was really quite deaf, shouted but did not listen. They were slipping away.

The small green plastic pots of impatiens were out in a neat row along the porch; her mother had the gardening trowel in her hand.

"It's supposed to rain," Edie called, before Mimi had unlatched her seatbelt. Mimi rolled her eyes; her father laughed, knowing his wife's ways, knowing there was no possibility of change.

"You got some naked people in the living room or could I just go in and get a glass of water first?"

"Well, it is supposed to rain."

Mimi was already heating up, her cheeks flushed. "I'll plant in the rain."

"Not if it's an electric storm, you won't." Mimi's mother sounded amazingly imperious.

"Now, Edie, let the girl get a glass of water."

Mimi went in and headed to the refrigerator for ice. Sauerkraut!   She smelled the overwhelming odor. She realized that she had completely forgotten the meal her mother had promised for her. "Umm. Smells wonderful in here, but I need to call Link."

"Why?"

"Aah, something I forgot about . . . "

"I can't have anyone else to dinner. There isn't enough." Her mother was agitated, calling through the screen door; her voice was a new student sawing on a violin.

"You know your father and I don't have enough money to feed anyone but ourselves. He's retired, you know. Pork chops are dear now. All you're going to get is one pork chop as it is. Of course, if you're real hungry, I'd give you half of mine . . . "

Mimi ignored her, plodding on to the bedroom for the phone. She could hear Edie, in a strained voice, inquiring of Mimi's father, "Who is she calling? Theodore, we don't have any extra. Is Link coming here? Something's wrong with that girl, isn't there, to change her name like that to a piece of metal?"

As Link's phone was ringing, her mother appeared at the bedroom door, "I just saw lightning!" She continued to stand there as Mimi left her message.

"Link! I goofed up. At my mother's and realized she's cooked for me. Maybe later, drop by or phone. Gotta go. Bye. Hope you're okay."

The older woman had her hands crossed over her chest as if barring the door. "Is she a lesbian?"

"What, who?" How could her mother still manage to shock her? *I am forty years old!*

"Mary Margaret. Her hair's so short. And she wears strange clothes."

"Link's had tons of boyfriends. She doesn't want to get married."

"Why?"

It always ended in sarcasm. "She wants to be happy."

*   *   *   *

"Why does she have to use fifty pots for every meal?" The rain was just a sprinkle after all, allowing Mimi to remain free of the distractions of driving in a downpour so she could speak in the dark car.

"Two damn hours to wash the dishes!" It felt good to yell into the rain and dark.

"After I planted all those damn flowers . . . and that TV. Constant. Loud. I'll never have a TV. Never. Never. And reading from Cross Talk. Cute. Isn't that a cute name for a church bulletin? And it's a complete misnomer. Because there is absolutely no cross talk! Oh, and where the hell do you suppose Teddy and Mickey are? They don't live at the car wash. Couldn't they plant a flower once in a while?"

She thought of her brothers, their newest deadly duo venture, and snorted, but was surprised to find her eyes tearing. Alone. So alone. And for a while she thought of nothing. What a relief it was: this momentary quiet. She rolled the window down; rain sprayed her face. Occasionally, she passed by a row of sprouting forsythia, a green-yellow in the darkness and car lights. Spring. It smelled so . . . she couldn't think of the right word. Something about an ancient scent. Surely one of the earliest memories we have. A word. Is there a word for something that is both old and new at the same time?

When Mimi pulled up to her apartment, she noticed all the lights were on.

"Did I . . .?" She didn't know whether to go on in, but it was eleven o'clock. She could not go to a neighbor's. She entered her building and went quietly up the stairway. Shrugging, she opened her door cautiously. Nothing had been moved. Everything as she had left it. She went down the hall and looked in the bathroom, into the linen and coat closets, and then, walking into her bedroom, rolled back the closet door with a loud bang. Nothing. She went to the phone: three messages. She flipped the switch.

"Mimi. This is Father Ben. How are you?" He sounded completely normal. "I do have an appointment to see Bishop Bernard. I wanted to thank you for your support the other day. I don't think I behaved very appropriately and wanted to apologize. There we were, meeting to discuss your very difficult situation, and I made a real emotional pig of myself and well, forgive me. We'll talk soon, perhaps. Goodbye."

The machine said that he had called only a half an hour earlier. Ten thirty. "That's odd. An odd thing for him to do." She was somehow disappointed in his message, in his tone. But the next message was rolling on. Her mother.

"I don't know what we're going to do with all the leftover sauerkraut. You know your father's not supposed to eat pork and really, it bothers my stomach. I wish you would have taken some of this with you. Don't you remember? I said when we were drying the pots, 'Now be sure and take some of this with you.' I am wondering if you didn't like it this time? The flowers look so cheery. I went out and watered them again." All this at ten forty-five Saturday night!

"Oh, my god," said Mimi. "I watered them. She watered them. And it rained! She'll kill everyone of those little buggers and somehow it will be my fault."

Link was next. "Look. It's almost eleven o'clock. Believe it or not, I just got in from work. I'll call when I can. I'm okay."

Mimi went around the apartment, turning off all the lights. Then she dumped her coat, shoes, and dress on the bedroom chair, pulled on her flannel nightgown, despite the warm spring rain, and got a can of beer from the fridge. She took it back to her bed and switched off her bedside light.

"Life is wonderful and cruel. Spring is wonderful and cruel."

Things like this came to her.

"My parents are dying. I am dying. Harold is probably dead despite Boise to the contrary."

She took a long draught of beer.

"Link is going crazy. Jan's husband is screwing a teenager. Mary Beth's husband is lecturing her on fatness."

"And what? What pray tell, what are *you* doing?"

"I, Mimi, am okay. I am going to quit teaching. Somehow. I am going to make beautiful things. Every day. Rings, necklaces. I am going to bury Harold in my mind, somehow, once and for all. It had been really all so hard, anyway. Making it work. A terrible mismatch. God works in mysterious ways."

But before she could list any examples, she remembered that she had not brushed her teeth, then promptly fell asleep.

FIVE

SOFT GIRL

She reached across the bed and picked up the receiver. In her dream, she'd been hacking her way though a forest of huge, garishly colored flowers, sweeping a long blade shaped exactly like a cartoon stork. She felt she was being called from another world.

"Hello?" There was hesitation on the line while Mimi noticed that her star clock glowed two o'clock.

"Hello?"

"Mimi?"

"Are you alright?"

"Well, yes and no. Actually, I'm a little drunk."

She felt sick. "Father Ben, where are you?"

"Home. Just home, feeling sorry for myself — some kind of priest, huh?"

She did not know what to say. "Did something happen? I mean, something else?"

"Yes."

"Ben?"

"My father died."

"Oh, I'm so sorry. When did you hear?"

"I just heard. I'm leaving from O'Hare tomorrow, though they don't particularly want me there. Look. Mimi ... "

He's going to ask something that will frighten me.

"Yes?" She was whispering.

"Can I please come over. Can I come over there?"

"Now?"

"Yes."

"Well, of course," she whispered.

*   *   *   *

At the sound of his footsteps in the hall, Mimi swung open her apartment door. It was the first time she had seen the priest in street clothes—faded jeans, a light jacket, denim shirt. She saw he was a trim, fit man. As he came into the living room, Mimi realized she had not changed from her flannel nightgown; she had dozed on her chair until she'd heard him.

"Hello, Father." She nodded and gestured toward the sofa. She pushed the old stuffed chair in closer and plunked down in it, noticing as she did so, once again, the newly white square on the wall. The priest glanced at her and then at the floor.

"Can I get you some tea or juice or," she offered uncomfortably, "perhaps some coffee?"

"Actually, do you have anything to drink?"

"You mean . . .? Ahh. I have beer . . . I may have an old bottle of Scotch that Harold never opened . . . "

"Anything."

When she returned, he had removed his jacket and opened her window a crack. It was warm, she noticed. *April. Quixotic.* Not knowing exactly what he'd meant, she'd brought the

Johnny Walker and some ice and soda, a beer and some sparkling apple juice. He poured the scotch without measuring and eschewed ice.

"You?" he asked.

"I'll just wait a bit."

She had never before felt awkward with him. She could hear her kitchen clock ticking, and then heard a car pull up, its door shut, someone's heavy footsteps, and, finally, the key in a lock across the hall—Lorna, the nurse, she guessed.

Ben shuffled on the sofa.

"I didn't know who to talk to. I didn't want to be alone."

As the priest looked up at Mimi, she realized the simple truth of what he was saying. She was moved to cross the short space between them, to pat his back a bit as she would any human who had just lost a parent or child, but she fought this feeling, struggling, wondering how alone these men were expected to be. Mimi had never understood the scope of it before. How profound the vow of celibacy. She was not certain she wanted to understand.

He began to speak softly; Mimi had to lean closer.

"I loved my religion. I loved my father, who really embodied that religion. He was a rabbi. Good God, a rabbi! We lived in a mixed neighborhood—Evanston. My best friend was a very strict Catholic, Tommy Angelo. Their whole family. My father was pretty liberal. He permitted me to go to church with them. Then Tommy became an altar boy." He laughed quietly. "I always thought I would marry Mary, his sister. She was so beautiful! Tommy's family is Irish and Italian and she had just huge blue eyes and hair so black . . . and she was such a soft, soft girl. No bite. Just kind, very kind." Ben drained his glass.

"I knew that rule about raising your kids Catholic and all of it even though I was just a kid. I even asked her. I was twelve. Twelve, and that smitten. Can you believe it?" Ben stared into her eyes. Mimi stared back.

"What did she say?" Mimi looked away for a couple of seconds.

"She said 'yes' but not if I weren't a Catholic. You know, . . . " He leaned forward, tapped her wrist lightly and nodded his head. "You know, they say a little kid can't be in love—it's always just a crush or something. But I had to marry that girl!" He looked at Mimi intensely. "You probably know exactly what I mean."

Mimi cleared her throat. "No. No. I don't . . . not really."

Ben received this silently, searching her face.

She poured some scotch into a glass, added ice and soda.

"But Mary wasn't the reason, right? Somehow, you came to believe what they believed, Tommy and his family."

"And when I did, it killed everything between my father and myself. Between myself and my family. And it never got better. Can you imagine—all the things . . . "

Ben covered his face and began to weep. Mimi waited, her hands sweating, but when he leaned forward sobbing, she could no longer restrain herself. She rushed to him, placed her arms around his folded body and simply rocked him. He wept for a long time. When he pulled his handkerchief from his pocket, Mimi went back to her chair.

"I guess I am completely out of it. You know, I always thought that he would come around. A knock on the rectory door —I'd answer it . . . We can't afford these broken cords. They are so destructive."

"I know."

He took this in, she saw, and then he shook his head. "I must let you get some rest."

"What will you do now?"

"I'll go back to the rectory. Try to catch a few hours of sleep. Then I have to go."

She walked him to the door and helped him on with his jacket.

"It's cold now," she said, shivering slightly.

Ben placed his hands on her shoulders and they looked at each other. Then so quickly, she would always think she had dreamed it—one of her bizarre dreams—he kissed her on the mouth and swooped out.

SIX

COLD FISH

Grandma Tinker was one of those little old ladies often featured in coffee and fast food commercials, hair in a gauzy bun, small plate of a hat, its netting crumpled. Flowery ancient dresses, turned-down stockings and nun's shoes. Mimi thought of her as the last of a breed. And the thing was, she had looked this same way ever since Mimi lived beside her on Jackson, since she was six. Grandmas these days were more prone to be outfitted in Caribbean-colored synthetic matching pants and jackets, as if they were on their way to the gym. Their hair tended toward a bright lavender sparkle, brushed up away from their faces, fluorescent pink on their lips. She had even seen a group of tap-dancing grannies on the TV, their legs stick-slender in glitzy short skirts. Mimi hadn't been able to decide if she were glad or sad when she'd seen them. How much effort it took not to look one's age. The grace of acceptance was so admirable, so attractive in itself, and yet, now, when she met her own face in the morning mirror, she herself was inclined toward a fierce struggle against gravity and time. Tap-dancing, lipstick—whatever it might take.

After the bathtub incident, those vaguely attached nephews and nieces decided that Miss Tinker should be looked after in Sunnyfield House. Mimi herself was cynical about such arrangements, and as she consulted her map and drove out past her parents' home in Gilton, she found herself mumbling, "If she falls in the tub there, she'll be in the cold water half a day instead of two hours."

But of the places Mimi had seen of their ilk, it was not awful. When Mimi pulled up in her Metro, Grandma was waiting with her new cane, crisp white gloves, and book-like purse. Many others were waiting as well, but Grandma informed Mimi, that, for most of them, there would be no Sunday visitors.

"No. No. They just like to watch." She responded to Mimi's question of whether many of the residents would be going out that day.

Grandma had been talking about a walk around the reservoir for months, but Mimi had not been able to get her there, and now the cane and her sore leg seemed to make that destination look unlikely. But Grandma Tinker was insistent, and the day was fine. She did limp along, but told Mimi it was only awkward, not painful. The wind blew seductively, in little whorls; the groomed flowers planted here and there bowed and bent.

"How long has that man of yours been gone now?"

"Two years, Grandma."

"He's not coming back."

"Well, it doesn't look good, does it?"

"It never looked good."

Mimi stopped, but the old lady went bumping along.

"What do you mean, Grandma?" Mimi half-shouted into the wind.

"Well, you're a live wire and he's a cold fish," she called over her shoulder. "I mean he wouldn't hurt a flea, but nothing to pine for, either. Remember, I knew both of you from then." She gestured down towards her knee.

"Then you never liked Harold?" Mimi had caught up.

"Now, I didn't say that. I don't have a problem with the man. But he's not your man."

Mimi looked out over the water. *What makes it go in those little waves? What makes it move and why doesn't it all sink into the ground or evaporate or do the things water does? What is a reservoir, exactly? What am I going to do?*

It seemed Grandma wanted to walk all the way around the reservoir and would not hear Mimi's concerns, so they walked in silence for awhile.

"You could get one of those men . . . " Grandma Tinker announced suddenly.

"What kind of men, Grandma?"

"One of those men you pay to look for somebody."

"A detective?"

"Yeah. A mean, sneaky character. You need to know what's what and get on with your life."

Why hadn't she thought of this before? Why hadn't anyone? Mimi was shocked and ashamed, but she supposed that that's what waiting did to you. You just kept waiting and any day things could change and, waiting—well, it gets to be a sort of life all its own.

The old lady was pulling at Mimi's sleeve.

"Get me back now."

When Mimi took her arm to guide the old woman back to the car, she could feel that her skin was so thin it was as though she could have rubbed it off like an onion's skin.

"But what about your sundae!?" Mimi had been looking forward to the splurge.

"They have them at Sunnyfield—and don't forget, I'm ninety!"

"Well?"

"An hour or two's all I can do. When will you come back?"

"When do you want me to?"

"Well, I want you to come back in a week. If the sun's out."

And then, as Mimi was unlocking the car door, Grandma stopped and pulled once again on Mimi's sleeve.

"I never married, but I know a thing or two about men."

Mimi helped her into her seat and was snapping the seatbelt over grandma's bulky pink coat when she looked up at her and laughed. "Such as . . .?"

"Looks are nothing. Money's nice, but unnecessary. Health is very, very pleasant, but heart," she placed a small dry hand on Mimi's cheek, "a man with a heart is the one you want. It's got to be big enough to put you in it.

SEVEN

LOAVES AND FISHES

With Mr. Weekday under her arm, her briefcase clutched in her left hand and two small goldfish in a plastic bag hanging from her right, she leaned against the doors of Lincoln school and went in. Smiling "good mornings" to the other teachers, Mimi wondered what had happened to her weekend. *It must be the full moon,* she pondered. *We're all going crazy. Except Grandma. She was my only sane moment of the last three days.*

This is when she loved her classroom. Early morning, when she stood behind her desk and "assembled" herself. It would be a tough day, she knew. The rain. *They won't want to sit for more than a few minutes!* She would have them talk immediately, asking each one to stand if they wanted to. Tell what their weekends had been like. It might expend some of the rainy day energy. She opened her lesson plan and squeezed a note under 8:30. *Rain. Do brief sharing before lessons.* As she jotted this down, her peripheral vision caught something in the doorway, and she looked up. Gerry Mertz in his awful kelly green jacket, waving his hand like a windshield wiper. "Oh, Gerry."

"Didn't want to disturb you."

"No. I . . . "

"Your weekend okay?"

"Well, kind of weird, but okay. How about yours?"

A mistake. He walked up to her desk, and began to tell Mimi about the new car he'd bought. A Corolla, green of course, and she should come out at lunchtime and see it. Just then, little Billy Merchant dashed in with a bloody nose, and Mimi had to take him to the office. She was able to remain uncommitted.

*   *   *   *

As rainy days go, it hadn't been a horrendous one. The awkward discovery of the hole in the bottom of Nickolas Lubovitch's shoe and his soaking wet sock and foot—trying to take care of that as casually as possible. And then Bobby and Byron's fight at recess. Their brawling was beginning to seem well beyond mere sibling rivalry; she had been set against the fraternal twins being in the same classroom, but their parents had insisted. There would be another discussion with Gerry and their parents as to the question of "Ms. Malone's not being quite in control of her class." She sighed.

One Barbie doll, two rocket things that came apart and could be made into interstellar weaponry, the usual lunchbox, and a small folded piece of manila art paper were the leavings of the day. She opened the paper and scanned for a name; there was none. Then she noticed something odd about the picture; she had never seen one like it. It was almost entirely drawn with black crayon, and appeared to be a spider web. In the center, a stick figure, arms and legs splayed; the figure sported auburn straight hair with very long bangs almost hiding the face. She caught her breath. Which little girl might this resemble? She conjured her two redheads, Missy Boyton and Allison Magee. Both had rather orange hair. Missy wore old-fashioned braids down to her waist, and Allison had short loopy curls. Neither possessed bangs as such. Becky Hienz had brown hair that may have had some reddish streaks. Mimi couldn't seem to remember. *Did she wear bangs or not?* She did however, remember her mother, Cynthia Hienz. Cynthia, a nervous, dramatic sort of woman, had been in Mimi's high school graduating class; during conference, she had expressed quite a lot of sympathy for Mimi's difficult personal situation, but more in an information-seeking mode than any real demonstration of concern, Mimi remembered. And . . . yes, Becky —that's why she'd forgotten her. She was dead quiet. She simply never spoke, but she did draw; sometimes she attempted to draw during recess or even during lessons. Mimi would have to gently talk about the picture with Becky, if indeed it was Becky's. She felt disturbed by the figure, that a child should have such a dark outlook. She refolded the paper and placed it carefully in her purse.

*   *   *   *

When she checked messages that afternoon there was only one:

"Hi. It's me, Link. I quit my job and I am home and need a shoulder, a meal, and to talk. And we never did talk about the Lighthouse night."

Mimi dialed her number immediately. "Hello?" Link sounded upset.

"Hi. Sure, I can meet you. Sam's okay? Wait. Let me make you something. I'll just make some simple thing. Did you quit today?"

Link blew her nose. "Yes. Yes, it was the only possible option."

"Come on, Link. Why don't you come right now."

"I will."

*   *   *   *

When Link arrived, Mimi offered her a beer.

"No. Oh, no. I'll . . . do you have chamomile or something?" Mimi was surprised, but dashed into the kitchen to make the tea. Link, she saw, from the kitchen doorway, stayed in the middle of the living room, walking in small circles.

"Hey" she called. "Where's your wedding picture?

"Ah . . . " Mimi felt foolish. "I didn't want to see it anymore."

Link ceased weeping momentarily. "Does this mean you're ready for a change?"

Mimi yelled back from the kitchen, "I don't know what it means, but I feel better with it gone. Two years and all I could ever think of every time I looked at that damn thing was how tedious it all was. I mean, the relationship was not without its moments, but . . . " She returned with the tea and cups.

"Still, to have somebody . . . there everyday. To know he's there . . . "

"Yes, but I've been thinking a lot about all that."

"And . . . "

They sat together on the sofa.

"Link, except that I don't think he ever wanted to be *there.*"

"But fifteen years . . . "

"More than half of that time we were in marriage counseling, and most of it was really rock bottom. I see it now, finally."

Mimi paused to pour the tea. She sipped, remembering that she had never been certain how she felt about chamomile.

"Rock bottom means. . . ?"

"Means all the problems came down to one problem."

Link searched for a tissue in her jeans pocket and Mimi handed her the box by the sofa, suddenly thinking of Father Ben. A small wave rolled through her chest.

"Which was, Mimi, which was?"

"Oh, it was that Harold felt completely stifled. We called it various names. I called it unsocialized. He called it eccentric. I called it selfish. He called it benign introversion. I called it distant. He called it, having hobbies. But I think he was just choking and I never really knew it. Er, accepted it. I think accepted is the correct word."

"Have you any more mail from Paris/Boise?"

"Nothing."

"Oh, Mimi, what you've been through . . . "

"Come on Link. What about you? We've been going over this Harold thing forever. What is this quitting stuff? What happened?"

"Well, Jewel, my anal retentive boss—god, I hate that bitch!—called me in and said that my copy on the car ad was feminist in tone and would have to be rewritten. I kept cool. I kept my head. I suggested to her that she had no notes in the margin and would she indicate the areas of concern. She responded with . . . Oh god, I hate her, 'The entire ad was stridently feminist.'"

"I said, 'Do you perhaps mean my choice of the feminine pronoun, *she*, or the fact that . . .

" 'No.' She wouldn't let me finish. 'No.' "

"And then she went on, 'Can I ask you a personal question that you need not answer? Link, do you like men at all?' I asked her just what the hell that question was supposed to mean? And she leaned across the desk with this freaky glint in her green, marble eyes and said, 'Just think about it. You'll have to rewrite the ad.' I told that little bitch if she could not give a written indication of what she wanted that perhaps her criticisms were subjective rather than objective. And personal rather than professional."

Mimi was stunned. *What was really going on here?*

"Did you bring the copy with you?"

"No. I walked out of there so fast because if I didn't I would have killed her."

"Did you give notice?"

"I told Robert that that was it. I would come back and clean out my desk Monday."

"Link . . . " But the phone rang. It was Mary Beth, excited.

"Marty just called from the office. He's being promoted and told me he's coming home and spending the night with the kids and I was to make a night of it for myself. What are you doing, Mimi?"

"Ah . . . " Link was mouthing, *Who is it?* Mimi was mouthing back, *Mary Beth.*

"Mimi?"

Link nodded her head and gestured toward the phone.

"Oh, Mary Beth, actually I'm talking with Link. We're in a crisis conference. She's quit her job."

"Oh, my God. Oh . . . well, maybe, should we get a drink or something?"

"We're having dinner, but we don't know what that will be —did you want to come?"

"I could bring lasagna. It's already made . . . "

"Well, thanks, but we're just going to make something light, okay? Come on over, Mary Beth. But I don't know how much fun we'll be having."

Mimi hung up the phone and studied Link's face. "Look, if that's not okay, I'll call her right back."

Link shook her spiky hair. "No, no I don't have any problem with her coming over. But I'm not going to tell the whole story twice. Why don't we fix dinner?"

They trudged into the kitchen and both women peered into the refrigerator. "Lots of eggs," Link observed, taking charge in her way. "What is this?" She was removing plastic bags from the crisper.

"How the hell do I know," Mimi laughed. Some nights I have cereal for dinner so the inventory is sketchy.

"Parmesan cheese, mushrooms—a bit toady looking but . . . ah, green onions, a little grey, but we can cut off the outside skin. Got any canned tomatoes?"

"I think so."

"So, could you drain them?"

They were working thoughtfully when the doorbell rang. "Mary Beth," Mimi wiped her hands on a paper towel and went to answer the door. In fact, it was Jan.

"I just got home from work and got this note taped to the garage door." She opened it for Mimi to inspect.

Mimi looked sharply at Jan and then into the kitchen, silence. "Ah, Jan, ah, Link's here. She's had an awful day—with Jewel, and she's pretty upset. We . . . "

"Mimi, please read the note." Jan's eyes were commanding.

Mimi took it, a light sweat blooming beneath her bangs.

Dear Mom,

I always thought you were a good mom, so this has nothing to do with you, but I have to get out of here. Me and Donny A. are going to hitch to Atlanta to stay with Dad. I'm going to get a job, maybe in a radio station that I know I will like and be good at. Don't worry. Things are so messed up here, and I miss Dad, he's funny. I'll call you soon.

Your son,

Richard

"When do you think he left?"

Jan's face was white, the crease between her eyes deeper. Mimi noticed she had bobby pins holding her dark unkempt hair in place. "I called the school, he wasn't there today. I know he was home last night, because about eleven I asked him to get his dirty laundry. Donny A. was there . . . " Her voice trailed off.

Suddenly, Link was behind Mimi's shoulder, reading Richard's note. Jan looked above Mimi's head and said directly into Link's face, "Link, something I said upset you that night at the Lighthouse. I know I was talking crudely and in gross generalities. I guess that's how I de-stress . . . I'd like to talk about it some time, okay? And I know you've had a hell of a day, but I'm being selfish. I don't want to be by myself." Jan began to cry. Mimi and Link placed her between them and lay their heads against Jan's.

Around the still-opened door popped Mary Beth's head. Mimi almost laughed at her wondering, enormous blue eyes.

"What's wrong?" Mimi let go her embrace and went to hug her friend and to shut the door. She placed an arm about Mary Beth's plump shoulders.

"These two ladies are having a rough time of it, Mary Beth. You want to join in? Or we give you a chance to bolt now."

"Well, I knew about Link but . . . But Jan, what?"

Link responded, "She just appeared here a few minutes ago. We thought it was you. Richard's run away."

Mary Beth's fisted hands flew to her horn-rimmed glasses.

"Oh, God! Oh my God, Jan. Has he called you? What's happening?"

"Look everybody, I'm getting a beer." Mimi bolted for the kitchen.

"Does anybody want anything to drink, and I think we should just eat and then maybe talk. Jan maybe you should call your machine and see if there are any messages? Link, do you want a soda or . . . "

Suddenly they were all talking at once, and Mimi shook her head, which was throbbing a little, and put on the tea kettle, got out some sodas and orange juice, grabbed a few beers and then finally the Johnny Walker and placed it all on the kitchen counter with some glasses. She yelled from the kitchen, "Get what you like. I'm going to work on expanding the omelet." And she went rifling in the pantry for the last of her potatoes.

*   *   *   *

Mary Beth patted her pink lips daintily. "Well, you and Link did it—another Loaves and Fishes episode."

"Did everybody get enough?" asked Mimi. "I've got cookies. They're old, though."

Link responded, "I'm stuffed, but I sure could use a cup of coffee."

Jan had been quiet, her omelet barely picked over.

"Not me. Last thing I want is to be awake." She got up and refilled her glass with a hefty jigger of Scotch. Mimi and Link's eyes met briefly, then looked away. Mary Beth put in an order for tea and began to clear the table, her brows squinched.

"Jan, I mean, what do you do now, about Richard. Do you call Lou or . . . "

"I called Lou. He said he'll call me as soon as Richard arrives."

"Well, I mean, should you call the cops or something?"

Jan's eyes looked slightly glassy. "He wants to live with his dad. He's made his choice."

Mary Beth held a stack of plates, yellow puffs dripping off the edge of one.

"No, I mean you know—hitchhiking and all, and leaving school. I mean, you have custody."

Jan's voice was tight.

"I can't lock him up, Mary Beth. When he gets to his dad's I'll talk with him. But . . . I've lost, that's all. As always, Lou gets it all—new life, new job, nymphette, and now Richard too. You know . . . " Her hair had broken from the bobby pins and made a stringy curtain over the right side of her face. "Did you ever know somebody who was born with a silver spoon in his mouth—of course Lou had a silver spoon up his nose, too..."

Link, who was crossing from the kitchen through the dinette with the coffee cups, called over her shoulder, "That's a long time ago now, Jan."

"To you, perhaps. But to me it's like yesterday, like a fire in my stomach that can't be put out."

Link ignored this. "Come on, let's have coffee."

Mimi got several candles from a cabinet by the sofa, placed them on the coffee table and lit them. They all sat down. It was dusk. The open window displayed a grey-blue Mimi had never learned the name for.

"Remember when we'd sleep over?" Mary Beth, asked, looking dreamily into the candle-flicker. "My mother never wanted me to. She wanted me there to help with the little kids, but I came. Her face would be scowling when she dropped me off. I never said this then, and maybe I only know it now, but I lived for those nights. I mean, we were just getting interested in boys and all that stuff. I still remember Mary-Marsha, oops, Link, painting every one of my fingernails a different shade of red."

"Red, ha, you mean orange, and I do believe a pretty neat shade of chartreuse, too, and wasn't there a blacky-bluey metallically thing that somebody brought?" Link's face softened. "Everything seemed simple then."

"Did it?" Jan was scowling. "I mean we didn't know anything, but we knew there was something. My mother handed me a box of Kotex when I was eleven and told me that if I used tampons I would not be a virgin. That was the sex talk. But there were all these feelings we could not get our brains around. Like jealousy. It was always so strong."

Mimi felt blank. "Huh? You mean—who were you jealous of?"

"Everybody. Wasn't everybody jealous? Then? Well, for one, Mary Beth. I was jealous of her."

"Of what?" Mary Beth's eyes were enormous behind her glasses.

"Everything. Just everything. You had breasts, for one thing. Every boy in eighth grade wanted to grab them."

Link laughed, then stopped when she saw Jan was serious.

"What else?" Mary Beth was earnest. It was very quiet in the room. There was a strange quiet in the street. No cars. No dogs.

"Well, your parents didn't drink. Fight. Your sisters loved you. You had blonde hair. You had a brother who took you to dances . . . "

They were all looking at the floor.

"Are you still jealous?" Mary Beth looked at Jan evenly. Their heads flew up.

Jan reddened. She moved her head like something trapped.

"I . . . well, maybe of Mary—well, no. No." Jan cleared her throat. "No, I guess not anymore."

"I mean because that's how it goes doesn't it? Everybody gets their turn, maybe." Mary Beth went on. "Look at me now. I'm this fat hulk. This late-life mother. This former everything, cheerleader, most popular—wiping behinds and chins, married to a wonderful man who's never at home who wants a thin wife and now you, you're rich. You have that big house and you're rid of a guy who caused you grief and you're a fabulous nurse. I mean you actually know something—how to keep people alive and how to pay your taxes and all that stuff. You work because you love it and when you want to."

At the end of her small speech, Mary Beth flushed and took her glasses off. She had both hands around her mug of coffee.

Mimi spoke up.

"Hey, what's happening here? We've all had our share of shit. We've all had good times. There's nobody in this room who hasn't suffered plenty. None of our lives turned out the way we planned. Well, in my case, I had no plan, so what was there to turn out, exactly?"

Link ignored Mimi's question.

"I never felt really right at those parties. I came because I liked everyone so much, because I could laugh a lot but . . . "

Link was sitting on the floor. The candlelight fell full on her fine-boned face, firing the red flames of her hair.

That almost constant edge of anger in Jan's voice. "Well, what was it? Was it all too girly for you?"

Link looked stunned. "Why do you say that?"

"Well, you never wanted us to touch your hair; you never wanted to talk much. That night after eighth-grade graduation, when we were at Tina Anthony's, we were all practicing with Mary Beth's black eyeliner, lining the hell out of our eyes while you were reading, *The History of Dirt*, that was it exactly, you were reading about dirt while we were measuring our waists and globbing up our eyes and I thought you felt superior."

"I didn't." Link's green eyes darkened. "I felt . . . bored."

"Well, bored, superior, they're kind of the same." Nobody responded to Jan's summation.

Mimi looked across at Link. "Why were you bored, Link?"

"I don't know. I . . . well, I wasn't into eyeliner. I wanted to *do* something. I got restless."

"We *were* doing something." Jan kept her eyes shut and leaned back against the sofa as she said this.

"We were lining our eyes and giggling and trying to smoke. It seems to me that's what thirteen year olds do, pretty universally."

Link was silent at this, staring over Jan's head.

"Do you guys remember," Mimi wanted to break the tension, "when we put the electric popcorn popper in Mickey's room?" Mimi could see this very clearly.

"No," said Mary Beth. "What happened?"

"Remember, we sat outside his door and we could hear the popping start, you know one pop and then a couple more and then Mount Vesuvius!"

"What I remember," said Link, "was him screaming, I know exactly what he said, this little ten year old, 'Jesus-what the hell-Christ.' That's when Mimi's mom tore down the hall, in shorty p.j.'s no less, and made all of us go home at two o'clock in the morning . . . "

Still laughing Link piped up, "I'm going outside to smoke and nobody say anything about it. I've been good all night."

Suddenly Jan, eyes still closed, started laughing. "Remember when Mary Beth stole her mother's bra—excuse me, brassiere, we used to call them—for us to try, I mean this was way back, one of our first pajama parties. We were all crammed into your room, Mimi, pushing each other away from the full-length mirror.

"And," Mimi laughed, "then it got really out of hand and we started stuffing Kleenexes down these really huge cups—God, what size was your mother, Mary Beth? And then . . . "

Mary Beth let out a shriek. "Oh my God! Your dad, your dad!"

"Yep." Mimi surprised herself by blushing.

"There was the old guy, bursting into the room and . . . " Mary Beth pulled her glasses to the end of her nose to look like Mimi's dad. "And he immediately," Jan interrupted her, "without pause, turned tail and jetted out of there with this expression, this wide-eyed kind of . . . "

"I could not look at him the next day, and he could not look at me." Mimi shook her head and said almost in a whisper, "We're lucky we had each other."

LOAVES AND FISHES

EIGHT

PATHS OF FOOLISHNESS

The first of May dawned a miracle of a day, as warm as July with the sky, ribbon blue. Mimi had been staring out of the classroom window all day and now, as she walked up the steps to her apartment building, she noticed that the wind had sprung up and some spongy clouds were rolling across the sky. It was a blessed Friday, and she felt immense relief. Teaching was getting harder, the children increasingly restless. Mimi herself was restless. When she went into the apartment, she walked directly to her bedroom, to the old oak table she had retrieved from her mother's basement. The surface she'd covered with a piece of black velvet. She'd begun three different necklaces, months ago, a silver and crystal one, a wooden bead and copper charm choker, and a long seed bead strand of turquoise, olive and amber. She picked each of them up and arranged them on the velvet, dreaming them finished. Her new business cards smiled up at her.

CURRENT WISDOM,

M. MALONE,

BEADWORK AND JEWELRY.

She'd always loved her logo, a violet owl, halo-ed with lightning bolts sparking from his head. Four teachers at school had placed orders, and Jimmie, who cut her hair, wanted a sterling silver bead strand, but there never was enough time. "This, is what I want to do," Mimi said aloud.

The phone's ringing made her jump and caused a buzzing in her head. Forgetting that she never answered the phone on Friday afternoons, she picked it up.

"Hi, honey." Harold's mom, Alice. "Hi Mom." *Mimi, the dutiful daughter.* "Mimi, I've been talking to Pete, and he said he wants to see you."

"Oh, how is he? I just love that old man."

"It's hard to believe that Dean's own father outlived him. His heart's just good and solid, he says. But he says he has you on his mind, and would you come to St. Joe's to see him?"

"Well, sure. I should have been seeing him regularly, Mom. This is a good reminder. Did he say when?"

Alice "hmmmed" a few seconds.

"Well, I think he said he can have one guest to the home for dinner. Yes, and he wanted you to come this Sunday. Oh, and Mimi . . . "

"Yes?"

"Did you hear about Father Ben's dad?"

"Ah, yes, somebody told me . . . I need to send him a card."

"Well, yes. I don't know. Can you have a mass said for a rabbi? I just don't know."

"Well, mom, Jesus was Jewish. I don't know what God would say about it!"

"It's not God I have to ask. It's a priest."

"Yeah. That's where things get tough. Well, give me the number of St. Joseph's and I'll call Pete and confirm this thing. How are you doing, Mom?"

"I'm wonderful, just a little (here's the number, 847 272-1004) arthritis in my knees, but I still walk and garden, so that's all I care about. Everything would be perfect if Harold would just come home."

"Mom, I'd like to talk to you sometime. I hope you won't be upset somehow. Actually, it was Grandma Tinker's idea . . . "

"Yes?"

"Well, what do you think about hiring a detective? I mean to look for Harold."

"Well, now how could we not have thought about all this before?"

"That's the same thing I asked myself. I think we just kept expecting him to walk in the door any minute, but you know, two years . . . "

"I know he's alive."

"Well, so we should find him, right?"

"Except, what if he doesn't want to be found?"

"Mom, we want him to be found, and what we feel counts. Sometimes I think it should count more."

"Well, can you find someone to do that? I just don't have time."

Mimi swallowed. For a brief moment, she saw a red blackness.

"Mom, could you maybe try first? I'm up to my ears with school and my business."

"Oh." Harold's mom sounded vague. "Your business . . . Well, I'll try then, but . . . "

"Thanks, Mom. How about if I don't hear from you, I'll call you by Wednesday."

"Well, all right. Oh, and Mimi?"

"Yes, Mom—I gotta go, though."

"I love you, dear."

Mimi, you idiot . . . "I love you too, Mom."

By the time she had changed into her running shorts and shoes, grabbed her key, and let herself out, she felt like a puppy, bouncy and agitated. The wind would be a problem, and the grey sky looked chancy. Mimi's heart drooped. It had been such a beautiful day! But as she ran, warming up first with a slow jog, then sprinting, and finally slowing to a steady pace, she was ready to redefine "beautiful." The newly colorless world had become merely light and dark. Black trees with lemon-lit leaves, grey streets, buildings, sidewalks, dark or light grey cars. Scraps of white trash blew at her knees. The windows of houses were alight with the low sun. What had it said in the Tao? "If you carry your lamp outside into the sunlight, it does not illuminate." But the world had its own lamp, she thought, now silvering the clouds, now sending out its rays of grace, as her mother had called them, now blackened by a cloud as large as the sky itself. *The world was a thing of such piteous beauty if taken on its own terms. It hurts to look at it. We keep waiting and waiting and pursuing and here it is, God in his own heaven and we can't see it. Can't see. Blind. I am blind.* Mimi saw that every other footfall hammered out the word, Blind. Blind. Blind. And she ran, drumming the pavement with that word for a long while.

*   *   *   *

In the shower, she sang and sang and prayed that the phone would not ring again. Friday afternoon, Jan, or Link, or less often Mary Beth, called and they met somewhere for Cheep Eats (as they all called it), but after last week's strange crisis dinner, as Mimi now thought of it, none of them had called—except Jan, the next day to say that Richard had indeed arrived in Atlanta, was perfectly safe, but had remarked that 'Dad's girl was a babe.'" Lou had then wrestled the phone from him and asked Jan what she thought they should do. It was the first real conversation they'd had in six months. Link had left a message that she was job-searching and therefore 'laying low' for a time, and would call soon. Mimi was content with this respite. She loved her friends, but right now she felt distant. She didn't understand Jan's hostility. She was on the verge of thinking Mary Beth had become a whiner—and Link's volatile behavior and strange sort of growing secretiveness just plain annoyed her. *God, I need to meet some new people. What adult woman still pals around with her grammar school friends?*

*   *   *   *

The sky was growing dark when she went into the kitchen to prepare dinner, and though it had become quite cool, she opened the kitchen window wider to a view that included the old narrow alley and the locust tree and again, she thought of her new idea about beauty. The storm had blown out as it had blown in, with only a suggestion of rain. All was now still. *Lovely. Lovely.*

Cats were crying. It was that time of year. A cat was what Mimi wanted more than anything, a kitten. She'd brought home four books from the library about rearing kittens, but had gotten discouraged. She didn't have the money now, and she wanted to do it right. Her brother Mickey had a calico named Wally that she had fallen in love with; she'd begged him to let her take the kitten home for the weekend, but he refused to part with it.

She'd thought, driving home, *Give Mickey time, just a couple of months and then I'll swoop down on Wally and grab him.*

Staring into the dusky light, Mary Beth flashed across her mind, and for the first time, she realized she was an exceptional looking woman. Her milky skin and blushed cheeks, her lake-blue eyes, her Dutch boy cut blonde hair. She was a Rubens in a flannel shirt. But we were blind to people, too. *I think, ah, Mary Beth's getting heavy, and then what? Why aren't there varieties of beauty? Why so narrow?*

The phone was ringing. "Damn!" Mimi shouted out the window above her sink. She'd let it ring then, *even if it is Harold. He can leave a message like everyone else.* The machine picked it up. It was a man's voice—Ben's. She froze.

"Mimi. I bet you're there, it's Friday and you're probably sick of people by now. I wanted to let you know that I am going to be okay. My father left a long letter for me, one he had written a week before he had the heart attack but had not sent." There was a long pause; she thought he'd hung up, but he resumed. "I don't know what to say about my behavior. I'm sorry, but . . . I'm taking a leave of absence for a while. I'll be here with my mother and I'll give you the number. It's 703-447-1850. I guess I am asking you to call me. This weekend if you can. Let's pray on it till then. Bye."

She could not seem to un-freeze herself or move from the window. *What the hell is* ***it****? What* ***it****?* She didn't want to call him. Something like terror swam in her chest. *Look. We are friends. He has to understand that.* Standing there, it came to Mimi that his thinking they had some sort of *it* was the mind's way of repairing as quickly as possible its sense of loss. She wouldn't be used like that, even if he hadn't a clue that this is what was happening. A priest, oh Jesus, please help us. And without a thought, she blurted out the prayer she had been praying since the day Harold had not gotten off the plane.

"God be with us on the paths of our foolishness, guide us to the path of righteousness."

93

NINE

PERCOLATING MIND

Harold's Grandfather had been a man that people referred to as sturdy. And this adjective applied to his character as well as his physique. But what Mimi had always loved about him was his gentle humor. He laughed as easily as some people breathed, deeply, quietly; at himself, at the foibles of the world, at the curious turns his life had taken. Rosa, for example, his wife and Harold's grandmother,

"She was like a goddess with a devil inside," he'd say. Then he'd take out her picture, which he always kept with him in his shirt pocket. And leaning toward his audience add, "Oh, she had me dancing."

Mimi dressed for their dinner because he'd always said, "I like a well turned-out woman." And because he alone thought her beautiful. Squeezed always for time, she'd taken to her own bangs with less than professional results. When she observed the choppy outcome, she decided that what she really needed was pointy, wispy sorts of bangs, and she attempted these with a razor-type implement that had been fantastically sharp. Within seconds she was not exactly transformed so much as mildly mutilated, with strands that refused to lie down on her forehead but stuck straight out. With the brush, conditioner and her blow-dryer she was able to bring some order out of the chaos, but on her way to St. Joseph's, she could feel them beginning to rise in rebellion. Otherwise, she was satisfied with her appearance. Her suit was soft and rounded, a warm coral color, her silk blouse she liked to think of as a blushing cream. She was surprised at her happiness, and shocked that she had nearly forgotten such a wonderful old man.

Pete was waiting for her in the lobby of St. Joseph's which proved to be a kind of sagging mansion of former glory. He was dressed in a brown pinstriped suit, sort of Al Caponish, she thought, but nice. He hugged her and wiped a tear from his eye when he stood back to look at her.

"Oh, Pete." She had never called him Pops, as did everyone else. "Oh, Pete, it is so wonderful to see you." At the same time as she said this, Mimi saw what it was—why she had "forgotten" Pop. Harold resembled him exactly. The slight hook of his nose, the bushy brows, the same height, more or less, the same slight bones and serene intelligence in his expression. She put her hand over her mouth and felt her lips tremble, but he leaned on her arm and motioned toward the dining room, and as they walked, she recovered.

The food was awful; it seemed as if everything had been cooked for days and in the process, lost its color, so that the pork cutlet was the same grey brown as the green beans, but Mimi supposed the old folks needed their food soft for dentures and gums. The view, however, was lovely, Pete was in the mood to talk, and since the regulars at his table were not as alert as Pete, he kept her engaged the entire dinner hour. It seems that Harold used to go with Pete to his brother's—Uncle Harry's place every summer for a number of years. Uncle Harry had a farm in Idaho, and there Harold and Pete would fish and take care of the animals. Why hadn't Harold ever mentioned this? Pete had simply closed down his candy store, and they took off for an entire month.

Pete placed his fingers gently on Mimi's wrist, interrupting her reverie. "Now, how about a little stroll around the park, honey?"

But they made it only a short distance, to the first bench in the park behind the dining room, and Pete was ready to sit down.

"Now, here's the thing," he said out of the blue. "Alice is well provided for. Dean left her a shitload of money. Don't let that house on Elise Avenue fool you."

"Pete, you really don't have to tell me all this. I know Harold's father was well fixed. Don't you think it's a good thing that Alice will have enough?"

"Yes, and so does she, but she doesn't need anything from me, so we've gotten to a little understanding."

"Pete, you sound so conspiratorial. What do you have up your sleeve?"

Mimi was amazed at the percolating mind the old man had. She knew he was in his mid-eighties.

"Here's *my* question. What about you?"

"What about me?" Mimi was becoming confused and flustered.

"Rumor has it that you're pretty good with your hands."

"You saw Alice's necklace!"

"Yes. She tells me it's her favorite."

"Really?" Mimi was shocked. Alice had merely thanked her politely. She felt dubious suddenly, about Pete's remembrances.

"Mimi, I want to give you a gift. I have the money and I can do that. Alice is fine with it, and I wouldn't care if she wasn't. I wanted to be the one to tell you, but Alice will give you the check. I don't want you waiting for Harold to get your life straightened out."

"But Pete, I, I . . ." Mimi started to cry; suddenly she felt tired. Pete gave her his handkerchief and spoke.

"I won't hear any argument. You call Alice and pick up the check. I'm going to die soon; I can't spend it. Now, you need to get on home and make something for me, a stick pin or some such."

The old man leaned on her arm, and they walked slowly back to the mansion. They embraced, and he said, "Now, I want to see you soon. I don't have any other beautiful young ladies stopping by."

Mimi smiled at her Grandfather-in-law and nodded. "Take care, Pete. There's no way I can thank you."

He laughed, "Be happy and I'll be thanked."

Mimi looked back when she got to her car. Pete was waving; he looked all at once small and far away, framed in the huge doorway.

TEN

CIGARETTE

The last time Mimi exited the doors of Lincoln School it was not without misgivings and regrets. Pete's gift was generous, but she knew that any sensible woman would invest the money and keep working. If everything went along in the best of all possible worlds and she got enough substitute teaching jobs, she would be able to keep Current Wisdom going for two years. But the jewelry she created was not really the stuff a business was made of. She could produce, max, ten pieces a week, and she didn't know the first thing about placing her things or advertising. That was more expense. She thought of the old saying, "The two worst things that can happen to a man are that he pine after his heart's desire and that he receive it." For a brief, panic-stricken moment on the way to her car, she thought she should perhaps move in with her mother, but by the time she plunked down in the Metro, she was laughing out loud.

"Oh no—no, no, no," she said aloud. "That, Mimi, would be the death of you both." She started the engine. *I wonder if there's ever been a simultaneous mutual homicide?*

It took her a half-hour to unload the car; looking around the box-filled apartment, she felt again the thud of finality. She retrieved her mail from the mailbox; among the ads and "you may have already won's" was a thick letter from Father Ben. She had never returned his call, and this is what they seemed to have settled on, this friendship by letter. He did make noises about her coming to D.C., but she ignored these and he did not press. In his letter he often mentioned grace, arguing that grace is so mysterious, that often right in the midst of what had been taken something was given. He had written, *Here I am in the house I grew up in, in some ways closer to my father than ever before. I have been given time. I did not realize that I had no time to think of anything. That I am exhausted. That I am lost.*

She had one phone message from Mary Beth ecstatically detailing her fifteen-pound weight loss with Jenny Craig this and that and counselors and such, but with no request that Mimi call her back. She decided to take herself out to Bead World and to dinner. She couldn't look at the boxes yet. *Too Creepy.* She hadn't eaten a really good meal in quite a long time. As she was pulling on slacks, the phone rang.

"Damn. Damn, damn," she whispered, as if someone might hear. "Hello?"

A woman answered—she imagined her to be blonde and very tall, and despite the hour, which was five o'clock, dressed in a satiny thing, such was the smoky jazz of her voice. "I hope you got my postcard."

"Excuse me, do you have the correct number? I don't recognize your voice."

"Oh, you don't know me, but I have seen him." She could hear the woman exhale breathily.

"Who? Whom have you seen?"

"Look, woman to woman. I don't think he should get away with it."

"What? Get away with what?" Mimi was aware that her voice was shrill, and despite the crisp click on the line, she continued to repeat the question. *I have an unlisted number, how could someone I don't know call me?* As she hung up, the phone rang immediately. She was furious, and bellowed into the phone, "Who is this?!"

"Why Mimi, this is Mom, Alice. Is anything wrong?"

"Oh, sorry, oh no Mom, just some kids on the phone being annoying. What's up? How are you?" Why could she not tell Alice about the call, or even the postcard? Didn't she need to know? Isn't that why they had hired the detective? Often, Mimi confused herself. "I have my first report from the detective, Mr. McClosky. It's not much, but we have information from a hotel in New Delhi that Harold never checked out. He never returned to his room one day after having stayed there a month . . . "

"Well, that much, I already know, Mom." Mimi felt crushed with disappointment. Jack McClosky had come their way enthusiastically recommended.

"Well, yes, but what I don't think you know is that his bill was paid in full two weeks later."

"By whom?"

"Well, Jack doesn't know. They didn't care who paid it. It didn't matter to them, but the clerk who entered the payment says that the check came from the States. You know the envelope and note, unfortunately he doesn't remember what the note enclosing the check said. From the States, Mimi!"

It was such a little bit, such a shred . . . "Well, what does Mr. McClosky say he's going to do now?"

"Well, he said he wanted to interview Harold's sisters next."

Mimi could not keep the annoyance from her voice. "Harold's sisters? Why? What could they know that we don't?"

"Well, I, I don't know. He's very experienced." But she sounded hesitant.

Mimi thought of telling her about the card and phone call, but something held her back. "Well Mom, I have to get to Bead World before it closes. Please let me know if you hear anything else."

"Of course, and I want you to come for dinner. You'll have more time now—oh, and I talked to the guild president last Sunday and would you be interested in a presentation?

"Oh, Mom! That's just what I need. Yes! Oh, thank you so much."

*   *   *   *

In the distance, an ancient farmhouse lay sagging into the flat land. The snow was falling softly, pigeon feathers from a dun sky. A few guernseys and a bay were bowed, searching for grass, but they stopped as she approached the fence. Smoke puffed from the chimney, and when she pushed opened the door to the ranch house, she found she was looking directly into a knotty pine kitchen. A woman in a turquoise evening gown with silver blonde hair was pulling iceberg lettuce apart with her melon-painted nails. A long cigarette lay in a chipped saucer to her right on the counter, its slender thread of smoke climbing into the chilly air. On the kitchen table lay a backpack with travel buttons pinned to it and a compass beside it—the large antique compass that had belonged to Harold's father, that he had given to Harold on his thirteenth birthday.

Mimi shot straight up in bed. Her heart was pounding. She stumbled out of her bedroom and threw open the living room window and sat on the sill. She was sweating profusely. After some moments, she lurched toward the kitchen to get a can of beer. But there was none. With a heavy sense of guilt, she yanked the Jack Daniels from under the sink, frowning as she noticed the dent Jan had made in it, poured herself the last bit into some diet ginger ale and returned to the sill. She wiped the sweat from her face with the back of her arm.

"Damn. How am I supposed to survive all this? Damn you, Harold." But she didn't cry. There were no tears left.

ELEVEN

ONE MIND

It was four in the afternoon exactly on the huge round clock over Detective McClosky's desk when Mimi was shown in and given an old oak chair, worn shiny by many an agitated client's bottom. Jack McClosky had the face of a man who had crawled through a lot of dark places, red and full. He possessed a beefy physique and dark, intense, mobile eyes. He looked to be on the less exciting side of fifty. His office resembled those of classic, slightly sleazy detectives depicted in films of the forties, right down to the fat crooked venetian blinds on the windows.

"Mrs. Piccolo." He spoke her name with a surprising amount of feeling in his voice as he searched her face. She could not say whether this was an announcement or a question.

"Well, actually, it's Malone—Mimi Malone."

"But, Mr. Piccolo's wife."

"Well, that's seems like something I dreamt, now."

"What's that?"

"Well . . . " She felt herself frowning and smiling simultaneously "Well, being Harold's wife, Harold, the whole garbanzo." (She could not remember the whole whatever it was supposed to be.)

"Well, I'd like to hear what you can tell me about your husband. And if you don't mind, what can you tell me about the relationship?"

Mimi noticed that his tongue seemed to stumble over the word *relationship*.

"Harold . . . " *What was he like?* No one had ever asked her. Everyone she knew, knew him.

"Well, he was a scientific sort of person, you know, kind of that stereotype of a nerd. I mean, you know what he looks like. You have several photographs. He was tall with a slight build."

Suddenly, she could see him naked as he emerged from the shower, droplets of water, the long muscles of a dancer. Her neck muscles closed.

"Could I have some water?"

Jack was fast on his feet, out the door and back again with a large pink plastic glass of very cold water.

"Is this hard for you? I'm sorry."

"Well, I didn't think it would be. We didn't have a dream marriage. You might as well know that. Why do I feel like I'm going to confession?"

As he smiled, she noticed he had dimples on each side of his mouth.

"Actually, it was all probably a mistake. We were in marriage counseling half of the fifteen years we were married."

"Can you summarize the basic problems?"

"Well, he felt closed in by the marriage. He had a lot of good will. We both did, but . . . he would try to share his time, but I could feel the effort. I felt rejected and lonely."

His eyes traveled over her face and then very discreetly over the rest of her. "And yet you didn't divorce?"

Mimi felt foolish. "No. In some crazy way neither of us understood, we loved each other, were part of each other. Maybe it was sick. Probably it was . . . we didn't make each other happy."

"Anything else you think is important?"

She looked directly at Jack, unable to keep the intensity from her eyes.

"We wanted a baby." She took a drink of the water from the pink glass. "We were desperate for a baby. About that we were of one mind."

McClosky was leaning forward, his face at attention, an expression that was a cross between a father's and a hawk's.

"And . . ."

Mimi pulled at some imaginary lint on her skirt. She whispered, "We could not have a child."

The room was airless; the wooden floorboards exuded heat. For a few moments, time stopped. The hands clung briefly to the face of Jack McClosky's clock and then, to all clocks. Traffic hesitated, the waves on the far-off ocean leapt up and forgot to come down. Mimi, sitting in Detective Jack McClosky's office on June 28, 1995—the Year of Our Lord.

TWELVE

ANGRY BEE

About twenty minutes after her presentation to the Lady's Guild of Saint Timothy's, as she and Alice were packing up her necklaces and earrings, she heard the footfalls of a man among the dwindling klatches of women. She looked up as Father Ben strode toward her.

"Hello, Alice."

"Father Ben."

"Hello, Mimi."

He put his hands on their shoulders briefly. Mimi only stared.

"I am so sorry for your loss," said Alice. Her eyes were moist.

"We each here have our losses," said Ben. "But you know, I came to know my father and to feel forgiven by him through his death. Maybe someday I'll understand how all this happened."

The priest turned toward Mimi. "Well, I understand you dazzled the ladies. If you can spare a few more minutes, I'd like to look for something for my mother. After some moments of scrutiny, Ben chose a sterling chain with freshwater pearls an inch apart, and a small crystal heart dangling from the center.

"Do you suppose this is too young for my mother?" He asked, blushing faintly above his white collar.

Mimi felt a pain in her stomach. This was her favorite piece; she had to fight her instinct to reach out and grab it from him. She held out her arms and shrugged. *You can make another one, she thought.*

He then asked her mother in law, "Alice, what do you think?"

"If I received that from my son," her face was very serious, "I would be very happy to wear it often." He turned to Mimi.

"I'll take it." As he paid, Mimi noticed his eyes were wandering over the table.

"Did you want a box?"

"Well…"

"You were wishing we would wrap it, is that it?" Mimi looked up at him.

"I, yes, is that possible?" He looked suddenly boyish.

Mimi felt a wave of that same fear she'd had the night he'd called.

"We don't have any gift wrap here, but I have some at my apartment and could drop it off on my way to five o'clock mass. I'm going home to rest."

"Mimi, thank you so much. I'm a real bumbler at things like that. I'll see you then."

*   *   *   *

At home, she counted her earnings, her heart beating quickly. One thousand, fifty dollars, and thirty-five cents. She could live on that for nearly a month, investing the money that Pete had given her. Meanwhile, she could make another collection and see if she could garner another guild. Perhaps Father Ben knew another pastor well. Or what about the PTA? *Ugh, I'd have to call Gerry Mertz.* At that moment, Mimi yawned so hard that tears dribbled from her eyes; she lay down on the checks and bills and coins she'd organized on her bed and fell asleep.

She awakened to the sound of a huge angry bee, and was startled to see the dark outside her window. Her door buzzer . . . she moved unsteadily and without asking who was on the other side, swung her door wide.

"Mimi!"

"Oh." Mimi felt her hair and dress. Her hair was puffed and standing out from her head. Her dress was wrinkled and damp.

"Father Ben, oh what time is it?"

"Nine o'clock." He was wearing jeans again and carried a bag of Chinese take-out and a bottle of wine.

"What . . . ?"

"I knew you'd fallen asleep and I came to claim my wrapped gift. This is my payment. You haven't eaten?"

"I haven't done anything. I slept. Like the dead. I'm sorry!" She was instantly awake.

But he laughed. "May I come in, then?"

Mimi's throat was tight. "Well, yes, of course, come in. Let me wash my face, please."

In her bedroom, she changed into jeans and a shirt. She washed in the bathroom and deliberately did not apply lipstick, but she did brush water into her hair and pulled it back with a band at the nape of her neck. Her bangs were growing; she watered them down.

When she got to the kitchen, he had the table set and the wine opened. Even with the boxes, to Mimi it looked beautiful. No one had done anything like this for her in such a long time. She got down a couple of her crystal goblets and washed them. All the while, neither Ben nor Mimi spoke. He poured a little wine in her glass and nodded. She tasted and nodded and then they ate ravenously and with poor manners. After a while, they talked. Ben told about his leave of absence, staying in his boyhood room. His mother's dignity and grief. He gave her the letter his father had written before he died.

Mimi told about the night at the Lighthouse Restaurant and her concerns for her friends. She then said how weary she was of them, but at the very same time, so fond of them and how she could not understand having both feelings simultaneously. She explained that she and Alice had contracted a detective but that they hadn't heard more than a shred. Then she told the story of Pete and the money and how he—an old man of 82—had seen into her heart. But that nevertheless she was tired all the time and had stopped running again. Then they washed the dishes, falling silent. A breeze flew over the kitchen sink, lifting Mimi's hair and blowing Ben's towel as he wiped each dish while he softly whistled.

She turned toward him. "Don't you know the Virgin Mary cries when you whistle?"

Father Ben laughed and shook his head. "A story invented by cranky old priests."

"Like yourself?"

"Exactly like me." He placed the towel neatly over the finished stack of dishes; she dried her hands. He turned and faced out the window. "Stars." Their shoulders touched.

"Stars." He bent and kissed her cheek like a high school boy. She turned her head toward him as if guided by an enormous hand.

THIRTEEN

NORTH, SOUTH, EAST, WEST

Mimi had set her new work table in front of the bedroom window where she had a blue/white north eastern exposure, her magnifying light on a stand and each tool nose-down in its own juice can. She had made a display board out of cardboard and a black velvet remnant from "Sew What!" and had her newest piece lying on it, a blackened silver chain from which hung smoky freshwater pearls. A second chain was attached in loose scallops to the first. The effect was a lace and pearl collar. Despite the fact that it was one a.m. and she needed to sleep, she was excited and just about to fasten the last scallop when the phone rang. *I want to make this loop, just one more loop!*

"S-h-i-t!" Mimi spit between her teeth and grabbed the cordless beside her, prepared to nest it between her chin and shoulder so she could keep working.

"Mimi!" It was old Pete. He had never called her before.

"Is anything wrong, Pete?" Mimi sat down on her bed.

"I don't know . . . Did you hear anything from Harold?"

Maybe Pete was beginning to have Alzheimer's. She answered him carefully and calmly. "I haven't Pete, have you?"

"I don't know. I'm not sure."

"Pops!" Why was she calling him that? "Pops," Mimi urged, "why don't you tell me the story from the beginning."

"Well, I don't know. I thought you might have heard, that's all. I'm superstitious or I don't know, but sometimes I get information."

Mimi was beginning to think she might have to run over to St. Joseph's and see Pete for herself. Maybe he wasn't being cared for. "What information did you receive, Pops, and how?"

"Well, they say I'm just old and don't know what's what, but I think I know a dream from the real thing. But I also know you dream for a reason. It's their way."

"Their way?" Mimi was up now, pulling her jeans on beneath her nightgown, the receiver squeezed between her head and shoulder.

"When people are lost or dead, and something prevents them from communicating, sometimes they get to you in a dream. You know this, Mimi."

"Well, I suppose that *could* happen." She sat down again abruptly.

"It happens. Ordinarily I sleep like a rock, I'm just lucky like that. But tonight I woke up. Exactly twelve thirty, if you don't know."

"Pete, what, what was it that awakened you?" Mimi's heart was pounding. *A dream—he's talking about a dream!*

"Harold! Standing right here! On the ground around him were letters—white ones just about as big as those on a Stop sign. They were in the positions of North, South, East, West. And that's what they were, *N, S, E,* and *W.*"

"So, Pete, you had a dream about Harold, right?"

"From Harold!"

"Okay, and did he look at the letters, did he see them?"

"Just about to tell you, my dear girl."

Mimi's body dripped with perspiration. Her head was beginning to ache.

"The *N* was behind him, the *S* in front of him and the *E* and the *W* to his right and left. He turned and placed his feet on the *N* and then walked to the *E* and sat down like an Indian. Then he got up and walked to the *S* and sat down and wept for a time. When he came to the *W*, he turned to me and opened his chest, parted it as if it were a coat, just like a heavy woolen coat, and there was his heart, right there—only, this is the really weird part, his heart was like one of those paperweights you see." He paused.

"A paper weight?" *I don't want to know this. I don't want to hear this.*

"Yeah. I think Alice might have one . . . a perfect fat heart but clear as a window, gleaming clean. You could see right through it to a little piece of sky."

"Pete, I can't think of anything to say."

"Now, there's just a bit more—almost the end . . . He stared right at me. I mean, you know how you can feel someone's stare— they want your attention."

"Yes, yes of course."

"Well, that was how. I could feel it, you know. And then the edges of him began to fade almost like he was being erased, more and more of him going and then . . . "

"Yes, Pete, what . . . "

"Well this part probably doesn't matter . . . it began to snow. Big flakes like goose feathers. And then I woke up."

FOURTEEN

MEDITATION

After Pete's call, something in Mimi's heart snapped open, something that had been lying closed and dark for a long time, months, ever since she had looked in the mirror on the morning of her fortieth birthday. Inexplicably, she found she believed Pete. That he'd indeed had a message, that Harold was alive, but this knowledge led her into a labyrinth of questions. If he were, why hadn't he called? Why wasn't he home? Why the tears? How literally to take the dream? And why that sky? And snow, in her own dreams as well. And the heart, why clear, why glass? And . . .

This is how her mind skipped and lurched as she twisted wire, beaded and clipped at a furious pace to finish her work for her mother's garden club. She could think of no one with whom to discuss the dream and her reactions to it except Ben, and she knew she must not call him. They hadn't spoken since the Chinese Food night. And mostly, she felt relieved.

"These things happen between people. It means nothing," she would tell herself when his face swam up in front of her work. "Look how vulnerable we both are right now. An accident."

Her stomach always responded to this particular line of thought with a roll and then a swift, heavy dip, which sometimes caused her to drop her pliers in the middle of wrapping the delicate wire. These responses, she ignored.

*   *   *   *

The invitation for a jewelry show at her mother's garden club was disclosed to Mimi accidentally. She'd been shoveling compost around her mother's iris border—the *flags*, her mother called them—when Edie proclaimed out of the blue, in her croaky former-smoker's voice, "The ladies at the garden club are so excited that you're coming, and they don't mind at all that the demonstration's not about flowers."

Mimi looked up, stunned. She was forever questioning her own psychic well being when she was in the presence of aging family members. She began to run through, in her mind, the last couple of conversations with her mother to see . . . could she have simply not recorded such an amazing opportunity? Perhaps she had lapsed into her Harold worries while her mother had been speaking to her over the phone. That was entirely possible. Perhaps she had written the date down while they were speaking, and it blazed happily on some number and month of her calendar, or perhaps she had not really taken in what Edie had said. To her mother, she must have looked blank as stone as she stuck the shovel into the compost and stared.

"Well, you said August first would be fine . . . didn't you? "

"It doesn't matter mother, August first *will* be fine. Somehow, I don't know, I can't remember that conversation. I'm just blanking on the whole thing."

Beneath her mother's rasp ran a small whine. "I know I told you. You young people are so busy, you never know whether you're coming or going. You don't keep us old folks in your mind for more than a minute. I know I'm a little forgetful, but I'd never have the entire garden party waiting for you to show up and you not come."

"Of course not, I just forgot, that's all. What time am I supposed to arrive?"

"I don't know. I don't know what I told them. You can't remember that, either?"

There was a real fear on her mother's face. *She can't face it. She's slipping and she just can't face it.*

"Mom, it's nothing. Look on your kitchen calendar. Just go on in and look. You always write everything down."

Edie looked instantly relieved. She would have been loath to call one of her gardening ladies to ask anything that might indicate she was not one hundred percent on top of things. Mimi knew this. Saving face had always been one of her mother's top priorities. Mimi watched her limping up onto the porch and through the front door. She remembered her mother doing headstands in the front yard when Mimi was six, when this housing plan they'd just moved to was surrounded by dairy farms. Her mother's dark hair tumbling over her face. Her loose black jeans rolled up to her calves. In a way, Edie had been one of them. They'd been on an adventure. Everything would be different. It had been different and the same. Her dad's schemes. The miscarriages. The bill collectors. Her mother on a ladder, pregnant, painting the attic bedrooms. Painting the new grey wallboard, yelling downstairs for Kool-Aid, lots of ice, which Mimi rushed up to her shaking on the ladder, sweat streaming down her face. July. This same month. Nicky and Teddy, locked up inside her.

Her mother returned almost immediately, a shadow behind the screen. Mimi knew she had a sheepish grin on her face when she called out, "Three o'clock! You're on at three o'clock." And then she turned and called back, "I'll get lunch! But all I have is wieners. I have good ice cream, though."

"She would." Mimi shook her head and flipped the wheelbarrow, rolling the remaining load of compost onto her mother's flag bed.

*   *   *   *

When she arrived home, she was sore, hot, and weary. Mimi thought herself capable of any physical challenge, but the endless shoveling had taxed her muscles. She mused to herself in the steaming shower that runners are not weightlifters. This annoyed her; she thought she might take up weightlifting. She wanted to feel invulnerable, ageless. It gave her hope.

Over the hair dryer, she could hear the phone, and she went scurrying into the bedroom to pick it up. It was Mary Beth.

"It's Friday!"

Mimi laughed. "And . . . "

"You know, Cheap Eats. I never see anybody anymore. What's wrong with us? What happened?"

"Maybe it's time to find out. Do you have time to call Link and Jan? I just have one more pair of earrings to make for the show and then I think I'll be finished."

"What show? I never know anything!"

"Well, I'll tell you everything when we get together. Can you call?"

"Yeah. Call you back!"

*   *   *   *

Freddy's Tacos was the last of a dying world. A Mexican restaurant where the owner was not Mexican and the food was wholly from the Pre-Lite Era. It was cool and dark inside (probably hiding the cockroaches), and it had that strange sort of liquor license whereby Freddy, if indeed there was a Freddy at all, did not serve any liquor; the customers could bring their own. This had led to astonishing sightings such as the evening a small man with glasses, it seemed his name was Jerome, lugged in a case of beer for a table of eight cronies. One evening a bottle blonde in a flame-red dress oozed by Mary Beth, Marty, Mimi and Harold, with a frosty-looking blender jar of Margaritas. Evidently, it fit neatly into the blender base in Freddy's kitchen. The crowd had cheered her in unison. Mimi and Mary Beth had sneered to each other that Freddy, himself, had given the woman a special Good Butt dispensation to enter his kitchen.

The tacos were stuffed with cheap hamburger, and the pinto beans were mashed; dime-sized puddles of liquid lard pooled across the top. And Freddy's made the only real nachos—everyone agreed. Smoky frijoles smeared across each huge wedge of corn tortilla, then jalapeños and layers of Jack cheese, baked until they had just begun to brown.

After Link had gone to L.A. to market the stars, and Jan and Mimi had returned from most of the exciting things they would do in their lives, Jan from Brazil, where she had taught basic prenatal care and inoculated the indigenous; and Mimi from Paris, where she had painted for a year. Then they had returned home. Mary Beth had continued on as an aide in Livingston Hospital, where she had not met a doctor, but an orderly with a smile as big as Texas who kept her "dangling on the line" for seven years. He had gone on to selling farm machinery, and his smile and choirboy sincerity had earned kudos and big bucks for himself and Mary Beth. The downside was that he traveled constantly—to Iowa or Kansas. Mary Beth remarked to Mimi that she got the feeling the kids had not been fathered at all but popped up behind pieces of furniture. Freddy's had been the place of their young marriages, hers and Mary Beth's and Jan's.

When Mimi adjusted to the light in Freddy's, she noticed someone familiar, red spiky hair—a woman resembling Link, in a pair of what looked like painter's pants. Then the Link look-alike waved her arm and beckoned Mimi to her.

"Mimi, it's so good to see you!" She came out from a booth and hugged Mimi heartily.

Mimi stammered, "Oh, I, I don't know why I didn't recognize you. Gosh, what is it?"

But Mimi or anyone else who had ever known Link nee Mary Margaret McCulhevy, could see what it was. Link had put on a lot of weight, she looked, well, almost pregnant. She wore none of her flamboyant persimmon lipstick, no makeup whatsoever. And instead of her angular red or purple suits, she wore a white V-necked Tee shirt and paint splashed overalls and shoes. And something else: there were her breasts, loose and uncovered under her flimsy jersey. Even for Freddy's, this was a step beyond. She sat back down, clutching what seemed to be orange juice, and smiled healthily, her Milky Way of freckles unhidden.

"Well, I've gained some weight."

"Oh, well, how are you?; it's been so long . . . "

Mimi hoped the other women would arrive, because when she looked at Link, she didn't know where to look, and she was afraid her surprise would show.

And there they were, except that Mimi barely recognized Jan or Mary Beth either, and she was beginning to feel what she and Mary Beth termed an "out-of-body experience," by which they always meant the feeling of flight the body experiences when what is being observed is either too threatening or completely at odds with the previously comprehended.

Mary Beth had let her blonde streaks grow out, and her newly light brown hair was very short. Was it shaved over her ears? She, in direct contrast to Link, was suddenly very thin, skinny even, and she wore a rose knit unitard with her sweat jacket tied around her waist. Her shoulders shone like a high school girl's. She too, had only a trace of lipstick and a slight flick of mascara on her pale lashes.

Jan, on the other hand, always the best groomed of their group, had bleached and grown her shiny, dark brown hair. She was paying lots of Lu's alimony for that job, thought Mimi, for there was still a swing and gleam to her hair, despite the chemical permutations it had been through. Obviously, she'd had some sort of extreme makeover. She had it styled like one of the myriad mop-tousled heroines of TV sitcoms. And she wore jeans, something no one had ever seen Jan in, not even in high school. She also wore what Mimi often thought of as a "small top," a little button-up number exactly the same grey as her eyes. Such an item, however, designed for those whose metabolisms run on the same frequency as a hummingbird's, looked a bit strained on Jan, as it would have on most forties-something-. Men would have liked it. Women might look away, or glance at their best friend with raised eyebrows.

As the friends greeted each other with screams of surprise and laughter, and hugged and found places to sit, Mimi reflected that she alone, these last months, had remained entirely unchanged. Not a whit. Nothing. Her life, too. Not a new job, nor man, nor apartment. She never had stolen Wally for a weekend. She'd chopped her bangs and then re-grown them. Her glasses were still the same burgundy plastic, sliding down her nose. She had never bought a different color lipstick or taken up kayaking.

She had a sense suddenly of being left behind. Clogged behind a boulder in the river of life, she couldn't move or see anything but grey.

Jan had brought some bottled sangria. She motioned to a small, perplexed-looking waitress to bring them some glasses, which she did after some moments, hurrying away with their order for double nachos. When their glasses were filled, Mary Beth, in a shy voice, offered, "Here's to our reunion!" They raised their glasses, but Mimi observed that Link did not drink her wine.

"So," Mimi questioned, looking round the table. "What's been happening for everyone?"

Link dragged her long fingers through her rough red hair. "I guess you all can see I've got a new career!"

Mary Beth was leaning over the table, squeezing her contact lens onto her napkin, and she looked up laughing. "Well, it appears you've chosen the visual arts!"

Chuckling and nodding, Link replied, "Yeah, I really did quit that bitchin' bulldog's office, but then, as I was typing up my resume *again*, I said to myself, just blam, suddenly, pop, 'I'm outta here.' I got up from the desk, called my brother Ian, asked him how the painting business was going and how was his heroin-head partner and just as I knew he would somehow, he said that Freaky had split for Key West and some alleged new money-making scheme of his brother's. I knew this all somehow; not like, each exact fact but that some kind of break was in store for me. And so I said, how would he like a new partner, and he said, you know, 'Ahh, M&M, you'll hate it.' And I assured him, 'Absolutely not.' And he said 'well, maybe just till I find somebody else,' but now it's three months and I have done eight jobs, and the lady across the street from my current house just asked me to do hers!"

Link's face shone like a child's with chocolate in her mouth, but the other women were completely silent, looking down or looking above Link's head.

Jan cleared her throat. "Is this sort of a leave of absence?

Link's olive eyes snapped wider. She looked at her friends' expressions just as the waitress plunked the huge nacho platter down in the middle of their table.

"Watch out, ladies. It's mucho caliente! Care to order the rest of the meal? Any sodas?" She peered myopically at Link. "More O.J.?"

"Ah, yes, please." Link glanced at the woman absently and then back to her friends.

"Well." The waitress's tag was labeled, *Louise*. "I mean, did you want to order your food?"

Mimi said softly to Louise, "We haven't looked. We'll just coast for awhile, okay?"

The small woman sagged at this and turned and walked away.

"Jan, what do you mean *leave of absence*? This is it. This is what I want to do." Link gestured, arms wide.

Jan was angry somehow. "Well now, come on, Link. I mean what will you do in the winter?"

"We paint the insides, too."

Mimi patted her friend's hand. "Will you have enough to live on, really?"

"Hey, what does everyone think I am? A flake or something? I have this figured out, really, I do. What I'm looking for is a little support, okay?"

Link's glow dimmed. "There's other stuff I have to tell you; I've waited too long already, and I'm going to need a hell of a lot of support."

The other three sat up straighter and mumbled various affirmative responses.

"I'm ... I'm. I ... " Link was flushed. Jan poured more sangria. Mimi removed her glasses and began polishing them slowly on her blouse.

"Well, what do you think I'm going to say? You all must know by now!"

Mary Beth remarked gently, "Well, you don't drink anymore."

"That!" Link looked stunned. "Well, yes, that's another thing I ... but, you really mean you don't know what I am going to say?"

Neither Mary Beth, Mimi, nor Jan said anything. They were looking at Link, waiting.

"I'm coming out. I'm gay."

Nothing.

Louise was back. "Do you ... "

"We'll call you," Jan replied without looking. Louise silently withdrew.

"I'm a lesbian."

After some long moments, Mary Beth cleared her throat and piped in a small high voice, "How do you know?"

To which Jan rolled her eyes and let out a croaking laugh that caused the people seated near them to turn and stare, and suddenly they were all laughing, their arms thrown over each others' shoulders until they formed a circle of arms and bodies, laughing.

FIFTEEN

THEY WON'T TELL ME

When Mimi entered her apartment, she saw right away that her message machine was blinking. She had forgotten to leave a light on. Standing at her door, she stared for a while at the image of the room going black, then red, black, then red. *It looks like the beginning of a Dracula movie.* She was so tired. Her head was pounding; she thought maybe she should leave it till morning. But then her mother's face flashed across her mind and she shushed over the rug and pressed the glowing button.

"Oh Mimi, it's Grandma Tinker." Her mother's voice was strained. "She's got pneumonia and she wants you to come and see her."

That was all. Mimi flicked on the lamp beside the telephone and checked her watch. Ten-thirty. She called her mother. Mickey answered. She could hear the TV and some cheering. "Where's Mom?"

"Well, she's been at the hospital since five o'clock. Didn't she call you? Grandma's pretty sick."

"Yes, she called. I don't know if I can go over there . . . "

Mickey interrupted. "Wait, there's another call," and he was off the line. She waited, agitated, scared. He came back on and said, "That was Mom. She's coming home—Grandma's stabilized. She wanted to know if you called. Naturally, I said 'no way'. Ha. Ha."

Was he slightly drunk?

"So how's the artist of the family? I never talk to you anymore."

"Well, I've been to the house lots of times, Mickey, to do all the physical labor that a real woman can do while her sissy brother waltzes around at his new car wash."

"Whoa, I just wrote you out of the will. You'll never get Wally now, man!"

"How is my kitty?" She asked, remembering the calico coiled and fat in her lap.

"He is one cool cat. And now we got him a wittle fwiend."

"Another kitty?"

"Whoa, your mind has always slayed me!"

"Mickey! Tell me about him."

"Her. Wailea. She is a little lady with an attitude." Mimi rode a wave of terrible envy.

"Well, I want to see her. Pronto."

"See and salivate at your leisure."

"I'll be over tomorrow after I see Grandma."

"Yes. But if any cat within fifty miles is missing, your life will not be worth much, hear?"

Mimi asked suddenly, "Mickey, what are you doing?"

"Me and fathersan and brothersan are just watching basketball and kicking back and stuff."

"And stuff?"

"You mean, Are we drinking, you little narc?"

"Well?"

"Ah, sissy, I've had two little beers in three big hours. I'm safe and sound."

She thought of Link's orange juice. "Still going to meetings?" She made her voice casual.

"No."

"Hmm."

"Well, you have a good little sleep, Mimi, darlin'. Goodnight."

It was none of her business, really. He was right.

"Oh, Mickey, despite you're being about the jerkiest jerk for a brother a sister could have, my magnanimous nature compels me to say, 'I love you'."

"I love *you*, Mimi Malone." Was that a crack in his voice?

*   *   *   *

Sunnyfield didn't have a single indicator as to the whereabouts of its infirmary, neither on the directory, nor on any of the doors Mimi had yet walked by. It was as though by this omission a positive statement of institutional health could be made. The receptionist was missing from her glassed-in cubicle, and finally she asked a little woman with jet black hair and dried apple skin seated in a wheelchair if she knew where the infirmary was. She'd looked confused and said as though to herself, "Infirmary? No. No. I don't think I have one. But listen, sweetie, can you talk?"

She grasped Mimi's hand in both of her shaking ones; her delicate fingers locked on as she asked a second time, "Can you just talk? They won't tell me where my husband is." Mimi looked at her, startled.

"I . . . " Finally she spotted a caretaker at the end of the hall, a white blaze in the setting sun by the window.   "Can you tell me where the infirmary is?" she called, still in the grip of the wheelchair lady. He turned and moved toward them, a giant Nordic-looking man, and placed his hand on the arm of the chair. "Now, Hannah, you're to let this lady go. She needs to find her husband." Hannah let go immediately.

"You let me know," the lady called after them. "You let me know."

The young man smiled warmly at Mimi as he walked with her down the hall. "Sorry. It's a white lie but it's the only way she lets go. The infirmary is on the fifth floor, the entire fifth floor. We don't have any signs because the ambulatory folks like to get themselves up there for a little extra attention, and it became complete chaos."

"Oh, of course," Mimi laughed and nodded. "And thank you for your help."

He waved goodbye, and she stood smiling after him.

When Mimi found Grandma Tinker, she was lying in her bed, a drying white flower. All her careful curls were gone, brushed into wisps on the pale blue pillow. Her onion-skin seemed pearlized. Her hands lay turned up, and Mimi's eyes sprung quick tears. The old woman was sleeping. Her eyes were rolling beneath her lids like blue marbles beneath piecrust. Mimi tiptoed, retrieved a chair from the corner and sat down without a sound.

"Mimi."

"Yes, yes, Grandma." Mimi started up from her chair.

Grandma's eyes opened slowly, heavy petals. "I'm so tired."

"Yes, of course you're tired. You've been pretty sick."

"Well," she spoke slowly, without her usual spark.

"It came on me, Mimi girl, like a sledgehammer dropped out of the sky."

Mimi was standing now, holding those finely made hands in hers.

"Just a pain so bad and all this coughing." With difficulty, she pulled her hands up and gingerly fingered her ribs. "Ah, they're so sore."

"How do you feel now?" Mimi asked, placing a hand on Grandma's small forehead.

"Oh, fine, fine now, just so darned tired. I can't even watch my shows. I just sleep all the time like an old pig."

"Is there anything I can get you, sweetie?"

"Nothing I could use at this point. Oh, maybe a couple of my nighties. No sense lying here with my rear end hanging out. But the ones that button. They're always listening to my chest. Goodness. This is a fine mess."

"You'll be out of here in no time."

Mimi leaned toward Grandma, who suddenly shut her eyes and seemed to have snapped back into sleep. She tightened the sheet below Grandma's light weight, fluffed the cover sheet and blanket, and pulled them up, folding them neatly under her chin. She then sat back down, uncertain as to what she should do next.

It was seven o'clock in the evening, and the sun was low in the September sky. Mimi could see the cool blue deepening in slices through the blinds. She thought of how the year goes on, how heartless it is, this cycle. How heedless of our need for time to be manageable, to be in our grasp. September. Children reluctant toward school. Apples. Groaning school buses. Then the holidays, and the snows, and the bitterness, and the wind—the hostile wind. The end and then the beginning. And a beginning trailing an end. She sat for a long time into darkness when a nurse came in and, sure enough, listened to Grandma's heart and took her pulse and her blood pressure and then her temperature through her ear with some high-tech throwaway thermometer. Through all this, the old lady slept. Mimi followed the nurse out of the room and asked out of earshot what the prognosis was. The nurse's name was Nancy; she was friendly and very young. She explained, gently reading Mimi's face, "Miss Tinker's old and weak. We also discovered that she's anemic, which has greatly lessened her energy, but she *is* on the mend and we expect a complete, although somewhat slow, recovery. You must be Mimi." Mimi nodded.

"She talks about you. She's much more alert in the morning hours. A remarkable woman!" Look, I'm here in geriatrics Wednesday, Thursday, and Friday — three to eleven. If you have a question, just call me." She patted Mimi's arm. "And don't worry."

Mimi tiptoed back into the room where the nurse had left an indirect light on above the bed. She noticed the heart monitor silently pulsing above the still-sleeping woman's head, a small green cartoon. Mimi sat again, feeling fear and something she could not quite name.

"Oh, Mimi." Grandma sat up in bed, suddenly alert, her old self completely, pale blushes on her cheeks.

Mimi jumped up and felt the woman's head for fever.

"Yes, Grandma? I'm here."

"Of course you are. I almost forgot. Harold had to get right back, but he looks fine, don't you think?"

"You saw him?"

"Didn't you pass him in the hall?"

"No."

"But he left not thirty seconds before you came in. You didn't see him? Alice told him about me and he flew in right away. He's still quiet as a rug, but he's always been a good boy."

"Grandma, Alice doesn't know where Harold is. Nobody does so . . . and actually, you were sleeping soundly when I came in."

"Wasn't. And we know where he is now."

"But . . ."

Now Grandma was quite red. She gestured and shook her head toward the sink in the room. "There, there, the white box. There was too damn much stuff on my bed table."

Obediently, Mimi walked to the sink; she saw nothing but a comb and a scraggly brush. But behind the faucets was lodged a slim white box.

"That's it."

The old lady's hands shook with exhaustion or emotion.

"Bring that to me; it's his present. I'm supposed to look at it to feel better."

Her pale fingers loosened the lid with difficulty, and she seized a silver picture frame from the white tissue. "There." She looked at it first, then held it out to Mimi. "That's where."

Now Mimi's hands trembled. She took the picture and looked at it, holding her breath. She felt crushed with disappointment. It was an old, old photograph, black and white; it was no place or house that she'd known. The house stood, an aging wooden cabin, on a frosted plain; towering in the distance were pale and darkish foothills. The sky was a flat medium grey, snow on the ground—not interesting, nothing memorable that she could note. It was some weird mistake, and she did not know how to respond.

Mimi took the box from Grandma's hand and tucked the picture carefully inside. She walked to the sink and placed it once again behind the faucets; when she returned to the bed, Grandma Tinker had lain back on the pillow and was sleeping soundly, her rosy cheeks paling, cool now to Mimi's touch.

SIXTEEN

MINNESOTA

"Mom?" She was never so glad to hear Alice's voice.

"Mimi, dear, how was Grandma tonight? I'm so grateful you went; I just had to get to guild and . . . "

"I . . . she . . . " Mimi suddenly found it hard to breathe and abruptly, she began sobbing.

"What is it, Mimi, what—is she doing poorly? Are you calling from the infirmary?"

"No!" Mimi struggled to stop, to breathe. "She's at least okay. She goes in and out of sleep so suddenly; it's scary."

"But the nurse, that nice one—she says that's normal. But . . . " Mrs. Piccolo's voice was strained, questioning.

"She had this picture. She showed me this picture . . . " Mimi resumed her crying, more quietly. "She says that Harold brought it in . . . "

"Harold!"

"Yes, she says he flew in as soon as he heard—she said you told Harold, but that he couldn't stay. That he was there, right there before I came in and did I see him in the hall? And that he gave her a picture of where he lives, but that can't be because the picture is so old. It's black and white, grainy; I don't know where she got it from, still . . . "

"Mimi, Mimi, listen to me. Listen. Grandma was probably running a fever and just thought she'd seen him. He isn't here. He probably isn't anywhere; who would have called him?

That's just not possible, and as for the picture—well, I can't explain that, but just suppose the patient before left it, or that kind orderly from the residence floor brought it to her. Maybe it's where *he* grew up and she was confused. She's ninety-six and running fevers. Mimi, dear, oh . . . I could come over and . . . "

Her voice trailed off. She never liked to drive at night. Even for the Ladies Guild—someone always picked her up.

"No. No. I, I'll be all right. I just, I don't know what it was. I almost hoped he had come, even if he'd come to see Grandma and not me . . . but when I saw the picture, I knew right away and I, I don't know what exactly I'm feeling except maybe—I don't know what it is."

"Mimi, you're exhausted. You need to take a hot bath and read something funny and silly." Alice was firm.

"You're probably right. Right. I just freaked. All of it, Grandma lying there, so weak, and that second, that microsecond of hope that shot through me like an arrow. You're right. A bath is perfect. Thanks mom."

Mimi was perspiring—her head, her arms, between her breasts.

"Look, call me after you go in tomorrow. Let me know how she seems to you. My mom's going in at eleven."

"Of course, dear. Will you be all right? I could come over . . . "

"No. No, actually, just telling you . . . No, I'm fine. I'll hang up now."

"Well, all right, we'll talk tomorrow then. Remember, you have an appointment with Mr. McClosky—soon, right?

"Monday. Yes, I haven't forgotten. Goodnight, Alice."

"Love you, Mimi, Goodnight."

Mimi hung up the phone and went around her apartment snapping off the lights she had only moments ago switched on. She went to the kitchen and retrieved one of two cans of beer from the rear of the fridge, went back to the living room and scrunched onto the windowsill to look out into the street. Like cards being flipped in front of her, she saw Grandma lying so still, white. Then sitting up, her eyes dark with feeling, gesturing so animatedly. Again and again. First one card then the other. Then the old wooden house, a crease across its corner. Nancy's hand on her arm, "don't worry." Don't worry. Suddenly, Mimi wanted to break something. To feel something shatter and rip from the force of her body. She crushed the can in one hand and then dashed to the kitchen for the last of the beer. She opened the kitchen window. A small breeze flew up into her hair. Grabbing the beer from the refrigerator, she almost ran back to her perch at the window. The streetlight directly across from her apartment buzzed. Insects stumbled into the light and out again.

"Well, what do they want in that light?" she spoke aloud, angry.

Diagonally, across the street, a small boy in torn blue jeans sat on his sagging wooden porch steps. He was perhaps nine. Mimi wondered why he wasn't sleeping. He pulled at his sandy hair repeatedly. *Now that's odd.* She swallowed. At last, he got up and went inside. His house snapped dark all at once, like a candle blown out. She crushed the second can and pitched it into the street, its tinny clunk completely unsatisfying.

Mimi rose and began to pace, touching things she liked in the darkness. The old glass doorknobs. The sculpture of the woman she had made in high school kneeling on rippling water, her shoulders thrown back, looking with longing toward the sky. How cold it was. The crocheted cover on the teapot her mother had made for her when she'd gotten her first apartment. The long chrome kitchen sink faucet, the Flokati rug in the bathroom. She sat down and ran her fingers through its long hairs, listening for bathtub drips. The world was still, but her heart flapped erratically inside her chest. Suddenly, Mimi jumped up, went into the kitchen and dialed the wall phone.

St. Timothy's message machine. "God Bless you, caller. " Please leave your message and number and Fathers Patrick or Ben will return your call as soon as possible."

Mimi smashed the receiver against the base, went into her bedroom and began tearing off her clothes. The cordless was ringing. *Where the hell is it?* She thrashed at the pillows and through the blankets that lay on the floor. *Shit.* Running into the kitchen, she plucked the phone from the wall just as her message machine clicked on, then off.

"Yes." She was out of breath.

"Mimi?"

"Oh!"

"The phone just rang here. I was on my way up to bed and I don't know. Sorry to call so late. I thought . . . that maybe you . . . "

She began to cry.

"What is it? What is it, Mimi?"

Ben's voice was as she remembered it, rumbling, fierce if you didn't know him. But it was useless. She was past words. She had surrendered to some great force. She was going down and could fight no more. Mimi hung up and went back to the bathroom and her hairy rug upon which she lay curled, and cried like something torn open, for Grandma, for the boy pulling his hair, for the log cabin picture, for herself the wedded widow, for the wheelchair woman with her jet black hair, for Jan and Mary Beth, and Link, and for her mother, forgetting and trying to hide it, for her father's brave smile and Mickey, slurring his speech, for the water that stays in the reservoir, for Gerry Mertz and his Kelly green jacket. The night was still and she was rolling inside of it, keening. She knew something suddenly, that she'd never known before—that life is for the very, very strong, which she was not. That life is for the brave and for the certain, neither of which she'd ever be. She was rolling, a lurching ball, and she did not know where she would end up. She did not care.

She must have fallen asleep, and in her dream, someone was calling her name; there was pounding, hammering—a building going up, but when she woke, the pounding continued and her name, over and over. She staggered from the bathroom in the dark and headed toward the living room door.

"Mimi, are you there? Open up. Please, Mimi. Please open the door."

She swung the door wide, dragging her hands through her damp hair. Father Ben stood there, a sweatshirt pulled over his pajamas.

"Mimi. Mimi, my god what's happened? What is it?"

Mimi fell to her knees and bent her head to the floor. "I can't do it. I can't do it anymore. And then she was screaming, "No. No. No. I can't do it. I can't live this life. I know God will understand. I'm tired. I'm TIRED!"

Ben knelt beside her and gathered her into his arms. "No. No. Mimi, no." He began to kiss her forehead. "No, no, Mimi. So many people love you. How would it be for them? Just as you feel now, so many you would leave behind would feel. No. No. Pain makes us forget all the other parts of our life. But you mustn't forget."

At this she called out, and raised her arms against him.

"Stop it. Stop it. Don't priest-talk me. You have all the answers. I don't want my life. You can have it. You do it for a while. You don't know what you're talking about."

She pounded his chest and struggled to get up. She was out the door and down the steps. She took off like a pursued Springbok, her bare feet slapping the sidewalk. Up Myrtle Hill— she knew he would never make it. But she could hear him behind her. She slid down the other side of the hill and slipped into Swanee Creek. The water was so cold that for a moment she stood rigid at the shock and then she plunged and the water drew over her, an icy blanket.

Very quickly, Ben was wrestling her; she struggled against him. "Stop it. Let me go. Let me go." She could see the stripes of his pajamas in the moonlight. But now Ben shook her, shook her so hard she could feel her teeth in her mouth.

"Can't you see what you're doing is so selfish? So Goddamn selfish." He shook her violently as he said this.

Surprised and enraged, she flung her hand up to slap him when she saw his face, his eyes.

"Don't Mimi. Don't." He dropped his head onto her shoulder and they stood there like children in the woods, lost and hopeless.

Finally, Ben picked his sweatshirt from the grass where he had tossed it and pulled it over Mimi's head. It was then she saw that she was in her half slip and bra. They stumbled back up Myrtle Hill and down the other side and then home. He placed her in her bed, removed her clothing, patted her dry, found an extra blanket and covered her. Then, falling forward on the bed, he collapsed.

When she awoke, alone in her bed, she lay still, thinking of these events as her latest dream, but when she went to the bathroom she saw her bra and slip hung neatly over the shower curtain rod, still damp as she felt them gingerly. Her feet ached and she remembered running up Myrtle Hill, surely faster than she'd ever run before. And the water. How cold, how it hadn't been deep enough. She got into the shower and let it rain hot water over her for a long time.

"I have to do something. I have to find out something." She kept repeating these words as she dressed. She then walked into the kitchen and stared out at the Honey Locust for a long time. Its leaves were the barest lime of early fall. She made coffee and took her mug to the table where there was a note from Ben, folded over the salt and pepper shakers. She scanned it. *Crazy broad.*

He had written the names and addresses of two psychiatrists and what he knew of their reputations. He begged her to see one of them and announced firmly that she needed more support for her situation. And finally, *Mimi, I've never known anyone like you. I would grieve forever if anything ever happened to you. You are in my prayers daily, hourly. Ben.*

She sat numb. She knew absolutely at that moment that she could not stay in this much pain and therefore, alive, for anyone. Suddenly, she started up from the table and ran to her bedroom where she pulled an old brown suitcase from her closet. She began to stuff it haphazardly with mostly underwear, a skirt, a sweater. She tumbled her bathroom things into a plastic bag and grabbed her winter jacket from the hall closet. As she sat warming her car, she looked in the rearview mirror and saw her own madwoman's face.

"Now what?" She called to whatever was directing her. Mimi drove to Sunnyfield and went to Grandma's room. She was sleeping soundly, with a healthier color on her skin. Mimi crept toward the sink and, just as her fingers had nearly closed around the box, heard, "You can have that, Mimi, if you bring it back."

It was Grandma Tinker's voice, but when Mimi glanced at the bed, Grandma had not sat up; her eyes fluttered open only when she'd spoken her sentence. Mimi stole out with the picture and drove across town in the hazy sunlight to St. Joseph's where she sat in her car a moment, combing her hair. She asked to speak to Pete Piccolo and was told he was finishing his breakfast. Could she wait for ten minutes?

"Yes," was all she could answer, and for several long minutes she paced the ill-smelling lobby.

"Mimi! It's not even Sunday and you're here!" The old man looked elated.

She hugged him briefly and dragged him onto a sagging sofa. She opened Grandma's white box and plunked the old photograph into Pete's hands.

He looked at it for some moments and then into Mimi's face, confused. Mimi's heart sank. She thought she'd been onto something.

"Why are you bringing me this old picture, Mimi?"

"I just thought. I thought it might mean something. I thought, I don't actually know what I thought . . . "

"But how did you get it?"

Mimi was blushing fiercely. "I, . . . Grandma Tinker loaned it to me."

"But I can't understand that. This picture is Harold's."

Mimi mumbled something about how Harold must have given the old photograph to Grandma and how she must have forgotten. This she half-believed herself, trying not to hear the "Why?" deep within her head. What the old man said next amazed her.

"Mimi, this is the place!"

"Pete, what place?"

His eyes were burning. "We talked about it. The old place in Idaho. Why, Harold took this picture himself as a little kid. Yep, my own brother Harry's place."

Mimi was stunned. "What . . . do you know what happened to it? I mean . . . is it . . . your brother . . . ?"

"Harry, no, he's been gone, why he was sixteen years older than myself. No. It's crazy, but I don't know what happened to it. I'd just thought his kids would sell it and that would be that. Probably a peck of houses on that land right now and a shopping mall out by the hills."

"Pete." Mimi heard the high tightness in her voice. "Where are Harry's kids? Now."

"Well, scattered every direction. None of them stuck around in Idaho. Hated it. And now, I don't think I know . . . there's one kid that made it kind of big in New York, on the stage. Joey. Joseph Piccolo. Him you might be able to find."

Mimi felt herself fragmenting, some of those fragments alive with the bright pain of hope, some dissolving into exhaustion, some shards of anger as she discovered she did not know her husband at all well. His history. His relationships. What had they talked about?

After excusing herself to Pete, who looked actually sheepishly grateful, probably because she had worn him out, Mimi sped to her car only to sit paralyzed under a darkening sky. *A storm is coming.* For the second time that day she stared, saying, "Now what?" She started the engine at last as the first tongs of lightning forked the sky. She drove slowly, empty, until she saw a sign, "Doolittle's Pharmacy" where she pulled in and turned off the motor. She yanked out her change purse, dumped its contents on the passenger seat and grabbed two quarters and four dimes. She then pulled down the visor where she had taped Jack McClosky's business card. Taking the change and the card, she found a pay phone and called his office. Jack himself had made the message.

"This is the J. McClosky Detective Agency. We answer your inquiries twenty-four hours a day if you remember to leave your number. Please leave your name unless you can refer to your case with extreme specificity. Thank you."

"Jack, this is Mimi Malone and . . . um, I think—it's a weird, weird thing, but I think I have something or maybe part of something. Um, about Harold. I'm . . . well, I'm actually not sure where . . . I'm driving . . . and then . . . Well, I'll call and check in with you later. She placed the phone in its chrome cradle and ran through the fat raindrops to her Metro where she again sat blank and uncertain. She got back out and called Alice.

"Alice," she breathed into the phone.

"Honey, are you out in the rain, what is it dear?"

"No. Yes, no. Alice, where in Idaho did Harold go with Pete for a month—a whole bunch of summers when he was little. Uncle Harry's. Do you remember?"

"Did Jack ask you that?"

"No, no. Do you know the town?"

"Well, I mean, I should know that, sure. Ah, well, let's see. Right on the tip of my . . . I'm a little forgetful these days. Harold loved it, there were mountains. Let's see. I know it had something to do with birds . . . "

Mimi felt exasperated. "You mean like Lark or Robinsville," she prompted.

Alice responded excitedly, "Yes, something like that. Ah, bird, wing, umm . . . Talk to me about something else for just a minute and I'll think of it."

Mimi dabbed at her eyes with her knuckles,

"Umm, ah . . . I just came from seeing Grandma Tinker. I can't believe how much better she is. She said you had been in last eve, . . . Downieville!" said Alice.

"Oh, Downieville. Where the farmhouse was—the ranch or whatever?"

Alice replied, "There, I knew it had something to do with birds, but why do you need to know, dear? You know Uncle Harry's dead, don't you?"

"Yes, I know. I don't exactly know why I want to know . . . Where is Downieville?"

"I've never been there. Oh, dear, umm. I think Pops said . . . "

"Pete?"

"Yes, ah, Pops said they stopped short of Boise. Other than that I can't say. But Mimi, you should come over here, I well, you sound funny. I'm worried."

"I'll be all right. I'll come over, maybe later. I'm just thinking now . . . and driving."

"Mimi?"

"Mom, I'll be all right. Don't worry."

Mimi reached her car just as the storm approached its zenith. She felt no fear under the carwash of rain and the booming thunder. *There is not one thought in my head. There is only this force which I cannot seem to fight.* When the storm began to lessen, she again started her car and began driving. She found herself approaching the North West Toll Road, reached one of the access lanes, and entered the highway. Mimi felt the sense of a gate having swung open. A sense that she was leaving something behind, something enormous and heavy, but beyond that she concentrated on her driving and listened to tapes that had been sliding around the car floor, unheard, for years. She sung in her pleasant alto, old folk songs, Dylan, Janis Joplin.

"I'm singing *driving* songs," she said aloud. "And I'm driving!"

Her mother's voice called inside Mimi's head, "Just where are you going? What are you doing?" But Mimi snapped off the tape player and sang out, "I'm driving to the sea of love. I'm driving to the sea of love. There's a great Red River valley flowing free and full of love; I left my home in the flatland. Driving to the sea of love. Sea of love. Sea of love. I left my home in the flatland and I'm driving to the sea of love."

She sang louder and louder until the hinges of her jaw ached and her eardrums began to vibrate. By early evening she had reached Madison, but something urged her on toward Minnesota. Finally, about ten o'clock, she began looking for a place to sleep and found one easily, a few miles east of Rochester, the Sleep Inn, which was serviceable, quiet, and clean. And most importantly, to Mimi, cheap.

SEVENTEEN

TWO THICK WHITE CUPS

TWO THICK WHITE CUPS

In her room and settled, she realized she had not eaten all day. Fear shot through her when she thought of looking for a place alone and late at night. But as soon as she locked the motel door and turned around, she noticed a silver diner with the name "Suzy's" in orange neon, directly across the highway. She walked to the intersection, crossed the wide road, and opened the door to the restaurant with a feeling of finding some great treasure in the back of one's closet. It seemed there was even a Suzy, a red-haired woman, barely tall enough to see over the counter. Her hair had been tinted and fried into neat fuzzy sausages. Her glasses were black and pointed at their tips; but Mimi doubted that Suzy knew nor cared that such fashion had come and gone and returned, that high school girls all over the nation now sported similar eye decoration. She wore a spotless butter-yellow uniform with a white ruffled apron and a little nurse-type cap on her curls. A pearly chain originated from her earpieces and danced along her pale wrinkled neck; it bobbed wildly as she came out from behind the counter to shoo Mimi with a menu into a small plastic booth.

"What's a pretty girl like you doing all alone on the road at night?"

"Why's a pretty lady like you working such late hours?"

Suzy laughed. Above her name badge she had pinned a tiny picture of some laughing toddlers, two boys. She pointed to them with a gloppy pen. "For these, right there. They're my sweethearts."

"Are they your grandsons?"

"Yep. Quinlin and Spence, kinda fancy names, I think, but their mother likes that sort. Fancy."

"Is she wealthy, then?"

"Ha." Suzy's head rocked back, and her glasses flew up a bit onto her forehead. She replaced them and looked directly into Mimi's eyes.

"Not where she is she ain't." Then nodding for added significance, she continued. "Jail. A woman and these little angels' mother."

Suzy shook her head side to side. Then she asked Mimi what she wanted to eat. Mimi scanned the specials on the old blackboard above the counter and ordered meatloaf, mashed potatoes, and green beans. She could have eaten the evening newspaper. The old waitress shuffled away busy, urging the Hispanic man at the grill. The group of men who had been sitting talking quietly to one another at the counter, crows on a telephone wire, Mimi thought—began to break up and gather their jackets from hooks by the door. As they said their good-byes, they called various terms of endearment (*sweetheart, Suzie-babe*), but the last man to leave called back from the opening door, "Sleep tight, Grandma Freud." Suzy laughed and made a dismissing motion with her hand; then she shuffled back to Mimi and dropped a meat platter-sized plate onto Mimi's table with an added salad and a hard roll.

"Oh, my! I don't know if I can eat all this."

Suzy ignored Mimi, smiled, and turned and went to the door and locked it, switched off some outside lights and turned the sign in the window to "closed."

She came and sat on the last stool of the counter kitty-cornered to Mimi's booth and pulled a pack of "Basics" from her apron pocket and a clear plastic lighter. She didn't ask Mimi if she could smoke but motioned the pack toward her.

Mimi shook her head.

"Maybe later," she said, as best she could through a mouthful of mashed potatoes. "Your food is good. Just so good. I feel like I could eat all night. Are you closed now? I'm keeping you, aren't I?"

"No customer keeps me. I'm just having my rest before I go home." She scratched at some loose food bits on her apron. The man at the grill gathered all the utensils and pots and began running them under a huge spray of steaming water, singing something in Spanish.

"Ya watch everything." The old woman commented.

Mimi wiped her lips with the napkin, the odor of bleach stinging her nose.

"Do you think so?"

"Yep. Them big eyes don't miss one anything."

Mimi laughed. "Maybe that's what keeps me tired all the time."

"I wouldn't doubt it. Whatcha looking for?" Suzy was trying to pick a piece of tobacco from between her teeth with her thumbnail. The ash on her cigarette was long and curved.

Mimi pushed her empty plate away. "That's what's funny. I don't know."

Suzy showed no reaction to this. "Where ya driving from?"

"From near Chicago, by Elgin."

"And to where?"

Mimi could feel herself blushing. "Umm. I think Idaho."

She sat, cheeks aflame, glancing toward the floor. Mimi could see the shine of Suzy's pantyhose, the purple and red currents of veins running the length of the old woman's legs.

The waitress ignored her *I think* and asked, "What's in Idaho?"

"Well, probably nothing. My husband used to go there to a boyhood place. His Grandpa, Pete, would take him for a month—a bunch of summers when he was little."

Suzie pulled the cigarettes from her pocket and fingered for the lighter. Mimi could feel her gaze on the top of her head. "Do ya want some coffee? Still good."

Mimi looked up and nodded. "Decaf," she requested.

The waitress moved across the floor. Mimi could see, by the way she walked, that her feet must be hurting. Suzy got down two thick white cups and poured from two different pots simultaneously. She brought them and placed them both on Mimi's table.

"Can I sit?"

"Please."

Suzy lit another cigarette and shoved the pack toward Mimi who awkwardly poked for one, but then could not get the lighter to work. The waitress mumbled over her cigarette that the child catch was engaged and finally took the implement and lit Mimi's cigarette herself.

Mimi was dizzy instantly, but it tasted fine.

"I don't know why, but it feels good to be here. Is the mother of Quinlin and Spence your daughter?"

"God, no." Suzy shook her head. She was my son's wife.

"And your son?"

"I see him sometimes. He's running parole, sneaks back into town to see the boys and drops me some cash if he isn't borrowing some. He was a good, good boy. He started driving a cab nights and just everything changed. She was a whore—claimed she was done with that. Found out she was pregnant with Quinlin and they moved in together, and quick along comes Spence and everything goes to hell. Seems they both got started on heroin. I had to take the kids. Poor things got to have a sitter most times. But now I got things so I don't come in here till eleven. Got a good lady for the afternoon and evenings for them."

"How old are you?" Mimi wanted to know.

"Seventy. Can't keep (here she waved her hand, ashes sprinkling) this up much longer." Then she turned back to Mimi. "What about your husband?"

"Excuse me?"

"What are you gonna do if you find him?"

"I don't plan on finding him."

Suzy looked off for a quiet moment.

And Mimi remarked, "I didn't say he was lost."

"Didn't have to." Suzy stubbed her cigarette onto Mimi's empty plate. "Why are ya driving to him then?"

"I'm not." Mimi rummaged through her purse and brought out the picture. "I'm driving toward this."

Suzy's face darkened, and she almost dropped the picture on the table. She cleared her throat. "Why are you driving to a house?"

"I want to see if it's still there. I want to see it."

Suzy was looking off again; Mimi wasn't certain she was listening. She spoke with a faraway sort of voice. "Sometimes, occasionally, I get feelings . . . about things, about people's stories."

Weakly, Mimi got out, "Feelings . . . ?"

Suzy looked at Mimi. She was at once startled by her eyes. Mimi had never seen anything like them. *Like glass. Like glass.* They were eerily pale.

"Today. Tonight when I saw you. Well, before I saw you. When I felt you come through that door, I had a strong feeling. A bad feeling. It was a bad feeling."

"Oh . . . " Mimi whispered.

Suzy patted Mimi's hand. "Not about you, darlin. What I feel coming from you's pretty good, sad and kind of frantic, but pretty good."

"Are you a kind of fortune-teller?" Mimi asked.

Suzy placed a magenta tipped finger to her wrinkled mouth. "Shh. Not that. I'm all dry most times. Just sometimes."

"When . . ."

"When? Well, for the bigger things. Then I get more."

"What are you getting, now?"

"Well, I had this dark feeling. Don't think you could tell, but when I saw this house—there is so much unhappiness coming from it . . . it's like this house got built from unhappiness."

EIGHTEEN

CLARET

Mimi could see the orange *Suzy's* through a slit in the curtains, but she did not get out of bed to close them. She sat leaning against the glued-on headboard of the hard bed in her motel room.

Unhappiness. A house built of unhappiness. What did that mean? And here she was, driving toward unhappiness as if she didn't have enough already.

*   *   *   *

Her mother was standing with plants in her hands, two clay pots of impatiens. The plants were dying in front of Mimi's eyes. The leaves first grew pale green while the fuchsia blossoms washed to pink. Then the plants began to wither, shuddering slightly in their pots, which then cracked and fell from her mother's hands. The loose dirt rained down through her fingers. Finally, her mother stood with her open hands full of yellow roots. When she glanced at her, Mimi saw tears streaming down the furrows of her mother's face, and her hair—how white, how white and straight it had become!

"Look, look at these. If only Harold had come home!" Her mother cried.

Mimi bolted upright in bed. She could feel that her jaws had been clenched tight for some time. Where was she? She glanced across the room to a small table with its single chair, to a picture of ducks rising toward the sky. Was it autumn? The picture was a palette of beiges; it made Mimi feel strangely sad before she was quite awake.

"I better call my mother," she said into the bathroom mirror. She splashed water onto her face. "I know a guilt dream when I have one."

When her mother came on the line, she asked where Mimi was and why she had not told her and couldn't she tell her own mother where she was going and what about Grandma Tinker—wasn't this a funny time for a fling? All this Mimi suffered her mother, remembering the white of her dream-hair— its strange straightness. Finally, Edie wanted to know, "Does this have anything to do with Harold?"

"Ah, yes, but I don't know exactly what."

"Well." Her mother was annoyed. "You don't have to be secretive with me, you know."

"Oh, Mom, I know that. It's just . . . I don't really know what I'm doing, myself, I mean."

"By the way," Edie went on as though she had not heard Mimi. "That Jack called. The detective. That's how I heard you were gone. But all he would say was that you were 'driving.' Looks like the two of you are keeping secrets."

"No, Mom, no, Jack knows no more than you do. Has he any input?"

"He asked if you had ever mentioned anything about Harold's Uncle Harry?"

"He asked that?"

"What's Harry got to do with anything?"

"Harold used to go to Uncle Harry's during the summers . . . as a child."

"Oh, goodness! That's so long ago. I think this Jack is barking up the wrong tree."

Mimi felt exhausted. "Yeah. Yeah, probably."

Finally, Mimi said she was famished, asked after Grandma, and managed to hang up the receiver though she thought her mother might still be talking.

* * * *

Back on 90, Mimi drove in silence, subdued with breakfast and the memory of Suzy's dark pronouncement. *A house built of unhappiness.* That's what she'd become. The day was cloudy, the wind gusty, blowing her small car to and fro, so that she had to concentrate more than she wanted to on her driving and the heedless semis rolling by. She drove on, forehead tensed, wipers slapping, till darkness began to fall. She had no more thoughts. Near Sioux Falls, she pulled off the highway and into a Howard Johnson's, where she registered and went to her room. Feelings of guilt began to collect in her stomach.

"Is this a fling?" She wondered, looking over the map. "Am I playing with my own fantasies? When will I be ready to face it, to say it? He's dead. Harold's dead. I must shake him off and be done with it."

She opened the old brown suitcase and took out her skirt and blouse. She had forgotten hose, a slip, and a jacket. She removed her things and dropped into a hot, foamy bath where she fought off sleep. Then she walked about a half-block down the highway, her bare legs nipped by the wind, catching sight of her ensemble in the store windows—cream-colored skirt, cream-colored silk blouse, cream-colored pumps and denim jacket, unsummered legs. She thought of those black bands over unsuspecting women in fashion magazines—their fashion faux pas. She was one of them.

When she happened upon Le Cafe Petite, she was surprised by its blue and white gingham charm, the cherry red front door. She walked in and realized immediately that she was its single patron. Looking about in confusion, she was just about to head back to her car when a man in a tuxedo, tall and foreign-looking, emerged from the dark rear of the restaurant.

"Bon soir, Mademoiselle," he said kindly, very quietly, indicating a chair beneath a picture of The *Kiss*.

I'm afraid my 'mademoiselle' days are but a memory, she thought.

"So, you *are* open?" She looked around, still uncertain.

"Ah, yes, but Sioux Falls does not seem to know this, eh? And for the favor of your trying our cafe we wish to bring you a glass of wine on the house. I think you are a Claret? Am I correct?"

She laughed and felt a blush bloom toward her ears.

"Why yes, that would be wonderful!"

She sat down quickly, pulling her white legs beneath the blue and white checked cloth and began to remove her denim jacket awkwardly. She had just finished wrestling with it when the waiter came back with the bright red wine in a clear bubble of a glass. He tugged at the wrists of the jacket for her and then hung it on the chair opposite.

"You will dine alone?" The waiter asked, avoiding her eyes and sweeping a crumb from the table.

"I'm afraid so." Mimi felt suddenly apologetic, imagining the kitchen crew summoned from their cloudy ponderings for a single (and additionally, unsophisticated) diner.

"But that must be an aberration, no?"

She knew this trick. He would charm her into spending much more than she should, all the while pressing her for small indiscreet confidences, and then not look at her after she had paid the bill.

"I'm a widow," she offered, ignoring her own instincts.

"Ah, but no, you are too young!"

Mimi saw that he looked serious, not wearing the look of mock horror she had expected.

"Perhaps sometime when you feel like it, you can tell me this story." He bowed slightly as he said this, and she could not help laughing.

"Well, actually, I don't live here. In Sioux Falls, I mean."

"No? Where then?"

"Ah, near Elgin, near, er, in Illinois, western, northern Illinois."

He walked to the desk, got a checkered menu and placed it in her hands.

"And are you going home or going away?"

"Well, I'm going away, but just briefly."

He offered his hand. "I am Henri. I will help you. I will give you some time, eh."

She opened the menu, but could choose nothing. The words swam. "Concentrate," she told herself, "Think."

Henri returned. For a split-second, his expression reminded Mimi of the monkey in the movie *Heidi* just before he'd begun throwing the candles down.

"What will you be starting with?"

Mimi was blank. She glanced up at the waiter and heard her voice come from far off, small and tinny. "I don't seem to know what I want. I don't have any idea. I . . . "

Henri grabbed a chair from the table next to Mimi's, sat beside her and held the menu, as if he was about to read to someone. He placed the fingers of his right hand on Mimi's left shoulder. Let me see you. Let me see."

She looked at the waiter's face. But there was no flirtation there. He was concentrating. After a moment of this, he stood up, snapped the menu shut and returned the chair to its table. He then faced Mimi and said quietly, "I will return shortly."

And he did with hot rolls, fragrant herbs emanating from their steam, and a largish glass of champagne that he placed in front of her, smiling.

"Oh, but no, I don't think . . . "

"You are on a journey, no?"

"Yes, and, but . . . "

"Every journey is an answer, don't you think?"

"Not, well not necessarily. Sometimes . . . "

"What is your name?"

"Mimi."

"Mimi, we all need champagne for our answers."

She laughed, and he skirted away once more.

Mimi buried her roll in butter and stared at *The Kiss* on the wall beside her table. She hated photographs of sculpture. She thought it was an insult to the artist. Thinking back to Paris, to the days she thought she would paint forever, maybe stay there, fall in love. Her own trips to see the Louvre and Rodin's work. How it never failed to thrill and terrify her simultaneously. She had had boyfriends, had made love, but Rodin's work she knew to be something else, something about power and surrender and weakness and force and then all those things getting mixed up, so that you couldn't tell which was which. They weren't actually two figures. They were some kind of storm. Some kind of storm at sea with the clouds and waves and winds tossed about and was it the sea that made the rain or the rain that made the sea? And how could terrible force be beautiful? She had understood, however these things were, that she had never known them. Rodin understood something of which she was completely ignorant. And with a start, she realized these many years later that that fact remained unchanged.

The plate in Henri's hand was crystal, faceted, and caught the candlelight as he, moving his arm like a dancer's, deposited a salad of small butter lettuce leaves, red grapes, pistachio nuts and bits of feta before her.

"Magic," she called out, "I love this!"

"Bon appétit!" And he was gone again.

There was no music. She ate, and smiled, unsure of quite why, except for the quirky nature of it all. Sioux Falls and French food, and bare legs and denim on silk, the empty room, the strange, pleasant feeling of being a kid alone at Grandma's house.

Mimi was already beginning to feel full when Henri returned with her second course, a plate of scallops, golden from sautéing, tossed with bits of browned red peppers. Potatoes, small as thumbs, made a half circle at the plate's edge.

"Ah, no. My favorite!" She stared at Henri. "Where did you learn to read minds, from being a waiter or from your mother?"

He only laughed at Mimi's question, and slipped away again. When he returned, he brought another bubble of Claret.

But this time Mimi was firm. "No. I cannot have any more. I must drive all day tomorrow."

But he placed the glass opposite Mimi and replied, "Mimi, if you permit me, I should like to join you for a few minutes. I will let my other customers wait."

A small icicle of fear slid through her, but she nodded, and Henri sat down. She noticed, in the candlelight, a rather large scar shooting through his right eyebrow.

"Yes." He fingered it lightly. "I am lucky to have my eye. This is from a very angry Portuguese woman."

She laughed and drank the last of her champagne.

"What is it that happened to your husband? Can you tell me, or is it too terrible to talk about? And I am a stranger, not really, but I respect your feelings about that."

Mimi cleared her throat and looked for a long while into Henri's remarkably serene face. "I don't know what happened to my husband. He went away and never came back."

"How long?"

"Two years."

"Then actually, he could be alive, no?"

"Well, no, I don't think so."

"Why is that?" Henri picked up the napkin by his glass and leaned forward to dab at Mimi's eyes. "Well," he said quietly, "of course he would have written to explain, something, of course."

She nodded. He softly stroked her hand while she sat dabbing at her eyes.

"I think you are bringing something to a crisis, with this trip, eh?"

"Why do you say that?"

"Because this is what I feel."

"But I don't. I feel aimless. Crazy."

"Because you are following your instincts."

She stared at Henri a long moment. "I guess so. I should be taking care of Grandma Tinker."

"Mimi must take care of Mimi." He placed a finger under her chin, and she laughed. "Speaking of which, you must go home and go to bed now. I will walk you to your door."

Again that same sliver of fear, but she did not want to walk alone in the cold and dark back to the motel.

"Won't you be missed?"

"By whom?"

"Why, ah the cooks, the boss . . . "

"I am the cook and I am the boss. See how convenient?"

"You made that dinner?"

"Yes, of course. Men do cook, you know."

She once again felt self-conscious as he helped her slip into her denim jacket. They walked across the room and out the door, which Henri locked behind him, and fought an icy wind all the way to the Howard Johnson's. Henri slipped his arm around her shoulders and held her tightly; she could feel his thin body shivering in the cold.

"You've no coat!"

He laughed and shouted, "That's okay, I've got my love to keep me warm."

At the orange-painted door, he asked for her key, and she gave it to him. He opened it and took her inside. "You'll be all right then?" he asked, turning to face her.

"Yes, yes. I will."

"Then I will say 'good night.' And you will sleep well, I know."

He stepped through the doorway and stood outside. The wind blew his dark hair in fits and starts. He again placed a finger beneath her chin.

"Mimi, you will find what you will find, and then you will begin again. You will be happy."

She looked at him, and somewhere inside, she could feel a small turning.

"Good night, then."

"Good night, Henri, and thank you for everything you've done tonight."

"What have I done? Spent some hours with a beautiful woman. No, there is nothing to thank me for."

He waved and then turned into the wind. She watched his thin body retreat. The night was suddenly dead. No people anywhere. The crazy lights of night—the sodium vapor street lamps, the green neon, the headlights of cars all seemed to illuminate emptiness. Mimi stood with the door open. When Henri was nearly out of her sight, he turned and they stood looking at each other, uncertain. Pain gripped Mimi's chest, and she held on to the doorjamb so hard her fingers ached. At last he waved once more and began to run into the night. She closed the door and slid to the floor, her arms round her body as tightly as they would go. *River of loneliness. River of loneliness.*

NINETEEN

NOTHING OR SOMETHING

When she awakened, it was all of a sudden. Her shoulder ached; she felt as though she'd slept in one position the entire night. Indeed the bed, except for her mussed sheets to the right, looked barely slept in. Mimi showered, dressed and went to the hotel restaurant for breakfast. It was not until she approached the cashier that she realized her mistake with Henri.

"I didn't pay for the meal!" This she said aloud to the cashier as she handed her the money for her breakfast.

"What, ma'm?" The old lady looked confused.

"Oh, no, I'm sorry. No, not this . . . well, here."

She stuffed the bills into the woman's hand and ran to her hotel, packed quickly and jumped into her Metro. She took the short drive to Le Cafe Petite and sat in her car writing a check, estimating each item and adding them up on some old papers she had in the car trash bag. Accounting for it being Sioux Falls and not Chicago, but then remembering to tip generously, she jotted the sum down on the check and then realized she should leave a note. She found she had no more paper, so she ripped another check from her book, marked it void and wrote on the back,

Henri, I want to be certain you know that . . .

Here she was nonplussed. Certain of what? Know what?

Certain you know that . . . She stopped again. "Jeesh!"

You were so good to me. And I don't know why. You made me feel cared about way down deep. It hurts me that I won't get to know you better. Mimi.

She folded the note over the check, found a bobby pin in the bottom of her purse and clipped them together, and then walked up to the little red door and popped them through the brass mail slot. She leaned her head for a few short seconds on the restaurant door, and then returned to her car.

*   *   *   *

Mimi traveled—driving, listening to music, a conversation here and there, on the radio. By the time she left 90 and headed past Yellowstone, she was thinking differently.

Turn back, turn back. She tried to shake off the persistent message. *Turn back. Turn back.* But she knew she had come too far. She contacted Jack, who said that he'd run into two dead ends in two days and could she be a little straight with him and tell him what she had in mind. She could not.

He said, "Look, if you're out looking for him, you need a plan, a carefully thought-out strategy. Suppose he's flipped his lid. He could be dangerous. Suppose he's become a child molester. You don't have any idea of what you're walking into. Well, frankly, not to let reality intrude too far into fantasy, you need to have a destination."

"I have that."

"You mean you actually know where he is?"

"No. I have no idea."

"Am I slow, here? Then you have a supposition."

"I have a nothingsition."

"Let me see, you have a destination with no indication of your husband's actually being there."

"I don't even know if there's a there." Mimi surprised herself and felt her throat close.

"AAAhhh. You seemed so . . . "

"Normal, " she whispered.

"Look Mimi, I'm being a little unprofessional here, but, I don't want anything bad to happen to you."

"It's a little late for that, Jack."

"Well no. I feel that you're sort of under my care."

Mimi was silent, confused.

"Mimi?"

"I . . . I'm just going on instinct, that's all."

"Well." Jack sounded exasperated. "When you get there, whether it's there or not and/or he's there or not, will you please call me? I'm really concerned."

"Certainly. I'll call you right away."

"Thanks, Mimi, and take care of yourself."

"Thank you Jack and . . . "

"Mimi?"

"Thanks for caring."

"You have a whole fan club back here who want you safe and sound, ya hear?"

"Thanks, Jack. Bye now."

"Bye, Mimi."

*   *   *   *

Her last night before reaching Downieville, Mimi decided to splurge a little, and pulled off the road at a sign titled The Three Bears Cottage, Bed and Breakfast. The sign itself was of three cocoa-colored bears sporting a wildflower bouquet in each paw. This made her smile; she pulled into the gravel drive, which proved to be about a mile and a half long. Giant, old pines rose on each side of the drive, an emerald/black wall. Now she became slightly uncomfortable, apprehensive, and would have turned back had she been able. But then there it was, a large log cabin, looking like a postcard or an illustration from a child's book. Fat honey-colored logs, copper buckets of wine and orange mums across the porch. The front door was cranberry, its center a large beveled glass oval curtained in lace. Mimi walked up the steps of the porch and rang the bell, half expecting an old grandma in a lace cap and shawl, or perhaps even a bear in an apron. Mimi started up then when an elderly, sturdy woman answered, wearing a long challis dress, lace cap and powder blue mohair shawl. She welcomed Mimi with a faint foreign accent and gravelly voice.

"Well, a visitor to Three Bears! Won't you please come in. I'm Melva Haines." Then, "Ida, we have a visitor."

At this, another elderly, likewise strongly made woman appeared in the hallway in farmer's overalls and red flannel shirt, reading glasses just about to slip off the end of her generous nose.

She came directly up to Mimi and offered her hand in a firm grasp. "Welcome to Three Bears, I'm Ida Haines."

Mimi cleared her throat. "I'm Mimi Malone. I'm pretty tired and I sure am hoping you have a room."

"Ma'am, we have one hundred percent availability at the moment," offered Melva.

Ida indicated a sort of log podium in the hallway, where she gave Mimi a sheet of paper with four bedrooms in colored pictures glued in place with typewritten descriptions and the prices of each. Mimi's eyes glazed over.

"You know, I'm too tired to decide. Look at me and tell me which one I should take."

The two ladies stood back and surveyed Mimi. Ida spoke up.

"The Newlybears' Room, I think, even though you're alone."

But Melva was dubious. "Isn't that," she said in a whisper, "you know, bad luck?"

"That's an old wives tale," Ida replied, all impatience. "There's no such thing as luck."

Mimi retrieved her suitcase from the car; Ida insisted on carrying it upstairs to the door near the end of the long hallway.

She could see that the inside and the outside of the house were one and the same. It seemed strange to Mimi to see interior walls made of logs with pictures hung on them. They were old black-and-whites of ghost towns, horses and buggies. Women and men pioneers, their expressions dour, jaws locked. Hay wagons, steer as big as three men. Ida dropped Mimi's small case and began to unlock the powder blue door with a plaque, *The Newlybears*, when Mimi noticed one picture at the very end of the hall, to the left of the window. Though she felt suddenly frozen, she forced herself to walk there. Melva had been following at a distance with blue towels and soap for her room when she noticed Mimi—her hand to her mouth.

"Why, my dear, oh, what is it?" And the old woman picked up her pace.

Mimi turned briefly, but long enough to observe from Melva's hobble that she suffered from a troublesome knee.

"This house . . . " but that was all Mimi could get out.

Ida pocketed the keys in her overalls and came near.

Mimi stammered, "I, this, do you know anything about this house?"

Ida's and Melva's eyes met, then looked quickly away, then again at the picture, an imposing old ranch house on a plain. Mimi wasn't certain this was the same house as the one in her own picture, because this photograph showed a frontal view instead of the side, and a porch that was sagging, even then. Her house had no porch, but in all other ways was an exact match.

"Well, no," Ida spoke firmly. "Not really. What I know to be a fact is that all these pictures were taken by the same man. We actually got them from an estate sale. But we did notice that some of them are titled on the back. Not all, though. Let's see about this one."

Ida gently popped the photograph from the nail on the wall and slid the velveteen back from the frame. A greying fountain pen script floated across the bottom of the picture: *Piccolo Ranch, Unhappiness Valley, Downieville, Idaho 1888*. Mimi's arm shot toward Ida's shoulder; she held on to keep from swaying. Melva took the picture from Ida and replaced it.

"Come, come into your room and sit down."

Mimi, her hand still grasping the woman's shoulder, went with Ida into the room, where she was gently deposited onto a blue love seat in front of a small woodstove. She heard Melva thumping down the hallway, quickly, and then her feet on the wooden steps. Ida sat opposite Mimi and held her hand. She was completely still.

"Why do they call it that? 'Unhappiness Valley'?" She peered into Ida's grey eyes.

"Well, ya know, it's just a local name, not official. I don't have any facts on that, but there are lots of rumors. They add up to something like this. Around the turn of the century a couple bought the spread. They were young. They built the house themselves and moved in. The man wanted to raise cattle, and the woman—she was a schoolteacher. Back then there were only two teachers, this lady, and another guy from, I think, Deer Flat, doesn't matter, within fifty miles of Downieville, and they taught in a two-room schoolhouse. He lived in the teacher's cottage at the rear of the property. Well, hard to say this delicately, but after half the school year was finished, the woman found she was in the family way and, evidently, well, it goes that she and her husband, for whatever reason, had not yet known each other in the biblical sense. She didn't tell him, but of course she eventually showed. Then one Saturday night, the husband lands up in town at the Trails' End Saloon and drinks steady for about three hours till the bartender refuses to serve him any more whisky and he rides on home. The next morning, they were both gone. Nobody ever saw either one of them again, but about ten years later—and this is the only fact anybody has—hunters way up behind the ranch in the foothills, they found a couple of skeletons. Well, one was medium-size and one was real tiny, a baby skeleton. Ever since then, everybody calls it Unhappiness Valley."

Melva entered just then with a small silver tray holding a linen napkin and a crystal vial of amber liquid. "Take this, honey, it's some brandy. Calm your nerves. You're overwrought. How long have you been driving?"

Mimi ignored her and squeezed Ida's hand. "Their name? The couple's name?"

"Why, now this is all just a story . . . "

"But then, in the story, what's their name?"

Melva piped up, as she placed the tray on a small table to Mimi's right. Why the same as on the picture I'd guess. What was it, Pocatello, Ida?"

Ida was looking directly into Mimi's eyes. "Piccolo, unusual name out here."

Mimi picked up the crystal glass and drank it down in one gulp.

"Mimi, what's your name?" asked Ida. "We forgot to ask you to sign the guest book."

She felt trapped; she opened her mouth but nothing emerged.

"Piccolo, isn't it? Is that right, Mimi?" Ida was patting Mimi's hand, still looking at her with that penetrating gaze.

"Well, Ida, whatever . . . ?"

"Malone," Mimi said firmly.

Mimi stared over Ida's shoulder. Melva shook her head. "Was that a relative, honey, a great, great grandpa or something?"

"The name is my husband's. It's his family."

Ida, still patting Mimi's hand, said, "And that, this place in the picture, is that where you're bound for?"

"Yes."

"And why are you going there?"

"I don't know for sure. I feel something in here." Mimi indicated her lower right side.

Melva said almost to herself, "Well, it sounds like you have your own story, dear." And then, "How about you washing up and coming down for some nice pea soup? Share with us what you want to. I think I'm seeing a woman who could use some food."

The women left her, and she picked up the towel and soap and went to the little bathroom inside her room. It was so pleasant. Everything in the room and the bathroom was the same pale shade of blue, some cranberry trim here and there but mostly blue. *Color of the sky, early morning.* Even the claw-foot tub was shiny sky-blue. As she washed her face, she could see that she had grown thinner these five days. Dark circles had bloomed beneath her eyes. Her bangs straggled past them, but she'd never noticed.

"Oh, dear," she said to her face. "Oh, dear. What am I doing here? What am I doing?" Her voice echoed from the tub, the room. A sense of hopelessness and darkness overwhelmed her as she grasped the sink, swaying. But to the mirror she said, "Maybe I do need food. Of course I do."

*   *   *   *

Melva and Ida fussed and clucked over Mimi through dinner, listening to her story, her journey, her unfocused mission. Then Melva filled the clawfoot tub while Mimi devoured Ida's peach cobbler with a voraciousness that shocked her. When she returned to the Newlybears' room, her bed (huge, king-sized) had been turned down—sky-blue sheets, cranberry woolen blanket. Various chubby teddy bears, in place of a headboard, cuddled above several pillows. Steam rose from the tub, and candles were glowing from all corners. Ida spoke firmly, "Now then, let's get in that bath before it gets cold."

She pushed Mimi gently into the bathroom and toward the tub. "You slide down in there and rest. And stop all that thinking."

She did as instructed. Mimi slipped out of her jeans and into the deep hot water. Like a small miracle, her mind floated and went blank. She breathed deeply and smiled.

*   *   *   *

In the morning she hugged the women goodbye and thanked them effusively. But they shooed her into her car. Just as she started the engine, Melva hobbled down the porch steps with something in her hand. It was the address and phone number of The Three Bears.

"I want you to call us if you need anything, hear now? And if you don't, well, Ida and I would love a note when you get back home. We can't help feeling, well, sort of connected."

Mimi patted Melva's hand.

"I will do that, and thank you again for everything."

She turned the little car around in the gravel circle and rolled past the dark pines.

She spoke to herself as she pulled out onto the road. "This is it, Mimi, you kook, you crazy woman, you impulsive lost dreamer. This is the day either nothing or something will happen.

TWENTY

ANGEL'S FACE

She drove on, skipping lunch, her stomach full of movement or lead at varying moments. She had to backtrack, for she had somehow driven right by the town. At 3:30 she saw the sign, a small brown wooden one with a yellow arrow painted on it and the announcement, *Downieville, 5 miles.*

Her throat constricted. She leaned over, popped the glove compartment, pulled out her binoculars and placed them on the seat beside Harold's picture of the old house.

But Downieville proved to be so rural that there were few street signs. How would she find anything? What had she expected? She had not, until now, realized the extent of her foolishness. Driving down one rolling road after another, stands of trees or meadowland, an occasional ranch, she knew that all she had to go on were the mountains. They were the same as those in the picture. Big camel humps, dusty brown or covered in pines, becoming bluish toward their soft peaks. After a long hour of this, with the sun already sinking, she spotted an old white Jeep stopped along the road. Slowing the Metro and pulling alongside, she grew heartened when she saw *USMail* in large letters on the door. She stopped her car. *Good news and bad news.* No postman inside. She looked in every direction; finally, she nervously searched the mailboxes beside the Jeep where, sure enough, the missing mailman had deposited fresh letters and catalogues.

She would wait. After some seconds had passed, she heard sticks breaking and shrubbery schussing till, quick as a vision, a chubby, small, dark man appeared from the trees and bushes across the road, zipping his slacks.

"Yo!" she yelled and waved.

The man looked sheepish but put up his arms in a shrug and yelled back, "Heh, when ya gotta go, ya gotta go!"

He crossed the empty road and mumbled, as if to himself, "Late today. Goddamn half sick all day, think I'm coming down with some bug. Didn't expect no welcoming committee." He peered up at her. "Whad'ya need, lady?"

"Well just some information."

"I don't have much, but I'll give you what I've got." He began sorting through a huge stack of white envelopes.

"Well . . . " She opened the door of her car and pulled out the picture. "This house, have you seen it around here?"

"Well." The man was scratching his head. I never delivered mail to any place like this. Let's see. Well . . . "

From the distance an old rusty truck appeared, and the mailman waved his envelopes in the air. The truck slowed and creaked to a halt. A skinny young man, chewing at least a pack of gum, quit the motor and rolled down his window.

"You're late today, Carl."

"Damn bad day. Coming down with something."

"Well . . . "

"Ya ever seen a place like this?" The mailman stretched out his hand. The young man studied Mimi's picture and likewise, began scratching his oily brown hair.

"Seems so. Seems like that old ranch house off Truman Hill, don't it?"

He slapped the photo for emphasis.   "I didn't think nobody lived up there anymore. Kind of a creepy place, I'd say. You the one looking, lady?"

Mimi nodded.

"Well, there's one light in Downieville, down here." He pointed in the opposite direction from which she had come. "Oh, I'd say about a mile. There's no sign, but you hang a left and that'll be Apache. Go approximately four miles, and then, hang a right. That'll be Truman Hill. Just as you get on Truman, like fifty feet or so, well actually, you should be able to see it right from the road. It ain't dark quite yet."

He stuck his head out and squinted at her.

"You planning on buying it?"

She was startled. "Well, no. No . . . but maybe." She realized she should have some reason for being there.

He winked. "You ought to know it's haunted. That's what they say, despite what some old, fat real estate fella like Jackie Drumond will tell you."

With this he waved, swooping his hand downward from the truck and starting up the clanking, snorting vehicle, which lurched forward.

"Nice kid, Frank, but kind of rude." The mailman looked apologetic.

"Well, I better ride out there before it's dark. Thanks. Thanks so much for your help."

"Didn't do nothin', but you stay safe, you hear?"

"Okay," Mimi called over her shoulder as she opened the door of her car and climbed in. She drove as instructed, but was forgetting to breathe and soon had to pull over in a driveway. Long breath in, long breath out. *Almost there, honey.* As soon as she turned on Truman Hill, she could see it, black and old and settling deeply into the sparse meadowland. As she got closer, she thought she saw small slits of light behind black window shades.

"They must be from World War II," she said, sitting back in her seat for a moment. Her heart was knocking out of her chest. Mimi did not pull in the driveway but parked the Metro across the road on a narrow but flat part of the shoulder. She could not turn her body, nor get her legs to move. Her fingers rested on the chrome handle but could not seem to press down to open the door. Frozen.

Finally, now nearly dark, she heard her hand clunk down the handle, felt herself emerging from her seat. She was in a dream, she thought, but she also stood outside the dream watching. Then she remembered the binoculars, and ran back to get them. Mimi stood on the gravel drive, almost grown over with dry brown grass, for another long moment. Then, thinking better of it, she stepped instead, gingerly, onto the meadow.

"Oh, God, please, no dogs. Oh, Holy Mary, oh, Jesus," she breathed. But there were only crickets and occasional scurrying sounds not far from her feet.

The black shades covered every window it seemed. She could see nothing. But definitely, there were threads of light peaking out from the edges of the old shades. *Definitely lights, Definitely people. Must be.*

When she stood about fifteen feet from the ranch house, she began to walk its perimeter. Finally, a window at the rear of the house that looked toward the mountains, appeared before her, open, unshaded, but small, the light dim. She could see no one. Nothing appeared to be happening. Opposite Mimi and to the right of the window, about twenty feet away from the house, stood a very old, half-dead apple tree; without thinking, Mimi climbed quickly up into the crotch of the tree. From there, her view was excellent. She could see a kitchen with an ancient black cook stove and shelves for dishes and pots. She thought maybe the floor might be dirt or very old planks. The tiny light that illuminated the scene must be over the sink, Mimi thought. Someone left it on. Perhaps doing the supper dishes, watching the sun set. Someone *was* there!

No sooner had she woven this scenario for herself, than a door softly creaked open. A narrow shaft of brighter light washed into the room, and Mimi was shocked to see a woman, slender, in ragged jeans and plaid shirt, walk in. She went to the far wall, the fittings of which Mimi could not see, and returned to the beam of light with what must have been a bottle of beer. The woman was attractive, her blonde hair moving, a slow curtain across her back, her face pristinely pale. Mimi thought her young, maybe twenty-four or twenty-five. She walked the way a dancer walks, upright and graceful. Mimi had seen her before. Had seen her but did not have any idea where or who the woman was. Though she had tried to expect nothing, it never occurred to her that a woman would be here in this place. Her mind raced. Perhaps Uncle Harry's grandchild. A writer of mysteries come to do battle with another book about pets and murders. At the doorway the woman turned back, moved to the small window. Mimi could see a plaid arm reach up, hear the light's chain being pulled, but before the light went black, Mimi saw clearly, an angel's face, the ivory skin, its youthful sheen, the soft eyebrows like wings. The only completely perfect face she had ever seen.

She waited ten or fifteen more minutes. Would anything else happen? The crickets' urgent love calls ratcheted louder and louder. No sound came from the house, and Mimi began to doubt what she'd seen. *Perhaps nothing. Needing to see something. Not this, though.*

Finally, Mimi staggered down. Her feet ached from being stuck in the tree, but she made her way to the car, racing, suddenly aware of dog-like howlings in the distance. *Lock both doors!* She reached to her neck to remove the binoculars, but they were not there. *God!* She must have dropped them from the tree. *God!*

She would not go back for them. She could not. "Now what?" she wondered aloud. "Now, what the hell what?"

TWENTY ONE

GIFT HORSE

You have to eat and sleep. Mimi's mind spoke to her. She called this part of her the mother-mind. *But where?*

Go back to the light at the end of Apache. Where there's a light, there must be something more, the mother-mind continued. She drove to the intersection and turned left. It was eight-thirty and deeply dark. Soon, some lights appeared, a slender strip—a Seven-Eleven, a K-mart, a small dark bank and a tiny saloon, *The Cattle Drive.* She opted for the saloon, praying that they had food. The lights of the Seven-Eleven would have irritated her right now.

The Cattle Drive proved to be the darkest public room Mimi had ever been in. She could make out five or six round tables, all of them occupied. Annoyed, suddenly, she realized she would have to sit at the bar; someone might talk to her. *Oh, please, no.* Mimi decided first to speak to the bartender about the possibility of food. He was intimidating. Huge chest bursting the buttons of his western-style shirt from which long, black hairs sprung. A saucer-sized metal belt buckle flashed as if frequently polished; it displayed a man strangling a bear. His thick forearms, made visible from rolled-up shirtsleeves, made her think of pork roasts. His hands were paw-like, fingers thick and he wore a black folded bandana around his large head upon which she could detect, despite the dimness, skulls. His hair, long and Medusa-wild, frizzled about his head, an angry silver hair sticking straight out from the black coils every few inches.

"How can I do you, Ma'am?"

Mimi's jaw clenched. She whispered across the shining bar, "Do you have food here?" She pushed her bangs from her glasses.

"Now, what do you like?"

"Well, no I mean, a menu, a kitchen or . . . "

"On occasion," the man/bear responded and leaning closer rumbled, (Mimi felt roses bursting on her cheeks) "How would you feel about a *beef* burger?"

Frightened, she cleared her throat, but still could only whisper, "Fine. That will be fine. Yes, perfect."

He said nothing. Seconds passed. He was wiping a beer mug with a soft white cloth. Mimi took a stool to indicate her intention of staying, and then the bartender placed the gleaming mug with the others on their hooks and leaned again on the bar.

His eyes were bright flares in the dark. "I'm Hank." He held up one of his hands.

"I'm Mimi Malone," she replied, holding up her hand in the same sort of "hi" position.

"Excuse me for a second, ma'am." He then called, "Frankie!" to a closed door to the left of the bar. The door opened about five inches.

"Make the lady a burger, extra special nice, medium, Ma'am?" Mimi nodded. "Medium!" Hank continued to the open door.

"Oh, is that your cook?"

"No . . . my dishwasher."

"Oh, well, the cook . . . ?"

"Gone."

"Oh, no, I mean if the kitchen is closed . . . " Mimi began to rise.

"Frank makes a mean burger, Ma'am. Now what can I get you to drink?"

Mimi took off her glasses and used the bar napkin Hank had placed in front of her to wipe her face. "Oh, ah, well do you have a house Chardonnay?"

"Wine?"

Once more Mimi blushed. "Oh, yes, but ah, on second thought . . . "

"Lady." Hank leaned closer. "I'm thinking you need a real drink."

"I'm, well . . . "

Hank turned his back and got down a tall honey-colored bottle. He filled a beer mug with ice and water, placed it before her and then plucked a tall jigger from beside the small steel sink. He punched the jigger down into a bowl of salt and then poured the yellow liquid into it. Salt on the rim, a miniature Margarita.

"Now," Hank nodded his head in her direction, "drink."

Obediently, Mimi took a sip.

"Unh-uh," Hank shook his head in disgust. In a quick movement, he reached up and retrieved the bottle, poured himself a jigger and dumped the contents down his throat. He slapped the small glass on the bar and nodded in her direction.

She lifted the glass again and drank. Fire burned down her throat. She couldn't believe people drank such a terrible liquor.

"Tequila. Mexican," Hank told her. "Dark honest hands make this stuff. It's medicine."

Mimi held a hand to her heart, silently and firmly doubting this man.

"Why are you coming through Downieville?" Hank asked.

"Ahhh . . ."

"Uh-oh, one of those mystery women, I see."

Mimi smiled, hoping he would let it go.

"Check on that burger now," he said, but just as he started for the kitchen door, it opened and a scruffy young man with stringy air loped toward them with a plate. He was familiar, somehow. That boy! The one in the rusty truck. Mimi felt trapped. She looked down at the bar, but Frank noticed her immediately.

"You're the lady with Carl aren't you?" he asked, obviously astonished.

"Oh, um, yes. Yes, I am." She at once wished she had more tequila in front of her.

"Well," he said—the same head-scratching as before—"did ya have any luck?"

"Ah, not exactly."

"But you did find the house, right?"

Mimi nodded, her first taste of the *beef* burger in her mouth.

"Your directions were great."

This seemed to satisfy Frank. He turned back toward the kitchen. Then abruptly back to Mimi. "Anything funny going on out there?"

"Nope. Nope, just an old broken-down house, I'd say."

Frank, walking backwards, made an open-armed shrug, turned and walked into the darkness.

Hank was standing, his back against the shelves of bottles, whipping his towel forwards and backwards. Abruptly, he snapped it and then folded it neatly. Mimi jumped at the snap, and their eyes met. Without glancing down, she slid her jigger toward him. He refilled it, poured one for himself and gave her more ice and water. On impulse, she held her glass aloft and met Hank's with a chink.

"So, how long are you here for?"

"Actually. Well, . . . I need one more day, probably." Mimi's head felt suddenly heavy.

"And it's not okay to ask why, is that right?" Hank swirled the jigger on the empty bar.

"Well, I'm just not free to talk about it."

"Ooo, sounds pretty darned important."

"No," Mimi gestured, her mouth full of burger. And then, after she swallowed, "No, just personal stuff." She could see that Hank was somehow amused by her.

"You, know . . . "

"No, ma'am, I don't. But I figure everybody's got their secrets."

"Yes." Mimi nodded vigorously. "Yes. Certainly, they do. Don't you?"

"Sure do."

"Well, you see, there." She slapped the bar lightly.

"Speaking of which, it is now ten o'clock at night. Just where do you plan on staying, secret lady, for your one more day? "

Mimi had been rather sloppily dabbing at the mustard on her chin.

"Oh!" She held her napkin to her open mouth.

Hank was chuckling, his arms folded across his chest.

"Don't travel much, do you?"

"Well, no. Well, what about . . . I mean, where? Can I see your Yellow Pages?"

"There ain't anything in them."

"Well, maybe I, the next town or, I could call from here."

"And . . . you're just a wee bit tipsy, secret lady."

"Oh, am I? I feel all right."

Hank leaned on the bar once again. "Look, I'm joshing you. We have a room here. Just one, but it's convenient, and is mostly always empty."

"Oh, really, you mean this is a sort of bed-and-breakfast?"

Hank threw back his head and gave a short roar.

"More like a Booze and Snooze, I guess."

Mimi began to laugh, and then Hank. She had him all wrong, she thought. "So, what's the price? I mean it's clean and all, right?

"Well, lady, I don't think you're in a position to ask either of those questions, but the room's free to pretty ladies and yes, I clean it myself. No dust under the bed, and I keep the toilet seat clean."

She laughed again. "So you'd lock me up alone in this place?" She looked around; the saloon was empty now. "And free? How come free?"

"No, I would not lock you up, for God's sake, and it's free because it's mine. And you wouldn't be alone because this is where I live."

Mimi put down the water she had been sipping. "You mean stay with you?" Fear clamped her chest.

"Never look a gift horse in the mouth, my dear," Hank nodded. "No, not with me. That'd be pretty scary, huh? You have a room . . . to yourself and the commute," he slapped the bar again,

"well, you can't beat the commute."

"But, I don't know you."

"And I don't know you."

They stared at one another.

Mimi spoke finally, "Well, I don't seem to have any better ideas."

"Well, then welcome to Hank's Booze and Snooze." Hank held out his hand, and Mimi shook it.

*   *   *   *

The room was tiny, spartan. A monk cell. But it was clean. No covering over the small window; the full moon filled it and the room. The white spread was iridescent. The sheepskin thrown across it glowed. She had not brought her suitcase, and did not bother to retrieve it.   Mimi thought about placing the bedstand in front of the door and then noticed the latch. She could lock it. But she did not. She slipped from her clothes, leaving them to lie in a pool on the floor. She lay down and stared at the moon, and her life—how it had been for so long, came welling up from her bones, from her heart. She began to weep, then to sob. She knew she was making too much noise, but Mimi could not stop. She was thinking that she might never be able to stop, when the door opened and Hank, his hair slicked back into a ponytail and bare-chested in his old jeans walked in softly. He said nothing but caught the sheepskin at the foot of the bed, wrapped Mimi in it and gathered her in his arms. He sat down on the bed and began rocking her, slipping his fingers through her hair. She did not stop. In time, she sighed a deep, long sigh. It seemed she might be finished. Hank held her, scooped down the blankets and placed Mimi on the cool sheets. Then he placed the blankets over her, then the sheepskin. He stroked her head and eyes and left abruptly, returning with a cool cloth which he used to wipe her face, neck and shoulders. He then kissed her forehead and pulled her damp hair back onto the pillow. They looked at each other for a long time until Mimi reached her arms to his shoulders, then her hands to his head, and pulled him toward her.

TWENTY TWO

JEFFREY'S CASE

The following morning, Mimi returned to the house. The shades remained closed. A storm was coming up. Clouds like small lakes ran across the sun. She no longer cared if she were seen, and walked down the drive to the rear of the house. There was nothing anywhere that indicated life. She was thinking that the woman in the kitchen might have been a dream and then she stopped dead still at the small window where she imagined she had seen her. Then it came to her. The woman in the evening gown, smoking, making dinner. Harold's compass, his backpack. It was impossible. She had dreamed her, months ago. *Oh, my God. Oh, my God. What is this?* Mimi strode around to the front door and pounded on it. *The woman will answer, then I will see what's here. I will understand something.* Nothing happened. She pounded louder. Nothing. She tested the knob. Unlocked! Her heart flopping and banging, she opened the door and let herself in. Dark, so dark. Mimi stood immobile, but after a few seconds she could make out a sofa and chairs, their innards oozing. A coffee table made from a slice of log held newspapers and her dropped binoculars; she walked over to it. The paper held yesterday's date. Her heart thudded. She then walked to the door at the rear of the room and opened it. The kitchen. She did not dream this. The shade was open as before, and she stood for a minute staring at the mountains. Footsteps on the basement stairs. A door being pushed open. Harold standing in the doorway, wood in his arms.

"Harold!" Mimi's shriek was a whisper.

He walked by her and into the living room. She could hear wood tumbling onto brick. He returned.

"What are you doing in my house?" he asked.

"Doesn't that seem like a funny question?"

"Strangers do not walk into houses without being invited."

His eyes were empty, his face gaunt.

"Harold?"

"And why are you calling me that?"

"Harold?"

"Stop. Can you please leave now? I'd like you to leave."

She snatched her purse from her shoulder and pushed her hand into it. Pulling out the picture, she shoved it toward him.

"Where did you get that?" Pain in his voice.

"Grandma Tinker. She said you gave it to her."

"I don't understand. I don't think I know her."

A switch inside Mimi snapped. She grabbed the picture from him and hurled it at the small kitchen window, shattering it. Harold looked frightened, but something else . . . She grabbed him by the shoulders and began shaking his slight body.

"I am Mimi, your wife, god damn you. I am your fucking wife and you are my fucking husband and there is no way I can forgive you for this and there is no way you can fake your way out of this, so stop bullshitting me and start with the answer to 'why?' Why, Harold?"

With surprising strength, he pulled Mimi off and began dragging her toward the living room, toward the front door.

"Stop," she screamed. "Stop. I want to know why."

She began hitting him with her free hand, hard, everywhere she could reach. At the front door, he dropped her wrist. She attacked him with both hands till he fell to the floor, into a fetal position, protecting himself.

"Why? Why? When we tried so hard."

Mimi collapsed on the floor beside him, sobbing.

"Why? Why?"

Now, Harold was crying softly. At last he called out in the voice of someone she did not know, someone much younger.

"I'm not any 'Harold'. I'm not any anybody. I don't know any Mimi. I keep thinking I'll know. I don't seem to remember. Let Leda tell you. She's taking care of me till I find out."

As if on cue, the blonde woman, the one from the kitchen window, the one who'd been in Mimi's dream, slipped into the room with bags of groceries.

"Jeffrey!" She tossed the bags on the floor.

She squatted and began to help him up. Mimi leaped to her feet, embarrassed, confused.

"Who are you?" Mimi held her fists pressed to her hips.

The woman gave a shocked, icy glance while helping Harold to the sofa. Then she came back toward Mimi. Her angel's face rested inches from Mimi's own.

"I don't even care who you care. This is a sick man and you've walked in here to a private residence and have been harassing him, obviously, and pummeling him—there are hand marks all over his face—this man who would not hurt any living thing."

"Stop. That's where you're dangerously wrong. You see, I'm this man's wife! And he's very much hurt me. In fact, he is destroying me. I am destroyed. Now, who are you and how did you get here with my husband?"

The woman's eyes grew huge. She looked from Mimi to Harold and back again, searching for something in Mimi's expression. She then went over to Harold, who was still silently weeping, rocking himself, ever so slightly, on the decaying sofa, and looped her arms about him.

"Honey? Honey, what the lady's saying. Can you remember? Is this right? You told me you didn't think you were ever married." She placed her forehead against his.

A bolt of fury ran through Mimi, welding her to the floor.

Harold looked up at her, wiping his nose with his hand. He looked at her for some long seconds. Small waves moved across his face. The woman reached her hand into her jeans, yanked out some tissues and began patting his cheeks and eyes. She wiped his nose.

"I'm Leda Maus," she spoke quietly, not looking at Mimi, smoothing back Harold's hair. Harold blew his nose into the tissue she was holding. "I met Jeffrey at an Ashram in India. He said he had traveled from America to find himself, but in fact was having trouble remembering anything about the life he had left. He introduced himself as Jeffrey Reeves. The more we talked, the more he said that the one thing he knew was this house, this place in Idaho, and that perhaps if he went back there, here, the other things would come back to him. That was a year ago. But nothing ever seems to surface. Sometimes I hear him in his dreams, but he is always talking, arguing actually, with his father, dad, or pops. Nothing I could use."

"Pops is Harold's grandfather."

Leda looked hard at Mimi.

"Why did you never take him to a doctor?" Her anger made each syllable distinct and clipped.

"It's . . . ?" she said. Mimi thought she discerned an accent.

"My name? Mimi Malone."

"Please, can you sit? Can we?"

Mimi pushed one of the bulky old chairs around to face her husband and the young woman.

"I knew what was wrong. I'm a social worker. I did take him to a doctor, a psychiatrist in India."

Mimi snorted. "India?"

"The Indians are wonderful, thorough doctors. Dr. Jasuja confirmed what I had already diagnosed—something called Psychogenic Fugue."

"And that would be?" Mimi folded her arms over her chest. *What a scam,* she was thinking.

"Essentially, leaving home in the largest sense, suddenly, and with an amnesia for your original personality, all aspects of your former life. The condition nearly always spontaneously resolves itself before ten months are out, but Jeffrey's case is resistant, as you can see."

"And what do you support this man with? He has nothing."

The young woman folded her hands above her knees and leaned forward. She cleared her voice.

"Well, in fact Harold had in his keeping ten thousand dollars at the time we met."

"His savings."

"I didn't know."

"That's just it, don't you see? You didn't *know* anything, nor did you attempt to find out. You haven't stopped to realize that, in fact, you have stolen my husband and his money, and stolen my life."

"Jeffrey's money is safe. We haven't touched it. I live on my inheritance while I write my novel. That's why I went to India. My father died, cancer. I went to heal."

"So," her words spat from her mouth. "Which is your Jeffrey?"

"I'm sorry?"

"Is he your father or your lover?"

Leda's mouth flew open and she looked down, shaking her head.

"Can you go now?" she asked. "Would you please go?"

"How do I know you aren't lying? How do I know?"

Leda got up and went to an old roll top desk across the dusty room. From one of its pigeonholes she extracted a large white envelope and returned to Mimi, who was now standing.

"Can you come back tomorrow when we're all a bit calmer? Read this in the meantime. Please. Will you do that?" Leda's voice had grown kind.

231

*　　　*　　　*　　　*

Mimi was starting her car when the largest bolt of lighting she had ever seen struck one of the mountain tops, a tympani of thunder rolling in a half-second behind.

TWENTY THREE

BEGINS WITH A "V"

Mimi had slipped in by the back door, not bothering to tell Hank that she would need the room again; she was too anxious. Her monk's cell was cold. She wrapped herself in the sheepskin to read the psychiatrist's report. The same words: "Psychogenic Fugue." A number, "300.13." Harold's supposed illness had a number. She read the doctor's cartoonish script, "Presumed, precipitating episode—severe psychosocial stress, i.e. marital discord, natural disaster. Particularly resistant case at present. Of duration six months, estimated by patient. Possible suicide attempt, a year or so previous to presenting with Fugue. Scarring—anterior of both wrists, but records cannot be sought since patient is amnesic for his name or family of origin. Outcome is uncertain but usually resolves spontaneously. Patient will return to U.S.A under care of friend, Miss Leda Maus."

Hank shadowed the doorway.

"Oh . . ."

"I thought you might have up and gone, mystery lady." He was not smiling.

"Like that? Just, fyoosh . . . " She waved her hand over her shoulder.

"It happens, my dear."

"Yes . . . " She placed the report on the spread and stood up. "You know . . ."

"Not really."

She was having trouble meeting Hank's gaze.

"I don't . . . I've never . . . "

"Will you just come over here?"

Mimi was obedient.

"I know all that. I know what kind of person you are; you're a walking advertisement for the virtuous life." He said this, a hand on each side of her head, lifting her face. "I want you to believe me. I had no idea anything like that was going to happen. You were not set up. Can you believe that?"

She pulled her head away and looked down. Well, the tequila, I mean and the room . . . free."

"Mimi, did you want that drink?"

"Yes."

"Did you need a room, shall we say, in a big way?"

"Yes."

"Did we honestly need each other?"

She could not look up. "Yes." She faced him then. "Yes, but . . . "

"But it's not right?"

Mimi nodded her head slowly.

He placed a finger beneath her chin. "Are you certain of that?"

She noticed for the first time that his eyes were not brown; they were a deep navy blue. She looked into them for some seconds.

"No. No. I am not certain any more. My heart, my heart feels good, not bad. Good."

He held her in silence. They began to sway, and then he kissed her hair. "Come on . . . the cook's roasted a mess of chickens."

*   *   *   *

Realizing the next morning that she would need more time, she called Melva and Ida to tell all that had happened, and they insisted she stay at The Three Bears, gratis. Mimi accepted; she could think of nothing else to do. Then she drove again to the old ranch house. Leda opened the door at once, but the room lay in darkness. Harold was on the sofa, looking pale, unwell. She wanted to go to him.

"What . . . why do you keep him in darkness? I'm worried about that."

"Jeffrey." Leda went to him and placed a hand on his shoulder. "What do you say about pulling the shades up—a little sunlight."

"No!" Harold cried out with the strong voice she remembered. And again, "No!"

Leda returned to where Mimi stood. "He says that someone bad might find him."

Mimi brushed by her and knelt in front of him. She placed her hand on his knee, and he did not protest.

"Can you please look at me? Directly. Can you, please, just for a minute or so."

He did as she asked, and for the first time, he looked less blank, a tiny bit like Harold. Looking at Mimi for some minutes, he at last spoke to her softly.

"I remember a ring," he offered hesitantly. "There's a word inside. I think it begins with 'V'."

She slipped off her wide wedding band and gave it to him. He began to weep. He held the ring firmly for a time and then opened his hand and picked it up to see. "Too dark," he said.

Leda rushed behind the sofa and flicked on a lamp. But Harold closed his hand on the ring again. He bent his head into his free hand.

"It says 'vous' doesn't it? Does it say 'vous'?"

*   *   *   *

In the days that followed, Harold remembered more and more. His appetite increased, and Leda allowed Mimi to fix spaghetti for him the way he had liked it, his old birthday favorite. On that same evening, after Mimi had been visiting a few days and they had been going for long, slow walks, talking or just loping along, occasionally holding hands. As they were seated at the rough table in the kitchen drinking tea, Harold reached across the table and grasped Mimi's hand in his.

"You've been through a terrible time, Mimi."

Quick tears filled her eyes. "I have."

"And I'm the cause of it."

"Well, you got sick."

Leda rose, patted their shoulders and left them to themselves.

"I think . . . I think . . . that,

Mimi looked at Harold sharply.

"Mimi," he said. "I cannot come home with you."

She looked away from him and toward the dark mountains. She rose from the table and went to the window and then turned back. Harold had tears in his eyes.

"You need care."

"I'm getting better now."

"But . . . "

"You know, Mimi, it was never right."

"There were right things . . . "

He got up, crossed the old wooden floor and placed his arms around her.

"Something about it, about me and our life together . . . it's part of why I got sick."

Mimi pulled away from him. She searched his face.

"Does Leda feed you that stuff?"

"Mimi, I might be sick, but I can still think for myself."

"But I've come so far to find you. I've been so lost without you."

"You did find me. And it sounds to me like you've done a good job without me. Mimi, we don't love each other, not the marrying way anyhow. I don't think we ever did."

"What about the baby?"

She allowed him to embrace her once more.

"That's hard, Mimi. That's very hard."

She began to weep, her head on his chest. He rubbed her back in small circles. She remembered this and moved in closer. They stood linked together for a long while. She heard the front door open and close and then those far-away dogs howling.

* * * *

She did not listen to the radio for any of the five days it took to drive home. The weather held steady and brought her the finest October could bring. The yellow leaves shimmered, the red leaves were a furious fire. Mimi thought of herself as a bombed-out building; she would look in the visor mirror from time to time, thinking there should be something on her face, some markings there, but she merely looked tired. She talked to no one. She saw that it was possible, given just the right avoidance of eye contact, just a lowering of her right shoulder toward her book on the table, to remain unconnected to the world. She thought of no one. Once, of Grandma Tinker on her bed pointing to the box on the sink, of her papery skin. It surprised her when she'd burst out with a laugh of derision.

"Will I dry up now? Along with my skin? Will I run haranguing small children playing with balls? Will I be nasty to the man at the filling station? And sit with blankets wrapped over my shoulders in June?"

She asked these things in the darkness crossing from Iowa into Illinois pressing toward home. When she saw the sign for St. Charles, it was two o'clock in the morning. Even so, she parked the car under the maple just beneath the window of her apartment and looked up. A small red glow emanated intermittently. She had not been forgotten.

TWENTY FOUR

HONEY

"McClosky Agency, Jack here."

She was still in her flannel pajamas and had not yet drunk her first cup of coffee when the urge to touch base with the detective made her shuffle sleepily to the phone.

"It's Mimi Malone."

"What happened? I thought I should start looking for *you* now. You said about a week; that was three weeks ago."

"Jack can I meet you? Could you meet me at the Sea Horse for dinner?"

"Well, I . . . I don't usually have dinner with clients . . . "

"I'm not your client anymore."

"I see. Six o'clock good?"

"Yes."

"Good-bye, Mimi. I appreciate your calling me."

Mimi thought her first day back she should not have to tell her story to anyone but Jack. So, she returned no calls. She did call Sunnyfield and found Grandma to be her old self, but asking for her often. Mimi thought she might go out there, but realized she had no energy to drive all the way to Centerville.

She trudged down the stairs to get her mail. It fell out of her box in a whoosh: she had not stopped the postal delivery. Bills, magazines, some letters and finally a terse note from the mailman indicating that she would find the rest in the Jefferson Avenue Post Office.

She had two letters, one from Father Ben and one postmarked Sioux Falls, South Dakota.

Mimi ripped open the envelope from Ben.

Dear Mimi,

Your mother tells me you are driving out west to look for Harold. She said you had some hunches you were following and that she was quite worried about you.

I have indeed been transferred to Oak Park, to St. Timothy's here. It's a nice parish, old, established—a mixed population which I will enjoy as long as I stay on.

I would love to talk to you when you return. I need to talk to you because I seem to be in a crisis with everything I am currently doing, and I find you there in the mix. Please call to let me know of your safe return and regarding the outcome of your trip.

Ever,

Ben

Mimi crumpled the letter and held her lips shut with it.

"Oh no! Ben. No! This just isn't right. He shouldn't speak this way. A priest. Oh, God, no."

She opened the second letter; a check fell to her feet. The note was written in a foreign sort of script.

Dear Mimi,

I hope you will not think me overly bold for choosing to write to you. I think you must be home by now. I think you must now know your life perhaps, a little better. Thank you for the check for dinner, but I enclose it here because I wanted to treat you, to do some little kindness for you.

She was incredulous. It must be the waiter! Henri!

I enclose a drawing I have made of the Restaurant, Le CafePetite for you. I retrieved your address from your check and thought you might enjoy having the picture. It was a special night—getting to know you a little. I hope you will honor me with a note from yourself. Thank-you,

Fondly,

Henri

Mimi examined the second sheet of paper, the drawing. It was very fine. A pen-and-ink, drawn with a larger point, a technique that she'd not seen before. It was the restaurant all right, the plastic flowers in their cold blue boxes beneath the shiny window.

I never asked about him. I was so self-involved. I wonder how long I've been like that?   She went upstairs to her apartment and stared out the window, through the maples to the house opposite with its sagging steps up to the porch. With a start, she noticed the same boy as before—*the night boy,* she'd thought of him. Was he wearing the same jeans and striped shirt? She jerked open the window. "Hey!" She called. "Hey!"

He looked around, confused, and then stood smacking the dirt off the rear of his pants, searching through the thinning leaves.

"Hey! Hi!" He caught sight of her finally, and squinted uncertainly. "Yeah, do ya need something?"

She hadn't expected that.

"Let's be friends," she called.

"How old are you?"

Mimi shouted back, "Forty."

"I'm eleven."

"Well, what do you say?"

"Well, you're kind of old."

"For what?"

The boy scratched his head considering this and then responded, looking up and down the street for cars, "Okay." Then he crossed and started for her door.

A rush of happiness seized Mimi. She ran down the flight of stairs to her front door and let him in. He was very thin, even bony. She held out her hand.

"I'm Mimi Malone. I noticed you before. Late at night."

"Yeah, I like to sit on the porch," he said extending a small, very dirty hand. "I'm Stephan Drubowski."

"I'd love to have you come up for tea. Should you leave a note for your parents?"

"Neh. They won't care." Stephan was looking at the wallpaper in the hallway. "Hey, this is a neat place. Kind of like an old house, fixed up, huh?"

She saw that it was true. She'd thought the same thing when she and Harold had come to look for an apartment.

"Yes. That's exactly what it is."

"Miss Malone—are you married?"

"Ah, well, I guess not."

"So you're Miss."

"Actually, Stephan, you can just call me Mimi, if that's alright with you."

They started up the stairs. When they were nearly to her door, Stephan cleared his voice. "Mimi, actually, I don't like tea."

"Oh, what do you like?"

"Coffee, do you have any coffee?"

She turned to look at him. "All right," she returned. "Coffee it is."

They went inside to the kitchen where Mimi ground the beans and poured the water. Stephan began opening her cabinets. Mimi said nothing, deciding to watch this curious boy. Finally, he discovered her cups and set out two on her plastic kitchen table. He did not place saucers beneath the cups, but began searching the kitchen drawers. He had an earnest furrow between his brows that made Mimi smile. She watched as he searched for the spoons, tumbling the pieces over each other.

"Almost nothing in there matches," she admitted.

He looked up at her. "Just the same as our house." And then looking through her kitchen window, "People are like that." He plopped the spoons on the table.

A great weight moved inside her.

"You mean people are not like each other?"

"Not that. I mean, you know, people who are different try to match. Match up."

"You mean like friends?"

"Yeah, sometimes. Like Billy Long. He wants to be my friend because I can run fast and I can knock kids down hard but, well you know, my mom and dad . . . "

He looked directly at Mimi. She saw that his eyes carried a much older expression than his age warranted. Almost tired, she thought.

He squeezed the backrest on the vinyl kitchen chair.

"My mom likes music and animals. But my dad—he's really my stepdad—I don't know my real dad—he likes sports and hunting. My mom doesn't like my dad to hunt. When he's gone we go to the museum or to see paintings. He doesn't like us to do that. My mom and I want a dog. My dad says 'no dog.' "

Stephan shook his head, pulled out the chair and plunked down. Mimi poured the coffee and got out some packaged ginger snaps.

"Sorry, I've got no milk," she offered.

He waved a small hand, then looked across the table at her. His hair, she noticed, was not quite red. "Do you know what I'm talking about?"

"Yes," she said. "Yes, I do."

"I mean, did you ever try to match up?"

"Yes, I think I have."

"Who'd you match up with?"

Mimi could feel herself blushing. "Well, I . . . "

"Was it Mr. Malone?"

"Oh, my husband's name is Piccolo." Mimi met Stephan's gaze.

"How'd that work out?"

She looked down at her coffee, the steam, and then back at Stephan.

"Actually, Stephan, it didn't work out. We didn't match up. We thought we did at first, and then we tried to, but in the end it didn't work."

"So, do you have to get a divorce?"

Mimi dabbed at her eyes with her little finger. "I think so. Yes, I think that's what's going to happen."

"Oh . . . " He played with the grain in the plastic tabletop a few minutes. When next he met her glance he asked, "Do you believe prayers work? They don't seem to, but everyone says they do."

"Have you tried them?" she asked.

"A couple of times."

"Nothing so far, huh?"

"Nope."

"Is it something expensive?"

"It's not a thing . . . " Now Stephan blushed and looked away. "I want my father to leave. I want him to go away."

And suddenly the boy bent his head to his folded arms and began to cry.

Mimi rose and went to him, uncertain of what to do, of what was appropriate. She placed her hands on his shoulders and rubbed them. *Such small bones!*

"Stephan, God has his own plan, his own time schedule."

But Stephan broke from her hands and leapt out of his chair.

"I don't believe in God, but if there is one, well, He better hurry up, that's what I think."

Mimi drew back, shocked. "Why, Stephan? Why should God hurry?"

Stephan looked at her, red-faced and wild about his eyes.

"Because . . . because . . . " And then he tore from the kitchen and through the living room door, clattering down the steps, banging the old Victorian door with his exit. Its glass panel, Mimi could see from the top of the stairs, shook for some seconds.

*   *   *   *

The Sea Horse was depressingly old, with ocean paraphernalia draped over the walls: ropes and nets, lanterns and plastic fish, and the requisite swordfish, a silvery faded blue in perpetual need of dusting. The mauve carpet was polka dotted with catsup and tartar sauce. The waitresses, without exception, were well past fifty—women with bleached or dyed tresses wearing the makeup they'd worn in high school forty years ago: fat black eyeliner, aqua frosted across their lids, and pearly lipstick. They called everyone "honey" and stood in groups when it was slow, discussing men and their grown children.

Mimi loved it. She loved every "honey." She loved the fish and she especially loved Myrtle. Mimi thought of her as "my waitress" and always requested her booth. She was glad she had preceded Jack so she could enjoy Myrtle's special brand of wisdom and affection.

"Where ya been, honey? Missed ya. You've not been chasing any men? Remember what I told you."

"Well I have. I didn't listen to you."

Myrtle sat down and stroked Mimi's hand.

"Did you go looking for that man of yours?"

Mimi could only nod.

"You found him, didn't you?"

She nodded again.

"And he didn't want to come back."

It was not a question. Mimi shook her head.

"I'm getting you a drink." The waitress rose abruptly.

She returned almost instantly with the martini. "On me, honey." Mimi knew it would be lethal, mixed by Myrtle herself, and she was grateful.

"Thanks, Myrtle."

"Can't talk now, sweetie. Too busy. I'll stop back if I can. And Mimi,"

Mimi looked into the eyes of the woman's cracking face.

"Yes?"

"I know it's real corny and overused, but everything *does* happen for the best."

When Jack entered, squinting in the near-darkness, she waved her arm at him. He smiled, lumbered over to her and plopped down into the booth, a little uncertain of just where to place himself.

"Mimi, my God, you appear to be safe and sound. I guess you're the real detective. Is he back here with you?"

"No."

Myrtle appeared. "Jack, this is Myrtle, the best waitress in the whole world."

"Well, I don't know about that . . . What can I get you, Jack?"

"Chivas Regal on ice. Thank you, Myrtle."

His eyes were intense in the darkness.

"I'm sorry, Mimi."

She searched his face. "I guess you must be accustomed to such stories."

"Yes. And no. There are some basic situations, but because every person is different, every situation is different. I want to hear your story." He patted her arm.

Mimi talked on and on through drinks and dinner. She realized at a certain point she had been talking for some time with only an occasional nod or question from Jack, but she could not seem to help it. When she finished, he looked down at his coffee, stirring sugar and cream into it slowly.

"Do you believe him?"

"Believe him?"

"About this fugue thing, his story?"

Mimi stared at him.

"Well, I saw the psychiatrist's report."

"No, but what's your gut feeling? That's more important, I've always found. What's in here."

It was her turn to look into her cup.

"I don't know. I don't suppose it matters now."

"Yeah, it matters."

"How so?"

"Because you trusted him."

"You mean as a husband?"

"Well, yes, as a person, as a would-be father."

"Well . . . "

His eyes burned. "You're going to need to trust somebody again someday."

TWENTY FIVE

SOFT

When she got home she saw two messages blinking on the message machine. She pushed the red button and heard Mary Beth's breathy childlike voice.

"Mimi, your mom said you would have to be home by now. Are you? We all are very, very concerned about you. Can you please call as soon as you get back? We love you."

The next message was the one she dreaded, Harold's mom.

"Mimi, I've been calling your mother daily for weeks. She of course told me what you've done. I admit it seems like one chance in a million, but she thinks you must be home about now, and I am desperate to talk with you. Please call me, dear."

As she was standing there, the phone rang once more; she jumped. But she did not move her arm.

"It's me, Hank. Not to hassle you, but you said you'd call when you got back to let me know how the trip went. Call me, Mimi."

Mimi changed and sat in the dark living room. *On the windowsill again. Alone.*

Stephan on his porch. She wanted to see him better, so she pulled the old woolen blanket from her bed and threw up the window. It was too cold to be sitting out. He wore an old-fashioned pea coat but no hat. Trying to get his attention, she waved an arm; it too was too late to call out. But he was looking off into the distance, and she could not catch his eye.

"What's going on over there, really?" Mimi wondered aloud. "And where the heck is his dad—his real dad? He didn't say. You're never too young for trouble."

Becky from her classroom popped into her mind. She had finally realized it was her drawing—the one of the girl at the center of the spider web, the glasses drawn overly large, but that exaggeration making the figure seem more trapped and frightened. She grabbed hard on the sill and sat up straight.

"Oh my god, oh my god. That was not a picture of a student. That was me!"

*   *   *   *

In the morning, Mimi popped on her running shoes, knowing she was in for a miserable jog. It had been a month or so, she reckoned. The last run had been to the creek.

Not knowing is *worse than knowing, at least I think so,* she thought, going down the stairs.

She started up her street and noticed the sky, darkening and heavy, a certain scent to the air. Snow, she thought. Snow, winter. Absolute loss and winter, she thought, and for a while she jogged along chanting, "Loss and cold. Loss and cold."

How had she come to live in this suburban place? She should live in a city with cafes and shops, not here with families and dogs. Why had she never thought to go to California? No forty-year-old woman should go to the same church she had as a child.

"Child and stuck," she chanted. "Child and stuck," with each foot strike.

She noticed a pattern in the houses.

"Garage on left. Garage on right. Garage on left. Garage on right."

Nearly all had picture windows that glared into the street, and on nearly all stood a lamp on a table. Most of the lamps were elaborate. She thought they might be French Provincial or some such. Many featured dancing figures in seventeenth century dress. The houses were small and the lamps so large.

A young woman, lanky, was running from the opposite direction. Her face was brown from the sun, a new pregnancy blooming beneath her sweatshirt. She yelled to Mimi across the street, "How's it going?!"

Mimi merely nodded. Her heart seemed to rise into her throat and, she stopped abruptly to steady herself—hands to thighs.

"A baby," she heaved out loud.

Suddenly the tanned woman was at Mimi's side.

"Are you okay?"

Mimi looked up into her young face, at her belly.

"Are you happy?" Mimi asked.

"Excuse me?"

"About the baby and your life?"

"I just stopped to see if you were faint or something," the woman replied, looking unsettled.

Mimi straightened. She was the same height as her fellow runner.

"I know. I know it's weird, but are you?"

Mimi had an urge to shake her. The woman looked around, up and down the street, and finally into Mimi's sweating face. Her eyes were the color of bachelor buttons. She placed a hand on Mimi's arm.

"Very happy. Yes, I am."

She patted Mimi's shoulder and turned and ran on.

Mimi walked home. She already had a blister. *Time for new shoes.* She felt small pinpricks of cold on her nose and cheeks as she stopped and looked at the laden clouds, the silvery light. Snow. She stuck her tongue out.

"Child," she said aloud.

*   *   *   *

As Mimi limped toward the old Victorian, she spotted the blue lights of three police cars and heard another siren screaming toward her street.

"My God," she cried, and broke into a run.

When she was still a half-block away, she could see that all the activity centered on Stephan's house. She stood still a second and then tore up the street, searching the crowds for Stephan. He was not in sight. Neighbors she hadn't seen for years crowded the front lawn. The police were yelling, "Get back! Make way!"

An ambulance pulled up to the house; the paramedics jumped out and rushed up the sagging steps with a stretcher. Mimi felt panic roll through her body.

"Has anyone seen Stephan?" she called to the crowd. "Has anyone seen the little boy who lives, here, Stephan, his name is?"

Those in small groups bent their heads, evidently discussing Mimi and her question, but no one responded. She finally noticed a young chubby boy, licking a lollipop and watching the front door of Stephan's house with keen interest.

"Do you know Stephan?" she asked him.

"Drubowski?" he responded, flatly.

"Yes."

"He lives here?"

It was hopeless.

"Beats people up," the chubby boy offered as an afterthought.

"What?"

"Yeah."

Finally, she spotted a frail old lady the police had overlooked, standing directly beside the porch.

"Excuse me, do you know what's going on?"

"Oh, my dear, I'm Pearl Witsund. I live upstairs, you know. We've been waiting for this, something like this. Just a ruckus all the time. I'm the one who called the police."

Mimi placed a hand on the woman's gesturing arm.

"Please, what happened?"

"Don't know." She glanced around. "Just a terrible scream like I never heard, and I've heard a lot. Maybe some pots being thrown. I heard the man," she nodded toward Stephan's front door, "shout right before, but that's nothing unusual. Then dead silence, till the police showed up."

Just then, the old wooden door of the house banged open and the paramedics emerged with a blanketed figure on a stretcher. As they rushed by Mimi and Pearl, she saw that the figure was a woman, maybe late thirties, sandy hair, nearly red, with splashes of blood on her face. Two policemen came next with a man, handcuffed, a nearly finished cigarette in the corner of his lips. A stench of whiskey blew from his body. His full head of black hair and bushy brows suggested youth, but he looked old, used up; there was no telling his age. A huge, prune-colored bruise bloomed on his forehead. His navy filling station or car repair uniform displayed his name in white, *Al D.* Some people in the crowd drew their breath when they saw him; excited murmurings ensued.

They were placing the woman in the ambulance and the man into the patrol car when Mimi heard, "There she is, my friend! The lady I told you about!"

Mimi turned to see Stephan, speckles of blood on his T-shirt, break from a policewoman's hand and streak toward her.

He was screaming, "Mimi, I told them. I told them you'd be here."

Stephan was shaking her arms, and then he buried his head into her belly and began to sob. A policewoman came up to them. Kneeling down beside him, she spoke softly but very firmly, "Stephan, I know this woman is your friend, but we need to find someone to look after you. Someone the court appoints for you."

Stephan clutched his arms harder around Mimi's waist. Mimi held him tightly, her mind whirring.

"I'm not coming. I'm not coming."

The police woman stood up to address Mimi. "He's going to need special care, a counselor. His mother could . . . " She looked at Stephan and then called, "Officer Kemp, could you please settle Stephan in a patrol car?"

Stephan screamed and fought the officer; another policeman had to be called to help Officer Kemp get him into the car.

The woman waited a few seconds.

"His mother was stabbed, with pinking shears, if you know what those are. She could survive . . . but I've seen some of these incidents and . . . well. He witnessed everything—tried to stop the assailant, his stepfather, with an iron pot. Made a nice dent in his head—the kid is strong—but couldn't stop him.

Stephan said the man didn't like his beans cooked so soft. Soft."
The officer shook her blonde head.

Mimi's mind raced. "Where will he be taken?"

"Well, I don't know. Sometimes it's immediately into foster care, sometimes a juvenile facility. We'll try to find relatives . . . "

She spoke without thinking. "I will take him."

The woman officer looked down, hesitating.

"Released temporarily into my custody." Mimi had no idea where these words came from.

"Well, normally, we . . . "

"I'm a first-grade teacher. I'm not going anywhere. Temporarily. Check me out tonight. I'll give you references."

"That's not for me to decide."

"Well, right now, this very minute, after this kid has been practically destroyed, you want to take him away to strangers? Because it's not for you to decide? Because *you're* uncomfortable?"

"You don't get it." But the woman did not sound angry. "I could lose my job."

They stared at each other. Stephan was calling her name.

"You know," Mimi tried to sound calm, sensible. "He could lose his life over this. He might."

The women locked eyes and then, "Officer Kemp."

The policeman looked up from his paperwork.

"Bring Stephan here, please."

*　　　*　　　*　　　*

The first thing Mimi and Stephan did was to get a kitten. Mimi went to the same women who had supplied Mickey's cat, and Stephan picked out a calico. They sat her on towels on the kitchen table and, leaning on their arms, thought about a name.

"Boo hoo," Stephan offered.

"But don't you think that's kind of sad?" Mimi suggested.

"Yea, but she looks kind of sad," said Stephan.

Mimi couldn't see this but replied, "Well this is a big adjustment, don't you think?"

Stephan said nothing, just sat petting the kitten, somewhat tentatively. Mimi had a million ideas, Patches, Cloudy, Buttons, Pippy, Yin Yang. She liked Yin Yang the best, but she kept silent.

"Opal."

"How do you know that word?"

"My mom's ring. It has lots of colors in it."

Mimi looked at the kitten, now curled in sleep. *Opal.* She got up from her chair, ruffled Stephan's hair and kissed his head.

"You must be the best name-giver in the universe!"

Stephan looked at Mimi as if he were waking from a dream. "Do you think so?"

"I know so, Opal. Just look at that cat—Opal——amazing!"

Stephan's smiling face was a small sun. It was the first happy expression he'd had in the three days he'd been with her.

TWENTY SIX

WHY

This was a new life for Mimi, and the ride was not smooth. She wanted to be supportive, but not to smother Stephan. She knew nothing about football, which he was crazy about. She found the game boring and brutal. He was not a natural student. He was a curious, perhaps brilliant child, but academics held no interest for him. He claimed nightly to have finished his homework when, in fact, when Mimi checked, he had only begun each subject.

When Mimi took Stephan to the library she did not know what to expect, but he was impressed—first with the building itself, its columns and sparkling granite steps. At the entrance, he turned and told Mimi that he had never been to a library. She squeezed his shoulder.

"I think you'll find it interesting."

Inside, he stood very still and looked around him.

"How does it work?"

"Well, you get a card, a library card, and then you check books out."

"Anything? Any book?"

"Just about."

Mimi showed Stephan to the junior section. But soon he pulled on her sleeve, saying, "Where's the painting section?" So they went to Art and Art History up the winding staircase.

"This is the coolest place." Stephan's pale face bloomed a rose in each cheek. "I never saw steps like these. What kind of wood is this?"

He had stopped to caress the banister. "Let's see." She peered at the wood. Mahogany, yes, I think mahogany."

"This is the best wood in the world," he replied excitedly. "All those colors."

She smiled at this observation, wondering. He and Mimi then separated to comb the stacks, pausing here and there to open a volume. Each was lost in his own search for some time. When Mimi found Stephan, he was sprawled on the floor with several huge books and one smaller one.

"Do you know this Michelangelo?" he inquired.

She plopped down beside him. "Why yes, I do."

"He's the coolest. He likes strength."

"How do you feel about that?"

"Well, you've got to be strong."

"Not everybody is, you know."

"And that's how they get hurt."

"Even strong people get hurt, Stephan."

He looked at her, wide-eyed, and then snapped his book shut. "I don't think so." And then, "Can we go now?

*   *   *   *

Stephan asked if he could make dinner. Mimi felt dubious, but he looked so earnest.

"I want to make it for you, because you're taking care of me and everything."

"Well, Stephan, what if I help just a little? You can tell me what to do."

"No." He shook his head vigorously. "No, I can do it."

So, Mimi sat down at her work table and began twisting wire around some spherical amber beads. Stephan came in to her bedroom to ask where Mimi's spices were. "Spices?" She looked up from her work.

"Yeah. I need some garlic and onion powder."

She could not help laughing. "You little chef, you."

Stephan laughed also, but then said, "I'm not little."

She peered at him through her glasses. "No, no you aren't."

At this he walked over to her table. "This the stuff you make?"

"Some of it." She handed a couple of the wrapped beads to Stephan. He rolled them over with a delicate touch.

"Why do you do it?"

No one had ever asked her this question. She had not asked herself.

"I . . . " She looked down at the work table, at the beads. She picked up one of the amber beads and held it to the halogen work lamp.

"When I see these beads, Stephan, especially, the glass ones, when I hold them up to the light, it feels like everything changes. Suddenly it's the blue world or the red or the amber. And somehow this change, this light coming through makes me very, very happy."

He held one of the beads up to the lamp.

"Color is something like God."

Mimi's mouth fell open; she felt as though she had received a small blow somewhere inside. Mimi turned Stephan to face her. She shook him softly. "Stephan, you are a very remarkable young man. You have some kind of special gift. I don't exactly know what it is yet. But what I am asking you is to believe me, to believe that. Can you do that?"

Stephan was looking intently at Mimi, a grave expression in his grey eyes.

"My dad said, lots of times. 'Kid, you're gonna have to work damn hard in this life.'"

Stephan's eyes filled with tears and he looked down.

"Why, Stephan, did he say that?"

She patted his cheek.

"Kid, you're gonna have to work hard, cause you just aren't bright."

Mimi put her arms around him, and he wept hard onto her shoulder, then stopped abruptly, lifted his head, picked up his enormous T-shirt and wiped his face with it.

"I have to finish dinner."

Mimi turned him away from her and swatted his back. "Okay, Chef Stephan." And then she called after him, "Don't forget Opal."

"Been there. Done that," Stephan called in return.

Stephan would not allow Mimi into the kitchen, but when he finally called her, she was shocked at what he had done. Two mismatched candles were in the silver holders she'd forgotten she had. He'd carefully placed paper toweling over the whole table in lieu of a cloth and more folded towels as napkins. He had found the wedding crystal she used with Father Ben and had ice and water in them. Two matching plates for each of them; one was chipped. She clasped her hands together.

"I don't remember anything looking so lovely!"

He pulled out her chair for her, and she sat down. Then he took the plates to the stove and placed the dinner carefully, attractively on them, and brought them to the table.

"It's just hamburgers, fried, and baked potatoes, and I found this frozen spinach in your freezer."

"It's all wonderful! But . . . you like spinach?"

"Not much, but I want to be like Popeye, you know?"

She looked over at him, wondering; he winked, and they both laughed.

"Now I know what you wanted the garlic and onion for." She had bitten into the meat. "This is very good."

"Yeah," Stephan responded. "I like to cook."

"Why do you?"

"Because it's like an invention. You just make it up. You never know how it's going to be."

*　　*　　*　　*

Mimi took Stephan to see his mother once she was out of intensive care. Catherine was her name. Every time they went to the hospital, the woman cried and thanked Mimi again and again.

"You should be paid something," she insisted. "But I'm not in any position . . . "

"No," Mimi always responded. "You see I'm doing this because I'm selfish. I like to have Stephan around."

To Stephan, Catherine would say the last thing before they left: "Now Stephan, you won't forget your mother?"

One day after Stephan had been with Mimi a couple of weeks, they were leaving the hospital, and Stephan called to Mimi as they were getting in her car. "How could my mom think I'd forget her?"

Mimi considered this.

"I think it's just her way of saying she misses you."

Stephan clamped his seatbelt.

"Then why doesn't she say that?"

Mimi was startled. She patted Stephan's hand.

"Sometimes people have trouble saying what they really mean. They're not used to it."

"You don't."

"Well, I'm sure I do sometimes. You just haven't caught me at it yet."

Stephan was quiet for some moments as they made their way through the snow-dusted streets.

"I'm not homesick."

She did not reply at first, but as soon as she could she steered the car on to the side of the street and shut off the engine.

They looked at each other.

"Well, home was pretty rough wasn't it?"

"My dad's an asshole."

"Well, when your mom gets better, just think how nice that will be. You two will have an all-new life."

He turned away and looked out of the window; his reply was lackluster. "Yeah."

*   *   *   *

Mimi was relieved when they arrived at her apartment. They'd skidded the last two blocks on Fern. She collected her mail and then heard Stephan shout from the top of the stairs, "Whoa!"

When Mimi approached her door, Stephan was standing with his arms full of Calla Lilies and red roses. His eyes were sparkling. He hadn't noticed the card propped against her door. She bent to retrieve it and noticed, startled, Ben's firm handwriting

—*Mimi*—across the white envelope. When they were inside, she instructed Stephan to get a vase from the below the kitchen sink and place the flowers in it. She scanned the card. The same flowers were on the front, a message from Ben inside.

Mimi, I think it's been nearly a month since we've spoken. Much has happened to me, and from what your mother tells me, much has happened for you. I hope to talk to you soon. These flowers reminded me of your spirit.

With affection, Ben.

When Mimi went into the kitchen, Stephan was bent over the flowers in a vase, that furrow between his brows, arranging and rearranging the grouping. He'd placed Opal on her blanket on the table to watch.

"What are these big white things?"

"They're called Calla Lilies."

"They don't look real."

"No, no they don't."

"Is it your birthday?"

Mimi was looking out of the kitchen window, distracted.

"No, Stephan. Why do you ask?"

"Well, I never knew people gave flowers for nothing."

She ruffled his bent head.

"Not exactly for nothing Stephan. But yes, sometimes people just want to give you something."

"Why?"

"They want to remind you in an impressive way that they care about you."

"Who cares about you this much?"

She jumped slightly at his question.

"Oh, my friend, Ben."

"I didn't know you had a boyfriend."

She lifted his chin with her finger.

"Not a boyfriend, Stephan, a friend."

He went back to arranging the flowers. "Humph."

*   *   *   *

After her first day back, she realized she needed time, blank space, and then, when Stephan came to stay, knew she must concentrate all her energy for a while on him. So she'd answered no messages for days. Now, after Stephan's dinner, as they were poking through her bookshelves for something that might interest him, she noticed that the annoying machine was blinking. Someone must have called when they'd gone walking. She poked the red button with mixed feelings.

It was Mary Beth. "Your mom says you needed some time alone and that you found Harold—that's all she would say, and that somehow you have a little boy living with you. Please get in touch, Mimi. Everyone's frantic about you."

The next message caused her heart to rear up inside her chest.

"Mimi, I'm calling to tell you how much better I've been. I have no more amnesia. I am rethinking everything—my whole life —and would love to talk by phone when you can. I've called my mother as you suggested; but that was difficult. I love you, Mimi."

Stephan entered the living room and heard the last couple of sentences.

"Oh, is that your friend?" he asked.

"No, Stephan, my husband."

TWENTY SEVEN

THE KEY

Mimi had taken Stephan to Alice's so she could see her friends for dinner and a movie. Alice had enthusiastically accepted a grandmother's role with Stephan; the evening would give her a break from the growing intensity of their relationship. Link had invited all of them to dinner at her funky Evanston stone cottage that Mimi always thought of as "The Witches' House." They all wanted to hear the complete "Odyssey," as they termed Mimi's search.

As Mimi finished, they were weeping and blowing their noses into their paper napkins. Then questions began to fly, many and all at once.

"But, I still don't understand why he didn't come back." Mary Beth looked pained. "Is he in love with Leda? You didn't say."

"You know," Mimi's voice emerged amazingly calm. "I don't believe Harold's capable of loving anybody right now. And remember, he didn't come back because he said we didn't have a good marriage. That we didn't have the marrying kind of love."

Jan spat out the next words.

"That's shit. You had some problems, but doesn't everybody? Gosh, you guys were sweethearts in high school. Men —they are such chickenshits."

Link burst in, "Now, wait a minute. Let's not be sexist. There are chicken-shits on all sides. The guy is sick. He has an illness." She opened her hands wide for emphasis. "What is it called again, Mimi?"

"The doctor said fugue—Psychogenic Fugue."

Mimi could see that Jan was her same angry self.

"Fugue, smoogue. The guy hauls his ass on out of here to find himself (give me a break), picks up with a young rich babe, and *forgets* he has a life. Come on!"

No one chose to comment on Jan's small tirade. Link patted Mimi's hand.

"Well, what's going to happen to you financially, in all this? I mean *Current Wisdom* is not going to have a 401.K plan. Do you need to leave the apartment? I mean you can always stay with me if it comes to that, if you don't mind living with a dyke."

Mimi lay her head on Link's shoulder.

"Mary-Marsha Maculhey, you have always had a too-big heart."

Jan offered, "You can always live with me. I've got room upon room."

"Hey, women, I told you Pete gave me some money. I'm okay for now, and I am a teacher, remember? I have a profession."

*   *   *   *

Mimi had set up a small work table alongside her own, but soon Stephan eschewed the beads altogether and began using her rosary pliers and wire to make shapes. At first they were rough. Stephan would let out huge exhalations of frustration, but finally, after a week's work he'd shaped a horse that looked quite magical—not the horse so much as the kinetic impression it created. She knew other children's art from her work as a teacher, but did not remember this striving for motion and power in any child's art she had seen before.

Mimi lay down the necklace of crystals and turquoise she was stringing.

"Hey, Stephan, we have to talk."

He had not heard her. He was shaping individual wires into the flying horse's tail.

"Your mom comes home in three days."

He did not look up. She tapped him gently on the shoulder.

"Stephan."

He met her eyes, but held onto the pliers and the horse in his hands.

"Let's get some coffee," Mimi suggested.

They sat at the kitchen table sipping thoughtfully for a while.

"So, your mom comes home Wednesday."

Stephan stirred more cream into his cup. "Yeah."

"Look, Stephan, it's going to be good. Like I said, you'll have an all-new life."

"Well, see, I love my mom . . . "

"Yes, I know you do."

"But . . . "

"But?"

"I just like living here, that's all."

"Hey, but what about sleeping on the lumpy couch, and no TV, and no real place for your clothes . . . ?"

"Yeah, but I'll miss you too much. The stuff we do. The stuff we talk about. I'll miss . . . " He dragged a hand across his eyes. "You don't treat me like a kid."

Mimi got up from the table. Stephan jumped up from his chair. She circled her arms about his small, skinny body, and he wept quietly for a while.

"Wait, Stephan." She held him briefly by the shoulders, and then dashed to her pantry and pulled down a key from a nail. Mimi indicated Stephan should sit down; she brought her chair around to his side of the table. His grey eyes were earnest.

"This is the key to my apartment. This little home of mine is your home now also. You've made it that way, Stephan. You're to knock always first, but when you need to or when you want to, you are welcome. I will be here for you."

Stephan wiped some fresh tears, but he clutched the key in his fist and smiled.

TWENTY EIGHT

TROUBLING

Mickey answered her mother's door, beer in hand.

"Well, big sister, brother and I have been slaving over a hot stove all day for you."

"Fat chance." Mimi gave him an affectionate shove. "Where's Mom?"

"What a question!" Mickey shot back.

Mimi found her mother in the kitchen, stirring an immense pot of chili.

"Oh, Mimi, I don't think this is quite right, and the boys are so hungry. Could you taste it?"

"Hello to you too, Mom and I didn't see any boys in the living room. Just one big lug, I'd say."

Mimi tasted the chili, knowing it would be wonderful.

"What made you want to feed us orphans?"

"Here Mimi, take this beer to your brother. He called for one a half an hour ago."

"He has one already."

"No, Teddy. He's in the basement looking through your dad's tackle box."

Mimi went past the refrigerator and opened the door to the basement. "Hey Teddy, get your stinking butt up here and get your beer."

"Bitch," he yelled back. But she heard him barreling up the steps.

"Oh, Mimi, you never want to do anything for your brothers." Her mother's practiced whine.

Teddy exploded from behind the basement door.

"Hey, Mimi, look what the wind blew in." He gave her a bear hug; she kissed his cheek and returned to her mother at the stove.

"Chili's great as always, Mom."

"I don't know. Something's just not right."

"Well, then we'll just have to fix it, won't we?"

Her mother tried to read Mimi's expression. "Smart mouth," she replied.

Mimi began rummaging beneath the sink.

"Got any medicine in here?" she called, bringing out a bottle of gin.

"I'll have a little of that." Her mom's face brightened.

Teddy called from his stool by the refrigerator, "Ha, if it's like any other night, you'll have a lot of that."

"Smart mouth," her mother said.

The door to the tiny kitchen banged open, and Mimi's dad lumbered in, a load of logs in his arms.

"Well, I see the boys have been helping both parents," Mimi remarked.

Teddy shot a refrigerator magnet at Mimi. She shot it back, hitting him square on the chest.

Mickey came in and went for another beer.

"Now, Mimi, don't start. This is the only day off for these boys. They should rest."

Mickey screwed the top off his beer and took a huge swallow.

"Yeah, Mimi Mouse, it's our day to rest."

Her father walked past.

"For God's sake, one of you buttheads help Dad."

Mickey took the wood, and her dad began yanking off his down parka, which Mimi observed had been mended with silver duct tape. It was the family joke—her father's silver tape repairs. Teddy had once taken a picture of a Volkswagen Beetle with its rear fender patched to the body of the car with this same magic tape. Underneath the picture he'd scrawled, "Dad was here." Her dad still had the picture over his Salvation Army-gleaned desk in the basement.

"Mimi, I'll have a little of that gin. And a glass of water," her dad requested. He wore that vacant look again, she observed.

She poured a shot for her dad and made her mother and herself a martini of sorts. Her mother always forgot to buy vermouth.

Teddy got off his barstool just as Mickey returned, and they came together in the center of the room, clinking bottles and glasses.

"The family that drinks together, stinks together," Mickey offered as a toast.

*　　　*　　　*　　　*

Mimi sat on her bed, going over her accounting book. Her landlord was raising her rent, something she'd never even thought of when she left Lincoln to do Current Wisdom full time. She had a show coming up for Sunnyfield; Grandma Tinker had set it up so that the older folks could purchase Christmas presents. They'd buy her cheapest, least inspired pieces, if anything, so she couldn't count on any real profit from that. She could possibly go to Alice for a loan, but that was a last resort. And she hadn't heard back from Gerry Mertz about whether the PTA would allow her to do a holiday show at Lincoln. She would have to call; she dreaded contact with him, but she was getting desperate. Mimi closed the book and switched off the light, noticing that it was eleven o'clock. *So late!* She pulled on her nightgown in the dark, making her way to the kitchen, where she boiled water for some chamomile tea. She then went to sit on the windowsill with her cup. No Stephan. Now it really *was* too cold for him to be sitting out. Mimi missed him. She missed Opal; she'd decided at the last minute to let Stephan take her home.

Alone. Alone. Alone.

"That's enough," she said out loud. "What I mean is," she was explaining to herself, "what I mean is, that's enough of being alone. Time to do something."

Mimi trudged back into the kitchen and pulled the Yellow Pages from the kitchen drawer. She copied the names and numbers of a couple of optometrists. Then she went into the bathroom where she flipped on the light, plucked the shears she used to trim her bangs from the medicine cabinet, rinsed her hair in the sink, pulled off her nightgown and, after carefully combing her hair and parting it straight down the middle, began to cut off her hair to her jawbone. Her bangs were nearly as long; those she clipped at an angle toward her face. She held her glasses up and looked through one lens to the other side of her face to see the effect—new hair, no glasses.

"Nice. Very, very nice."

*   *   *   *

Mimi stood in line at the Roman Theatre. No one had been interested in *Wuthering Heights*. Jan had merely snorted and replied, "I don't have to see it, I'm living it."

Mary Beth was taking night classes. She hadn't reached Link. But Mimi had never minded going to the movies alone. She and Harold only occasionally agreed on a film they could see together. She was feeling the need for a purge. A hand lay suddenly, on her shoulder.

"Mimi, is that you?"

"Oh, Ben!" Mimi was surprised at her rush of feeling, a confusing sense of relief.

"I didn't recognize you."

Mimi was reddening. "I needed a change."

"Hmm," Ben was searching her face. The man behind her reluctantly hung back to allow the priest into line.

"So, have you changed just your hair and eyes—where are your glasses?—or has the overhaul been more extensive?"

Mimi laughed. They were at the ticket booth. She felt awkward,

"Oh, were you passing by, or were you going to see the film . . . ?"

The ticket-taker began drumming her fingers and looking over Mimi's shoulder. She was a wan waif with spring green hair; Mimi noticed, *FREE* , one letter per finger, tattooed in black.

"Well actually," now Ben looked embarrassed, " I was on my way to a card game at Jimmy Dolan's just two buildings down, when I thought I'd see if you were you."

The waif spoke into the microphone,

"Two adults?"

Ben slid his wallet from his Levi's. "Yes."

*　　　*　　　*　　　*

Ben squeezed her hand a few times during the film as Mimi dabbed at her eyes and blew her nose into his handkerchief. How could she cry for Catherine yet again?

When they stumbled out of the darkness and onto the marquee-lit sidewalk, Mimi felt ill from sorrow. Ben placed his arm around her shoulders.

"How many times have you seen that film?"

"Eight. Eight times."

"Whew! A glutton for punishment, eh?"

"Guess so."

"Well, Mimi, I would like to talk to you, but I guess I can't take you anywhere, really. At night like this."

"Oh." She was still stabbing the corners of her eyes.

They were quiet, looking towards opposite ends of the street.

"Well," Mimi offered, uncertain of her voice, "we could each go home and talk by phone." This idea appealed to her.

"It's hard to talk at the rectory."

"Oh, of course."

He turned her toward himself.

"Look, Mimi, let me come over for a while, please."

*   *   *   *

Mimi had a bottle of good Chardonnay but not much else. She gave the bottle to Ben to uncork and dug in the refrigerator for some cheeses. Finding no crackers, she grabbed a baguette and sliced it diagonally. All this she placed carefully on a large wooden cutting board, and brought it into the living room.

"Oh, glasses," she realized. Ben took the board, and she went back and got some plain juice glasses for the wine. *Better to keep things non-festive.*

This time they sat on the couch together.

"Well," he said.

"Well," Mimi replied.

"Please don't take offense if I say you are looking very lovely."

"Thank you." She sipped her wine. "Where are you? You said you were transferred?

"Well, it's rough. I'm half-time at each parish. Father Moretti and Father Lyon need to learn the ropes at St. Mark's while I am doing the same at St. Timothy's." He tapped her shoulder. "Your mother said Harold did not want to return home."

"No, he did not."

They were quiet for some time.

"Would it help to talk about it?"

"I've done that. I've done it to death."

"Has it helped?"

"At first."

"What will you do now?'

"I don't know. It's a blank. But it's got something to do with changing."

"More changes."

They looked at each other. Mimi thought she saw a flicker of mild fear in Ben's black eyes.

"It's funny. In a way we're on the same path." He drank a large gulp of wine.

"How's that?" Mimi inquired.

"Mimi, I can't stay at St. Timothy's."

"But in your letter you said you liked it—the mixed neighborhood and all. And, I didn't think priests had a choice."

"They don't."

"So?"

"People do."

"People?"

He placed the small glass on the coffee table and refilled it, but did not drink. He drew her hand into his both of his.

"I, I don't think I'm a priest anymore."

She pulled her hand away. "But . . . no! Don't you say 'forever' or 'eternal' or something like that during Holy Orders? It's just like marriage, isn't it? And what in the world would you do?"

"Married people get divorced."

"But not in the eyes of the church."

"In their own eyes. It's finally, the place we live."

She knew this was true. It was what she faced with Harold.

He cleared his throat. "And what would I do? Like you, that's kind of a blank."

Mimi could not look at him. "Would you go home for awhile?"

"I really don't know. That's one of my options. Why don't you look at me?"

"I don't know."

"Do you think this is wrong, Mimi? That I am wrong?"

She played with the design in the sofa cushion.

"Well," she looked at him briefly, "I am not going to judge you."

"Then what is it?"

She struggled to see what it was she was feeling.

"It's troubling, just very, very troubling."

"Well, my God, yes, it's troubling." Ben was on his feet, pacing the small room. "Troubling?" He turned towards her startled face. "I'm dying, Mimi. I'm dying whether I stay or go. If my dying is troubling, I'm sorry. If you're uncomfortable with whatever way you may be part of this and you're troubled, I'm sorry."

His hands, she noticed, were closed into fists at his sides. He had never removed his jacket.

She was up and standing in front of him, pulling at his arms.

"No. No, I'm not part of this—any damn part of this. I have nothing to do with this decision. You can't make me part of this. It's like blaming me."

"What are you saying? What can you be thinking?" Ben asked, his eyes burning. He pulled his arms away sharply. "What would I blame you for?" He turned his back on her. "Of course you're part of this, don't you know that?"

"No! Look, Ben, you lost your father. You lost your parish. You've been treated shoddily. You needed a friend; I tried to be one, but in your loss and confusion, don't turn what we have into something you think you need—something much, much bigger than it is."

He wheeled around.

"What are you doing?" He cupped her face in his hands. "I'm astonished!"

Mimi began to weep. "I don't understand any of this."

"Of course you do." He placed his arms around her and kissed her forehead. "Of course you do."

Mimi pulled away from him.

"You should go Ben. I think you should go."

He searched her face for some moments, turned, and in a few long strides reached the door, opened it and disappeared down the stairway. Once again, she heard the glass shaking in the old front door.

*   *   *   *

"I did tell you he wouldn't come back."

Mimi couldn't help smiling at this. "You did say that, Grandma. You did. But how did you know?"

"Unhappiness."

"Unhappiness?"

Grandma was limping down the hallway at Sunnyfield. Nonetheless, she'd told Mimi she needed to pace a little, so that's what they were doing. She used a cane all the time now. Alice had bought it for her; the knob of the cane was a round owl's head. Its eyes were glassy blue and huge. She stopped and gazed closely at Mimi.

"I want you to have this when I'm gone." She tapped the cane a couple of times on the vinyl floor. "You like owls, don't you? That's what I remember."

Mimi was confused. "Why, yes, and . . . thank you. But you were saying about unhappiness?"

"I was?"

"Yes. Something about Harold's not coming back."

"Oh, yes. People say unhappiness is in here." The old woman lay a blue veined hand lightly against her chest. She gave the cane to Mimi and gestured, sweeping her hands over her body.

"But I've always said, unhappiness is something you wear. It floats around your body like a gown. It lifts off of you, and when you stand close enough to people, they can feel it."

"And Harold?" Mimi held her breath.

"Unhappy."

"You mean with me?"

"With everything."

TWENTY NINE

PETAL AFTER PETAL

Mimi was cooking a dinner for Alice; Stephan had offered to help. She was showing him how to cut carrots on the diagonal. He wanted to know why, so she was explaining the idea of aesthetic sensibility.

"Like when I set the table for you."

"That's it, Stephan. You have it too. You take care with the way things look because to do so pleases or satisfies something inside of yourself."

"That's another reason I like it over here."

"Because?"

"Because you've got these little lights on the tables and funny cushions on the couch. And your towels all match in the bathroom. And I like the furry rug in there when I get out of the shower, and things are kind of neat, you know, put away and everything."

"Well, tell me about your house."

"It's worse now."

"Um hmm. Worse?"

"Yeah. My mom is sad all the time. You know, more than before. She doesn't do much. She watches TV and cries a lot so, well, she even forgets to do the laundry sometimes."

"She must miss your dad."

Stephan's head flew up. "I don't want you to call him that anymore."

Mimi placed a hand on Stephan's shoulder.

"Okay."

"And I hate that. I hate that." Stephan's hands curled tight. The knife was pointed up. Mimi knew it was very sharp.

"You hate . . . ?"

"How can she miss that bastard? How can she? He tried to kill her. I hate that! I hate . . . " Mimi slipped the knife from his grip and took him to a chair at the table and sat beside him.

For a moment, Stephan stared out the kitchen window and then, abruptly, into Mimi's face.

"It's all right. I can take it, Stephan."

"I hate it, that's all. You said we were going to have an all-new life. Well, it's a bad life and I hate it!" He began to cry, then pounded the table hard with his fist.

"I hate it. I hate . . . I hate . . . her. I hate her for missing him."

Mimi was silent. Then she stroked his hand.

"The hating part . . . it's all right, you can't love someone all the time. But my take on this—you let me know if this sounds right—my take is that you are very, very disappointed in your mother, and that it's what she's doing and not doing that you hate, not really her."

"What she's not doing?"

"Well, yeah, like the laundry, like running the house, like giving you attention."

His eyes were alert, intense.

"What's your counselor say?"

"She's stupid."

"Why do you think so?"

Stephan threw up his right hand.

"She doesn't get anything." He looked at Mimi, searching. She nodded for him to go on.

"She says my mom has been having a hard time for many years and to be patient."

"That doesn't sound too stupid."

"Don't you even get it? I had a hard time for many years too."

Mimi threw her arms around Stephan's thin body. Without thinking, Mimi rocked him, and for a few minutes he allowed her to.

*   *   *   *

At six o'clock precisely, the doorbell rang. Alice on time! Stephan ran to get the door, where Alice let out a delighted cry, squeezed Stephan, and reached into her purse for one of the little candy bars she always kept there. What a wonderful mother she must have been for Harold. What had gone wrong?

They came into the kitchen, Alice patting Stephan's head.

"I hear you've had some excellent help with my dinner."

Mimi was wiping her hands on a kitchen towel.

"There's no better help than Stephan's." Stephan began to tear off the wrap from a Mars bar. "Hey, Stephan, could you wait? Until after we eat?"

"Oh, I can't stay, thanks. I've got to go home."

Mimi was puzzled. "So, your mom is still cooking dinner, then?"

"Oh, no! I do. I'm making a chicken. See ya, Grandma Alice. Bye, Mimi. And Stephan dashed out the door, leaving the two women to stare at each other.

"That boy is cooking meals?" Alice was indignant.

"Oh, I knew he could cook. I just never thought how that all came about. Let's sit down and eat, Alice. I need to talk to you about Stephan.

*   *   *   *

After dinner, the women were on the couch drinking tea when Alice looked up and said, "Oh, your wedding picture!"

Mimi blushed fiercely.

"Oh, yes, I just thought, you know, this is tacky. Nobody has a huge picture of themselves over the sofa. It was embarrassing."

"And sad."

"And sad."

"You know, Mimi, there's something I need to tell you. Harold's father left him some money. He was supposed to receive it on his fortieth birthday. But he went away and never got it."

"Harold said his father had disowned him."

"Well, that's what Dean said, but he just couldn't do that. He worried Harold would not do well financially."

"Well, he had that one right."

"I want Harold to have it but . . . " The woman was still beautiful. At sixty-five, only the front of her jet hair was streaked with grey; her face held a glow.

"What is it, Mom?"

"You should have some of that money Mimi. If there's a divorce . . . for all the years . . . I wanted you to know he has it."

Mimi cleared her throat and squeezed Alice's hand. "Would it be okay to tell me how much money Harold will receive? It would help me to know."

"Two hundred thousand. More now I guess, with interest. Now that he's come back."

"But he didn't really."

"No. No, he didn't."

*　　*　　*　　*

Mimi was doing the dishes when her mother-in-law re-entered the kitchen with her coat on.

"Mimi, that child is with you too much."

"Do you think so?" Mimi's heart sank.

"Yes, I'm sorry to say. He needs a man's influence."

"So do I," Mimi shot back. Then, "Sorry, I'm fresh out."

Alice's forehead wrinkled. "I had an idea."

"Umm hmm?"

"Father Ben. He should take him under his wing. It's a rather desperate situation."

"It's a desperate situation. But . . . Ben's moving parishes and working double time and . . . "

"Ben?"

"Oh, Father Ben."

"I know. I know but—please Mimi, will you call him . . . for Stephan?"

Mimi wrung her hands in the sudsy water.

"Yes. Yes, of course."

*   *   *   *

It was a man in a winter coat—the kind worn in the forties, thick, pebbly, heavy. His head was bare. Snowflakes were coming down like air-filled golf balls, round, floating. When he turned, she saw that it was Harold. He opened his coat, and a cloud of small birds flew out. She noticed that his entire chest was in the shape of a heart, but it was not red or beating. It was clear glass, and through it she could see the bluest sky above the black tree branches. And he was calling like a child, in the voice of a child, "Mimi . . . "

She sat up and looked at her star clock. Three o'clock. She calculated the time in Idaho. One. Throwing off her blankets, Mimi went to the kitchen and poured herself a glass of the Chardonnay Ben had opened. She set herself on the windowsill with the afghan from her sofa and looked out.

"It isn't going to be easy to leave this man," she said, steaming the window.

What was it that held Harold to her? She remembered being surprised by his tenderness. Most of the men she'd dated possessed a wild urgency that frightened her. The way he'd removed her clothing that first time, folding each item with a kind of quiet respect. It had been a long time since she had allowed herself to look at these things, at the good times.

"Stop, Mimi. Don't do this to yourself. What is the point?"

She took a sip of wine and shivered against the wide window frame. The dream. Was it a repeat of another she'd had? It seemed so familiar.

"Pete!"

Like Pete's dream, the one that made me want to look for him. Not exactly, but very like it. But I did look for him. So why does he call me? Or is it really me calling him? She had not returned his phone call. She had not written to him. Should she have?

The phone rang; she pulled in a sharp breath, leaped up, spilling the wine on her nightgown, and fumbled for the phone in the dark.

"Mimi . . ."

"What is it Mom?"

"Grandma . . . her heart . . . "

"Where are you?"

"Home, but I'm going over there right now. She's in the coronary care unit at Emery Hospital.

"I'm leaving."

*   *   *   *

When Mimi arrived at the waiting room, she saw that her brothers were there, her father and mother—none of Grandma's nieces or nephews. As she walked in, stomping snow off her boots, they all stood.

Her mother held out her arms, and she walked over to her. Mickey, Teddy and her father surrounded the two women.

"What is the situation?" she whispered.

Mimi's mother held her tightly. "Heart attack. Just about an hour ago. Sunnyfield got her over here right away. They told us she sat up in bed and punched the button, but she could not speak—the pain was so bad—but she had her hand on her chest and they just knew."

Her dad spoke, patting her head. "She's alive, honey. She's alive but . . . " Mimi raised her head from her mother's shoulder and stared at her father.

"What? What, Dad?"

Mickey spoke. "Mimi, it's bad. They aren't giving us any hope."

Mimi's legs were water. She staggered a bit to one of the couches and sat down. Teddy sat beside her and took her hands in his; she lay her head on his shoulder and wept. They all sat then, dabbing at their eyes, blowing their noses. Silent. Was everything going to go away? She looked at her parents. Her mother had given up tinting her hair. Her dad forgot to comb his anymore. She hadn't noticed before that Teddy and Mickey were nearly bald. All of them were pale in the fluorescent light. Was everything slipping off the world? Grandma, Ben's dad. Soon her own parents. They were all on a conveyor belt—sometimes it seemed to run faster than other times. They would do what they would do and roll off the end. Nothing meant anything if it all ended. What had Mimi to show for her life—what had any of them? Her parents' house folding and sagging around them, her mother's fake brass candleholders. Her father's collapsing piano. The things that held them, that they used every day, would mean nothing to anyone. It would seem as if they'd never been there— gone up in a puff.

"She's the best person I've ever known." Mickey's face was wet. "Did you guys ever get one of her Band-Aids?"

Teddy released Mimi's hands and leaned forward, staring at the floor.

"Yeah. She kept a bowl of them by the front door, remember, Mick?"

"Beside the Band-Aids," Mickey was wiping his eyes with his hands, "was an identical bowl filled with Tootsie Pops. After you got your Band-Aid, you got to pick any damn flavor. Two cuts —two Tootsie Pops.

Edie spoke in a whisper, "You children know that she sewed ever tear in just about anything we ever had, all the buttons, patches. She'd come over and bully me into another load of mending."

Mimi knew she could remember a hundred things, but it sounded like a funeral and she found herself resisting their memories.

"What are they doing in there for her?"

Her father replied, clearing his throat, "They haven't told us except to say they have her on intravenous medication and a heart monitor. They're giving her oxygen too. They've called Veronica."

Veronica Tinker lived in Madison, Wisconsin. As far as Mimi knew, she saw Grandma twice a year. On Grandma's birthday, she flew into O'Hare at about ten o'clock in the morning, took her to dinner at Imperial's and, by midnight, was back on the plane for Madison and some vague corporate job. Mickey had always claimed that Veronica's briefcase had grown from her hand and could not be pried loose. She'd also come every year until Sunnyfield, on Easter, with an armload of lilacs which Mimi had thought a nice touch, taken her to mass and brunch and returned to Madison by ten o'clock that same night. She was all the things

Mimi was not—tall, frosted, willowy, and beautiful, not so much as powder across her Roman nose.

"So, the Ice Queen's on her way." Teddy shook his head. "Probably called the Neptune Society before she left."

"Children!" Edie held a finger to her lips.

A small dark man in a pale blue cotton medical coat appeared from nowhere. They all jumped up.

"Are you the family of Miss Tinker?" he inquired.

Mimi's dad spoke. "Yes."

"Please, can we sit?" He indicated the couches, and they all sat down again. Mimi held fast to Teddy's rough hand.

"Miss Tinker has expired." He made certain to engage each of them with his intelligent, cool eyes, the briefest moment.

"I'm sorry for your loss. She was comfortable and not in pain, but really, her heart was too damaged for her to survive."

* * * *

Mimi started her car in the hospital parking lot, noticing, faintly, that it had snowed. It was beautiful; she felt nothing. She felt that winter had moved inside, that it had gotten into her vessels. Thinking of them as frozen pipes, she would need the hair dryer of July to make her blood move again. She was surprised that she could drive her car, that she could remember, clutch, brake, reverse, third gear.

Expired. The spirit exits. The breath goes elsewhere. Where? Was there really no such thing as death? Expired. What cannot be, is. What is living is not living. What you cannot live without, you will live without.

The words were torn from her. "The truth is, we are all dying, every day, and it stinks. That's what I say, do you hear me, God? It stinks. The whole idea. The entire cosmos. Stinks. The trouble with you, God . . . " She was shouting now in the small cold car. "The whole trouble with you, damn you, is that you are not human. Your efficient means of the removal of persons no longer capable of procreation is fucked. It's terribly fucked. But being God, with a ruby for a heart, you wouldn't dream you were anything but a genius."

Mimi pulled up to her apartment building. She looked up through the maple branches into her dark rooms, her answering machine pulsing red against the pale wall.

"I will go up there and I will rip that fucking cord out of the wall and who knows, maybe my life will get better."

*　　　*　　　*　　　*

Father Ben was to officiate the mass for Grandma Tinker, and Mimi, sitting in the cold pew with her family, reflected that this was the right thing. He was family, after all, and no one would

313

have felt right about a stranger offering meaningless, droning tributes from the altar. They were all grateful that the assorted nieces and nephews had allowed them to plan the mass and reception. Grandma's few family members arrived, subdued and tearless, dutiful guests for the relative they'd never really known.

As old Mrs. Peabody struck up the organ with "Amazing Grace," Mimi could feel a sort of movement, a kind of wave throughout the mourners behind her. Just as she began to rise, she saw from her peripheral vision, a darkness flash into genuflection. Harold moved into the pew beside her. He held a white rose. He opened Mimi's hand, gave it to her, placed his arm around her shoulder and shook hands with her astonished brothers and father. Edie began to weep loudly. But Mimi, as if nothing had happened, as if Harold had never left, lay her hot, wet face against his chest.

*   *   *   *

At her mother's, following mass, Mimi hurried about, getting drinks for people, passing the little sausages and cheese cubes. Teddy cut the ham. Her mother fussed in the kitchen. Nothing was right. The ham was fatty, the potatoes au gratin, watery. She'd made her green bean casserole—mushroom soup, fried onions from a can. No one ever ate it, but Edie never noticed. Her dad was warming the rolls in the oven while he nursed a shot glass of gin.

People crowded the small living room, sitting anywhere they could, on the tables, the arms of the chairs and sofas; the windows were opaque with steam, with the freezing temperatures outside. She caught sight of Harold squeezed into a chair beside his mother, his arms around her. Both appeared to be weeping. Mimi was dashing to the kitchen for more sausages, which were disappearing at an alarming rate, when the front door opened and Father Ben walked in. Many people stood when he entered, as had been the custom when Mimi had been a child. Placing his large hands in front of his chest, he directed everyone to sit, and the shuffling for places began all over again.

Mimi, the platter in her hands, met his gaze evenly. He bent his head to the right—an inquiring expression on his face, and then stepped up to her and lay a whisper of a kiss on her forehead. For a brief moment, the conversation ceased, movement was stilled—one beat, two, three, and then fired up again.

Mary Beth, Jan, and Link came in behind him. Mary Beth took the platter from her hands. Link was gathering their coats, and Jan went directly to the kitchen. She could think of nothing to do but hold out her hand to the priest.

"Mimi."

"Father, I very much appreciated your eulogy for Grandma. What you said about her heart—the way it continued to open, petal after petal all of her life—the way that opening kept her young and caring . . . that's her, that's who she was."

"It's not an easy process." Ben was standing quite close to her so that she would hear him above the din.

"What is not easy?"

"Opening. It's an art and a dedicated practice."

"Well, some of us are still learning."

He placed a hand on her arm, his dark eyes intense.

"We are all still learning, Mimi."

*   *   *   *

About an hour had gone by, and Mimi had finally had a chance to sit down at the dining room table, when the front door opened and Mickey arrived with old Pete and Stephan. She had not known Stephan was coming. He ran to Mimi with the flying horse in his hands.

"Your brother came and told me what happened and asked if I wanted to come and I said 'Yes.' He said it might cheer you up."

His face was radiant. Mimi realized immediately that Stephan felt included, part of the family. She was astonished that Mickey had thought of such a loving thing to do; she met his gaze and smiled. He shrugged, trying to look dumb and boyish.

"Here, Mimi, I want you to have *Iron Mist*."

Her throat caught; she rubbed Stephan's back, lifting his chin with her fingers.

"Stephan, it means so much that you would offer me your beautiful work of art. But there are some things, I think, that are too precious to be given away, and I really think *Iron Mist* is one of those. When you make something else, not your very first piece, something I know will be just as beautiful, then I will accept it. Okay?"

Stephan stared at Mimi and then at the horse. He looked back at her and she thought she saw relief move across his face.

He shook his head solemnly and then asked, still radiant, "Your brother says that there's ham here, can I have some?"

"Yes, yes, you certainly can, but first I want you to meet everyone."

THIRTY

THOSE CUTS

Across from Harold at the Seahorse, Mimi could not shake the sense that time had stopped, jerked backward and had come to rest here, where she and her husband had spent many a Friday evening bringing each other up to date on their week. Myrtle had said just to wave a hand when they were ready to order and then went quietly away, a concerned look on her face.

"I can't get over how different you look from just a couple of months ago."

"Yes, I guess I do." Mimi looked down, away from Harold's confused face.

"Well, what spawned the change?"

"I . . . I was lonely."

He reached across the table and held her hand.

"I'm sorry, Mimi, I wouldn't hurt you for the world. You're the sweetest person I've ever known."

She withdrew her hand.

"When are you going back?"

"Back?"

"To Idaho, to Leda."

"I thought we should talk about that."

Mimi noticed that, despite the crisp blue suit, Harold seemed vaguely disheveled. His glasses were lopsided and filmy. She could not be certain if he had combed his hair.

"What did you want to talk about?"

"Well, us."

"Us?"

"I've been thinking. Perhaps we should give ourselves another chance . . . maybe . . . "

She stared across the table and tried to keep her tone even.

"Harold, you've been gone two-and-a-half years. And not all of it was a fugue state."

"I was unhappy. We were both unhappy."

"But India? I don't think you left to gain knowledge. I think you ran away."

He stared back at her, wounded. "I think you're judging me."

Mimi looked down at her drink. "Well, in a sense you are asking me to. I can't think of how I could trust you, ever, ever again."

"I was sick, you know that."

"Fugues aren't supposed to last for more than a couple of weeks. And nowhere in what I've read has one exceeded ten months!"

"You *are* judging me. You are saying I was faking it. Even when you were there? Is that what you're saying?"

She could see the tears well up in Harold's pale blue eyes, and she felt a sudden shame. Mimi looked at him and reached for his hand.

She spoke more gently. "Harold you've been living with another woman. For quite some time."

"Leda just takes care of me."

"This beautiful woman almost half your age takes care of you? Come on, Harold."

Harold waved Myrtle over to their table. "Another round, Myrtle."

Mimi squirmed a little. "That's probably not a good idea unless we order."

He shot her an injured glance. "Sure you want to hang around that long?"

"I'm not sure of anything."

He took both her hands in his. "Mimi have I ever lied to you? I've been straight with you. I left on that trip troubled, it's true, but I left with good intentions. Leda's just a good-hearted, rich kid who wants to write. She writes in the ranch house and cooks and cares for me and makes me walk and move. In the beginning, when I was coming out of the fugue and got so depressed, she practically had to spoon-feed me. We're not lovers." He hung his head. "I can't be a lover; I'm not well enough."

Mimi shook her head slowly. "What did you feel depressed about? Here you were getting better, coming back into your real life and you got depressed? I don't understand."

He looked up. "I'd lost you. I knew I had lost you."

*   *   *   *

They drove to Harold's mother's in silence. Up the wide, curved suburban roads, the lawns white with snow, sweeping down an acre, a half-acre to the gleaming night streets. The houses, mostly long, brick ranches hugging their foundation plantings and small trees. The Christmas lights, sedate, white and unblinking, were lavish on the rooflines. Candle-like lights perched in many a dark window.

Finally, Mimi whispered, "Oh, it's so beautiful!"

"And *you're* so beautiful, Mimi. Not just the way you look, which I admit to mostly having ignored, but your spirit— that little boy you are helping."

"Oh, no. Stephan I am not helping. Stephan is helping me with my grief, my sense of aloneness, my sense of purposelessness. No, definitely, I get the better end of the deal there. But thank you for saying such nice things to me."

They pulled into his mother's long driveway—candy cane lights illuminating the length of it. Mimi wished the Metro were quieter, more appropriate. She paused and looked at him carefully, then cleared her voice.

"I know you've been through a lot. I don't even really know or understand it all. But if you could just devote some time to thinking about what my life has been, how crazy, how hard, how lonely and troubling these last years have been, I think it would help me . . . somehow . . . I think."

In the dark of the car, on the candy cane lit driveway, Harold leaned over and held the back of her head in his hand, and whispered, his lips on her ear, "How could I have forgotten how much I loved you?"

*   *   *   *

Mimi entered the apartment on tiptoes as if there were someone she might waken. Shivering, she realized that, in her morning rush to get to the funeral, she had forgotten to turn up the heat for the day. She hunted under her bed for her old electric blanket; she'd been afraid to use it because of radiation, or positive ions, or something that led ultimately to cancer. She found it beside the wedding picture she had nearly forgotten, spread it across her bed and plugged it in. She changed into her nightgown under the covers as the heat began to radiate, jerking with little fits of cold. When she was dressed and settled, she puffed the pillows behind her back and allowed herself the full brunt of shock she felt from her encounter with Harold.

He had told her they had not had the right kind of love for marriage. Was that the fugue, the depression or the truth? She had thought he'd been right. And this thought had left her feeling more empty than when Harold disappeared. Now he was saying he loved her. But he had used the past tense.

Jack had never really believed the fugue story, and she respected him. His doubt caused hers. That look in Harold's eyes. He had lost a certain steadiness of gaze. And yet emotions she had never seen in his eyes gathered there. Had Leda shown him how to feel more? Had his illness made him more human, but more frightened? Fear, yes, she saw a lot of fear in his eyes. He had never, as he admitted, noticed anything about the way she'd looked; except before the braces. Was he saying she was beautiful because he was frightened or sad? Had Leda finished her book and wanted to go home, and did he now need someone else to care for him? Her thoughts raged on. How would she settle them? Who could help her?

Throwing back the covers, Mimi jumped out of bed and headed for the kitchen. She punched 411 into the phone and waited.

"What city please?"

"Oak Park."

"Yes?"

"Saint Timothy's Roman Catholic Church—the rectory, please."

It was midnight. She shouldn't be doing this. *It's too late. Too selfish. Too convenient.*

Four rings. She couldn't really leave a message. She was replacing the receiver when she heard his voice, far away and small against the kitchen wall. Her heart knocking, aching, she pulled the phone to her ear.

"Ben!"

"Mimi! You've been so much on my mind!"

"Ben . . ."

"Look, Mimi, I can come over there. It would take me about an hour and fifteen minutes. Nobody's on the road. Is this about Harold?"

"Yes."

"Please, Mimi, let me help. I'm worried."

Without responding, she replaced the receiver. She began pacing through the flat, switching lights on and off as she went. She left the apartment, went down the stairs and stood on the sidewalk. She walked up and down the stairs until Laura opened her door and peeked out through the crack. The eye that Mimi could see grew large but was quickly passed from view when her door clicked solidly. She walked up to the third floor, went to the old stained glass window at the end of the hall, studied her finger along the leaded panes, washed her hand over the lime glass at the center and the single cranberry jewel at its heart. She could hear Irene Appleby coughing faintly in 3B. From Mr. Somers' a TV, muffled, canned laughter. People gossiped that he drank a lot since his wife died. *Must have fallen asleep in front of the tube.*

She went back to her floor, into her apartment, and closed the door. She searched the pantry and found a tiny gift bottle of Chivas Regal on the bottom shelf. Dusty, with a Christmas note attached: "Happy Christmas, dear Harold. You've been a wonderful friend! Toni."

"Hmph." Mimi grumbled, twisting the lid violently.

She dug for some ice, then poured a bit and took it to her bed, crawling forward into the heat. She drank the scotch in three large gulps, cuddled down and fell asleep.

*　　*　　*　　*

Hearing a voice from far away, she opened her eyes. Above her stood Harold. She sat up abruptly.

"Hi," he said in a flat, strange tone.

"How did you get in here?"

"I still have my key, but anyway, the door was unlocked."

"What time is it?"

"It's one o'clock."

"Harold, you have to leave. You can't just go into someone's bedroom at one in the morning."

He sat down on her bed. "It's my bedroom too."

She grabbed her glasses from her bed stand and switched on the light. Harold looked wild. He still had his blue suit on, but his tie was gone and his shirt was open to the waist. It looked as though his T-shirt was soiled.

"I thought we should try to make love." But he said this without conviction, and with no feeling in his voice.

Mimi recoiled. It was then that she saw the sleeves of his suit, his wrists.

"What have you done? What have you done?"

"They're only scratches. Just little scratches. I couldn't do it. I can't even kill myself."

"Sit down, Harold. Sit down on the bed."

She spoke firmly, she hoped authoritatively. She punched her pillows, placed them behind him and pulled off his suit jacket. His T-shirt was grey and dirty. She went to the dresser, found an old one of his and went to the bathroom for soap and water.

"What are you doing?" He looked ready to bolt when she returned.

Mimi said in a voice of absolute calm that surprised her, "I'm going to wash those cuts Harold, and have a look at them. Then I'm going to wash the rest of you, and then we'll see. Lean back."

She saw immediately that the cuts were, in fact, little more than surface scratches, but she noted as she worked that he had probably not been bathing regularly. She scrubbed at his scalp and body and then rubbed him dry with a thick towel. After this, she brushed his hair briskly, noticing as she did so his eyes wavering and closing. She pulled the clean shirt over his head, gave his hair another slick. His head began to nod. And she said abruptly, "Here, Harold, let's get rid of the slacks."

He groaned as she tucked him in but did not open his eyes. Almost immediately, he began to softly snore.

*　　　*　　　*　　　*

In the dark, she stood at the sink washing her glass. The honey locust glowed softly, its branches filled with snow. She was shaking, her mind dark and blank, when she thought she heard her front door creak open. Harold! She mustn't let him escape! She dashed into the living room and ran directly into a body.

"Harold! You mustn't . . . "

"Mimi . . . it's me! What . . . ? Your front door was standing open!"

"Shush. Shush, please, you'll wake him. Close it. Close it and lock the chain."

He came back to where she stood and grasped her wrists, but she pulled away, lay her hand across his mouth and dragged him into the kitchen, closing the door behind her.

"In God's name, what's going on?"

Now, it was Mimi who grasped the priest's arms.

"Harold's here! I called you because I took him to dinner and then home and I thought he behaved strangely, looked strange."

"I noticed his expression even at St. Mark's and then at your mother's. I couldn't . . . just well, unconnected and distracted, I thought. But how did he get here?"

"I don't know. I don't know. But I was sleeping, and when I woke up, there he was, looking disoriented and disheveled, peering down at me."

"Mimi!"

She explained how Harold had behaved at dinner and in the car, and then some of what he'd said in the bedroom.

"But that's not the worst of it!"

"Go on, Mimi."

"His wrists—blood and cuts but . . . "

Ben grabbed both her hands.

"But shallow, hardly nicked. As if . . . " She was struggling. "As if he didn't mean it or for . . . effect. For effect." She paused and stared into Ben's eyes. "And I had to wash him. I don't know why he's so dirty!"

"He's in there now?"

"Yes."

"Mimi, I . . . I think maybe Harold's lost his hold on reality. Don't you think? Have you seen him like this before?"

"When his dad died, you know, and he hadn't talked to him in such a long time. His doctor just gave him sedatives."

"You need to call Alice in the morning and get her over here. He needs to go to the hospital."

Mimi met Ben's eyes. "The hospital." It was not a question.

Ben gently dropped her hands and patted them, then rose and came around to her chair. He pulled her up and into his arms and rubbed her back for a bit.

"Come now, Mimi, you lie on the sofa for awhile. I'll sit in the chair and keep watch."

He took a pillow from the easy chair and tapped at the sofa cushions, indicating that she should lie down. She did so, and he covered her with the afghan. Then, softly, he went to the chair that faced the bedroom and bath and waited.

*   *   *   *

She sat up, abruptly, sun pouring into the room. She could hear someone in the kitchen and for a moment did not understand why she awoke on the sofa. When she investigated the soft noises in the kitchen, she saw Ben frying bacon, her Christmas apron tied around his waist.

"Harold?"

"Still sleeping like a rock, Mimi. Looks like he never moved."

"Did you call St. Mark's and St. Timothy's?"

"Yes, I explained . . . " He looked about to smile and then said, "It's fine Mimi."

She went to the phone and dialed Alice's number. Explaining as calmly as she could the events of the previous hours, she was met at first with silence.

"Alice?"

"He's there now?"

"Yes."

"Sleeping?"

"Yes."

"Well, that's surprising. I don't think he's slept at all since he came home."

*   *   *   *

When Alice arrived, Harold was still sound asleep. The three of them had a meeting at the kitchen table. It was, by now, eleven o'clock. Alice dabbed at her eyes, and Mimi held her free hand.

"Those cuts. He could have died!"

"Alice, no, they were too shallow but . . . " Mimi cleared her throat, "we have to take Harold to the hospital."

"What? Why?"

"He might hurt himself."

"Do you mean crazy? For being crazy?"

"I'm not saying he's anything except dangerous to himself and . . . well, have you noticed his eyes?"

"I thought they looked like that from not sleeping."

"That too."

Alice looked across the table at the priest; she searched his face for a few moments.

"All right." It was a whimper, but it was yes.

THIRTY ONE

LIKE SUPERMAN

Mimi believed it was the strangest December she'd ever lived through. She made a little money at Sunnyfield Christmas Sale after all and then at the Lincoln School PTA. Two thousand dollars. Completely unexpected. She'd had to have dinner with Gerry Mertz out of gratitude for the PTA show, but when he heard Harold was back and ill, he did not press her.

Among the Christmas cards she received, one was from Suzy whom she had written to as soon as she'd arrived home. Suzy wrote in her card advising Mimi that she would be in Chicago in the spring to see her brother, and would come and see Mimi if she would send her number and address. Did she mind her bringing Spence and Quinlin with her? She was adopting them at her daughter-in-law's urging.

Victor also wrote, enclosing another drawing of the inside of the Le Cafe Petite—he'd sketched a woman, glasses, long bangs, at a table. He titled it *The Only Woman in the Restaurant* and thanked her for her Christmas note. At the bottom of the card he scribbled his phone number, adding, "Please call, eh? Mornings are best."

She laughed when she opened Hank's card to see him in a red T-shirt, a green bandana on his head, standing behind the Cattle Drive's bar—the mirror behind him strewn with fat, brilliant Christmas tree lights. "Howdy!" ran across the bottom.

He had hand-written the message, *This town's not pretty anymore since you went away! Merry Christmas. Write! Hank.*

She had not heard from Ida and Melva, because she had not given them her address or number. Now, she was reminded that she'd promised to call or write when she got home.

She went to see Harold every day at the hospital. Nights she read until the late hours about bipolar depression, which was his diagnosis. She tried never to think more than a day ahead.

They did not bother with Christmas. Her family agreed on this without dispute. But Christmas Eve, Mickey and Teddy pounded on her door with an orange tabby kitten they wanted named Matilda, and she joyfully acquiesced. Christmas Day, she spent the afternoon with Harold, who, much of the time, silently gazed out the window while holding her hand.

Christmas evening, Stephan joined Mimi to open gifts in front of an iron-work pyramid of red and green candles that served as her Christmas tree.

"What did you get your mom?"

"I spent all the twenty dollars you gave me."

"I meant you to."

"Well, I wasn't sure."

"So, what did you buy?"

"I got her a blouse."

"Really? What's it like?"

"Well, you know her hair—how it's almost red."

"Right."

"So, the blouse is kind of orangy-pink."

"Like coral?"

"Yeah. It has pearls on the collar, they're probably not real?"

"No, Stephan. It sounds wonderful, though. It sounds perfect. What did she say?"

"I don't know. I mean, she didn't open it yet."

"What did you two do this morning?"

"Nothing. She was sleeping."

Stephan's eyes were somber.

"Did you have dinner?" asked Mimi.

"Yeah, I made a meatloaf with red and green peppers on the top for Christmas."

"A meatloaf? How do you know how to do that?"

"My mom gives good directions."

Mimi rose and sat down on the floor beside Stephan. She patted his head.

"Things are kind of tough over there, aren't they?"

"I don't want to talk about it."

"Why's that?"

"Because, it's Christmas."

*   *   *   *

It was Jan's idea to have the potluck brunch. The first morning of the new year, they met at her house with casseroles.

Jan had made spicy tea, coffee, and caramel rolls, and they all plunked down on Jan's wine oriental rug in the living room and talked, sometimes everyone speaking at once. But it was Link who had the biggest news.

"I'm getting married."

Silence. Was that a blush on Mary Beth's pale cheek? Mimi spoke at last.

"Tell us about her."

"Him."

"What?!" Jan shrieked.

"One of the painters who works for my brother."

Mary Beth *was* blushing. "But umm," she cleared her throat, "we all thought, well, remember when you said that ah . . . "

"I'm a lesbian? Yeah, but I'm not . . . I guess. I mean not totally." Mimi observed that Link was radiant.

"Look, quit stringing us along," Jan demanded. "He or she or it, we want to know everything."

Link explained that she'd been living with a woman whose brother needed a job. He was an artist, a landscape painter, but was completely out of money; he hadn't sold a painting in two years. Link knew her brother needed some help temporarily, so they jumped in her car and went on-site to the offices Neal was painting. There hadn't been a phone installed yet. By the time she'd returned to her cottage, she'd had known she wanted to see him again.

Jan spoke. "What the hell did his sister say to all this?"

"Ha. She was just as glad. She said she hadn't been attracted to me for months but hadn't wanted to hurt me. Geez. The things people keep to themselves."

"He didn't mind your, uh, your having been . . . ?" Mary Beth looked incredulous.

"With a woman, his sister? No. He did not."

"Well," was all Mary Beth could muster.

"Well, what happens if you get married and then . . . " Even Jan seemed at a loss for words.

What Link said next answered their common unarticulated question.

"One of us meets somebody we like better or a gender we like better? Joey is not a gender, he's not even a somebody. It's about him. All about him."

They all had some news to share. Mary Beth revealed her decision to become a nurse. Her Marty had changed positions and no longer traveled. He cared for the kids at night. This he did not like, but he did like seeing Mary Beth fired up and determined.

Jan said she was talking almost nightly to Lou, and that Lou and Richard were coming home for Jan's birthday in February. But Jan only shrugged after she'd relayed this information. His young "plaything," as Jan called his girlfriend, was still in the picture.

Mimi told them about Harold, his return, breakdown, and subsequent hospitalization. She talked about Grandma Tinker, and how awful Christmas had seemed without her. Then Mimi told them about Matilda and her small Christmas with Stephan.

Jan instructed Mimi, "You're going to have to go over there."

The others agreed. They all thought maybe Mimi should try to get a social worker out to see Catherine.

"I guess you're right, but if I do, they might take him away."

Jan replied, "Just bully them like you did before."

Link had an idea. "I don't know her, and I don't know how the system works, but I bet Catherine could request that you take him. I bet she could influence them."

Mary Beth plucked a strand of hair from across her nose.

"Because, I think," she looked up at Mimi, "right? You'd be lost without him."

*   *   *   *

Mimi took her parents to dinner New Year's Day. They wanted to go to a buffet; Mimi obliged them, despite her revulsion for what she thought of as "face-stuffing restaurants." When they were seated, her mother took everyone's plates off the trays and carefully laid out their silverware. She had long ago ceased telling Edie that she, Mimi, could sperform this simple act, because somehow her mother had refused to believe it. In the middle of sipping her noodle soup, Edie suddenly gasped and put down her spoon.

"Oh, Mimi. Have you seen Father Ben recently?"

"A couple of times at the hospital. Why?"

"Because, my dear, he's leaving!"

Mimi's heart dropped to her stomach.

"Again?" She felt a confused pain. "He just got transferred to St. Timothy's"

"No, Mimi, not a parish. He's leaving the priesthood!"

* * * *

"They're going to release me."

Mimi was walking the halls with Harold. The nurses had told her that he hadn't been up and about enough. She placed her arm around his waist, her head on his chest. Stroking her cheek he said, "It's over, Mimi. This hell is over."

But Mimi felt dread. Would he want to come home to her apartment? Of course he would. Would he want to sleep in her bed? There was no other bed. Would he become manic again and drive off in the night as he had from Alice's house to some unpredictable place, some unsafe place? She could not imagine any of it. She wondered if he had thought any of this through. She kept silent, waiting. When they returned to Harold's room, he asked her to sit with him a moment on the bed.

"Mimi, I don't want to hurt your feelings, but I can't go home with you."

"But, where else *can* you go?"

"My mother's already asked me. She wants to take care of me."

"Harold, Alice is not young. I think," Mimi paused and gripped the blanket, "I think you should come home with me. I'm the one who ought to take care of you, who *can* take care of you."

"Dr. Sinclair, . . . please Mimi, don't be upset by this, he doesn't think I'm well enough to be with you. He says he thinks I'm conflicted about our relationship, and he's right. He said if I'm feeling anxiety it would retard my progress."

Mimi flashed ahead to Alice cooking and doing laundry and running to the grocery store. She stared at him a while.

He picked up her hands. "Look, don't worry about my mother. I can do everything for myself. And . . . " He looked down, paused, and then continued. "Leda will be coming."

Mimi felt limp with anger.

"Couldn't she have come sooner? Why is she coming now?"

"She said she wanted to help me."

"Harold, you have a great deal to figure out."

He stroked her hair, watching her face.

"I know. I know."

*   *   *   *

"Mimi!"

The phone had rung six times before she'd jumped from the shower and wrapped herself in a towel. Maybe she should relent about the answering machine and plug it back in.

"Pete?"

"I missed you on Christmas!"

"Oh, Pete. I spent the afternoon with Harold. Were you disappointed?"

"Of course I was disappointed, but I had a nice time at Alice's. You have to be with your husband."

"Yes, Yes." She cleared her throat at this. "How have you been?"

"Good, just as fit as ever. I had another dream."

The bedroom walls shimmered.

"I want to talk to you about it, and I want to see you and I've still got your Christmas Present."

Christmas present. Damn. Damn.

"Well, ah, when, Pete?"

"Now. What are you doing right now?"

This was the first time Mimi had seen the lobby of St. Joseph's filled to capacity with residents. Pete had not come down yet. Some were in wheelchairs, but a couple of older women, she noticed, wore those shiny nylon or polyester athletic two-piece outfits, sparkling with beads and fake diamonds—brilliant tangerines and limes. They stood tapping their feet and moving to the music. A male resident, hunched and tiny, sat at the piano.

Must be what the excitement is about, she thought. What Mimi found disconcerting was that so many people motioned for her to come to them.

"Come on over here, young lady." The man on the piano bench made room for her.

One lady in a wheelchair with weepy eyes called, "Why Eleanor, you've come back!"

Another man, unshaven, also in a wheelchair, patted his lap, but did not speak. What was Pete doing here, anyway? He had prostate cancer, but it was progressing slowly, and he was more than fit.

"Young lady," the piano man called again. And before she could think, she found her feet propelling her, her body placing itself on the bench. The piano man threw up his arms in his enthusiasm and cried, "Can you sing?"

"A little."

"Go on darlin," the lime sports attired woman encouraged.

The man began to play and sing, Durante style,

"When somebody loves you, it's no good unless he loves you ... "

Mimi joined in, "all the way. Through the good and lean years and through all the in between years, come what may. Who knows where the road may lead us? Only a fool can say. So, when somebody loves you, it's no good unless he loves you all the way, all the way."

She noticed Pete stepping spryly into the lobby, grinning. He must have heard her before he'd seen her.

She and the piano man sang a few more numbers (she'd always liked her parents' music), but not until she'd corralled some of the others to join them. When she excused herself and thanked the pianist, who turned out to be Thorton something or other, the crowd applauded enthusiastically, and Mimi felt a surprising swell of happiness. *Others. Others*, she reflected.

She and Pete had a lovely visit. On her way out her door, she had snatched the candies that Stephan had given her for Christmas, and this she made Pete's present. He presented her with a small purple velvet box. She saw that it was not new.

"Oh, Pete! What now? I'm not even your real granddaughter!"

"You are to me! It was Rosa's. Go ahead now, open it!"

Mimi opened the box to discover a dark clear oval-shaped sapphire of a bluish purple hue. A small round diamond sat on either side of the stone, and the band itself was white gold.

"Platinum." The old man responded, as if reading her mind. "Now, let's try it." He withdrew the box from her hands, pulled the ring from its white velvet platform, and slid it easily onto the third finger of her right hand.

"I just had to do it that way. Just like I did with Rosa. Only the left hand. She didn't want to marry me, you know."

Mimi could hardly think.

"Oh, why not Pete?"

"I was dancing then. You didn't know that, did you? I was tap-dancing anywhere I could, for whatever I could make. She said she wouldn't marry a show business man."

"Oh." She looked away from the ring and into his still-bright eyes. "What did you do?"

"Why, quit. She made a decent man out of me."

"But . . . well, would you make that same decision again?"

Pete threw back his head and slapped his knee.

"Hell no!" he roared.

This time when they entered the lobby it was vacant. The afternoon sunlight washed the walls a soft rose. Why was this a sad scene, Mimi wondered?

Just as she was hugging Pete and saying good-bye, he gripped her forearms and cried, "Oh, I forgot."

"Yes, Pete?"

"That little boy, the one I came to your mother's with, that little . . . "

Mimi felt cold. "Stephan."

"I had this dream, Mimi. He was at an open window and he had a black cape tied around his neck—you know like Superman or something. He kept waving with a big smile on his face. Just waving and waving, smiling, which was so strange."

"What was strange, Pete?"

"Well, people don't usually smile and cry at the same time."

THIRTY TWO

ROOM AT THE END

Mimi drove home, a new anxiety pushing out the pleasure from the afternoon she'd just spent with Pete. He'd been so comforting and reassuring about Harold. Telling her that Harold was stronger than she might think. When she arrived at the apartment, she ate some cold chili out of a can, standing and looking out at the tree in the alley.

The buzz of her doorbell shocked her from her reverie. She walked hurriedly, but felt some trepidation.

When she saw that it was Ben, she cried "Oh!" and her hand flew to her mouth.

"May I?" He held a bouquet of buttercups and violets. "I thought we needed some spring." He handed it to her. But Mimi broke into tears.

"Why Mimi, what is it? We can talk about it." At this, he led her to the sofa and sat her down. He sat beside her for a long while, his arm over her shoulder.

"I've been waiting for this," he said. "You never saw a psychiatrist, did you?"

She shook her head against his chest.

"Tell me about it. Go ahead."

She wriggled away from him. He pulled his handkerchief from his jeans and gave it to her.

"Everything. Just everything. I don't feel I can handle it all. I've got something of a tight money situation—they raised my rent. The whole thing with Harold is just a mess. He's gone home to Alice's, and it should be me. I should be taking care of him. And he told me Leda is coming out here—she's the one who took care of him when he had the fugue. My mother told me that you're going to leave the priesthood. And that makes me so sad." She paused to look at him. He wore a gentle but unrevealing expression. "And now Stephan. He was so lost and alone on Christmas—it can't go on. And then Pete had this dream—this horrible dream about him —Stephan."

"Is that something you should pay attention to?"

"Oh, yes. Definitely. Yes. Crazy as that sounds, yes."

"Well, Mimi where should we start?"

"Well, you. Let's start with you. Since you're here." She looked at him.

"I don't want to argue again."

"Well, I'll try, but I can't promise you that."

"You've got to."

Mimi looked for a long while into Ben's eyes. "All right then. We won't argue."

Ben explained that he hadn't felt the call to the priesthood since his father had died. As he'd pored over the lengthy letter his father had left for him, which described his devotion to the Torah and to the duties of a rabbi, he had been stricken with a nearly disabling nostalgia for what he had known as a boy. And before the letter he'd had huge questions about the Church's stance on certain doctrines: Satan, for example, the concept of a physical embodiment of evil. The Rite of Exorcism had not been altered since the 1600s. And then, as he had come to know Mimi, yes, Mimi, he'd had to tackle and finally be defeated by what he now considered the senseless and cruel vow of celibacy. He explained that people outside the clergy thought that the priests wanted more and more offspring for their churches, but in truth, he said, from the early writings of many of the church fathers had sprung an attitude of extreme revulsion for the body and its act of procreation. What the hierarchy actually had wanted for its members was for them to refrain entirely from sex. Or to reproduce themselves and then become celibate. The Jewish tradition, he explained, rejoiced in all things physical, even to the making of the point in the Torah, that a man is not a man until he takes a wife.

After he had talked for some time, he simply opened his arms and shrugged, looking at Mimi as if asking for mercy.

"So, it's not just that you feel you've lost your vocation. You've lost your religion." She searched his face.

"The way you put it showcases my situation in a negative, judgmental light, don't you think?"

She felt she'd been hit, and looked away.

"Life just isn't the moralistic, little black-and-white arena that the church teaches us. I think I haven't lost anything. I think I'm finding out who I am and it's not this, not this suffering, this hocus-pocus."

"Hocus-pocus? What all does that word cover?"

"You know Jesus Christ himself never called any of his disciples to celibacy—never."

"You know, Ben, your experience is yours, but for myself, for myself . . . "

He placed his hands alongside her jaw and pressed them against her face. He moved a few inches from her and forced her to look at him.

"For you, celibacy has not been a struggle? Some of these tears are not about the terrible loneliness of never lying down with one you love and being held and being taken and losing yourself? Part of your sorrow—isn't it about the craziness, the complete insanity of being alone, not just in the spirit, but also in the flesh? This has not been a problem for you then?"

Mimi was startled by his anger, but also something else. What she felt was a pain so intense that a scream tore from her throat. But when Ben's lips pressed her neck, she could feel her own demons, she felt this exactly, flying from her.

*   *   *   *

One late January day, Mimi stood up from her work table, stretching her sore fingers and stiff back. She rubbed her neck hard and went to make some tea. Looking out the kitchen window, she saw that it was a fine day, fine enough for a good long run, probably warm enough for only a windbreaker. She smiled. *January is always the worst of it—the darkest, the most hopeless month.*

She nestled once again onto the wide windowsill in the living room, her think tank, she had begun to call it, and sipped her green tea, noticing its amber-olive color, feeling its warmth, the warmth of the sun on her skin. *Oh, Stephan is out to catch some sun.* She set the tea down and pulled open the window.

"Steph," she called, and waved. At first he did not look her way, nor move. "Stephan! Steph?"

Finally, he looked up and gave a limp wave of his hand, then looked away again. Hmm, she thought, and rose and got a jacket from the closet.

"Hey!" she called walking across the street.

The same limp wave. She sat down on the porch steps beside him, rubbing his head roughly. "Hey, dude," she said, smiling. "What gives?"

"Opal's missing."

"Inside or outside?"

"Inside. I don't let her out."

"Well, then we can find her."

"Well, I don't know."

"Sure." She touched his head softly.

He turned and trained the full light of his grey eyes upon her.

"No! You don't know anything! Anything!"

He jumped up, clattered up the steps and went inside, slamming the door behind him.

She was stunned and sat frozen for a moment, then went up to the door and rang the bell. Nothing. She knocked, calling,

"Stephan." First softly and then a little harder. "Stephan!" And then, "Mrs. Drubowski? Catherine? Mrs. Drubowski?"

Nothing. But a quiet that was less than normal issued from the house. A sensation poured over Mimi, a heaviness she could not name. She tried the doorknob; the door was not locked. She opened it a slit, feeling like a thief. Then she gasped. Nothing prepared her for what she saw—a room so chaotic and filthy she could not have imagined it. The rotting curtains in the living room were drawn shut and grey with dirt. In one corner were stacked five or six emptied tin cans. Cans of diet cola were scattered everywhere, about one to a square foot. The sofa had piles of clothing, clean or dirty, she could not say, but on the very top of one of the piles lay an orange lace bra with its cups pointed skyward. She thought she smelled old urine. The TV played on with a nearly inaudible tone, the picture so fuzzy she could see only that someone was being interviewed by someone.

She called out, "Stephan?" Nothing. She went into the kitchen. Dishes were stacked, food stuck to them, everywhere. Pots with black mold growing on the insides lay on every counter. Yet beside the sink stood a neat drainer of freshly washed dishes and one pot. A mouse skittered beneath a door. She thought she heard something scratching. Mimi stopped and listened. Yes. But she could see nothing moving. A brown supermarket bag lay sideways on top of the stained refrigerator; it was tightly closed. On impulse, Mimi reached up, noticing the blackened, oily dust atop the appliance, grabbed the bag and lifted it, feeling, as she did so, a light weight slip to the bottom. She had a sense of dread so enormous, she could not breathe while she opened the bag.

"Opal. Oh, my God, Opal!"

The kitten was lying in excrement and urine. She grabbed it from the bag and clutched it tightly.

"Oh, Opal, oh, my baby, Opal!"

Then she cleaned and dried her at the sink. Opal opened her mouth as if to protest, but no sound came out. She held the kitten to her chest and went to find Stephan.

"Stephan?"

She called loudly now, not caring if Catherine emerged from one of the rooms, angered by her intrusion.

"Mrs. Drubowki?"

She climbed the stairs and as she rushed by the bathroom saw towels everywhere on the floor, the lights on. One burnt-out bulb over the sink. Her heart twisted in her chest. On instinct, she went directly to the room at the end of the hall. It was closed fast. She tried the handle—locked!

"Stephan! Stephan! Open this door, please Stephan!"

There was a huge cardboard box in the hallway with a few socks and a towel at the bottom. She set Opal into it and went back to the bathroom, where she'd thought she noticed an old wooden chair. Grabbing it and running, she started banging on the center panel of the door. The wood was old and thin, a single panel. She pounded, something coming apart in her shoulder joint. The panel began to crack and then she pulled enough of the wood out so she could climb through. In the open window above a neatly made bed stood Stephan, his back to her. He rose on to his toes. He did not turn. He was perhaps ten feet away. Mimi spoke the only thing that leapt to her tongue.

"Opal. I've found her, Stephan."

He wavered and she flew to him. Clutching his waist with her left arm, holding onto the window jamb with her right hand, she pulled his thin body toward her, both of them falling to the floor where she embraced his trembling body, holding him as if she would never let go.

THIRTY THREE

ELMWOOD

It had rained an icy rain. *It is hard*, Mimi reflected, *for spring to break through.* But the forsythia was budding yellow; soon there would be color again. She had not seen Harold for a month, at his request, though she talked to him by phone a few times, so she was surprised when he suddenly wanted to see her, the urgency in his voice on the phone. Leda was staying in an apartment, he'd remarked; she'd felt a strange relief at hearing this.

When she walked into the Seahorse, Myrtle was at the cash register behind the bar. She met Mimi's eyes, rolling her own, enlarged by the lenses in her glasses.

"He's here, honey," she remarked with a shrug.

Harold stood when he saw her; he'd gained weight. *Alice's cooking.* His hair was close-cropped, and he wore a tweed jacket and new pewter-framed glasses. *Health and something else.*

She found she was blushing as she reached out to receive his embrace.

"Mimi." He stood back to look at her. "I've missed you!"

"Harold, you're looking so well. You're looking, well you're looking damned good."

"I ordered you a drink, Mimi, is that all right?"

"Yes but . . ."

"The medication."

"Oh, yes."

"Tell me how you've been, Mimi."

She told Harold how Stephan and she were adjusting to his living with her, that Catherine was making only slight progress. She had lost the house and was living with her elderly mother. Catherine had come to see her son once a week that first month—February—but Stephan and his mother had talked by phone only, this first week of March.

"You know there really isn't much else going on, Harold. Caring for Stephan, getting him to his counseling, talking things out with him—it's pretty amazing how consuming parenting is."

He stroked her hand tenderly.

"Mimi, I'm worried about you. I should have been helping you, but I wasn't ... "

"No, I know you had to take care of yourself. I understand that. Father Ben is helping me. He takes Stephan to his basketball practice and to his games. They go to the movies sometimes."

"How is Ben?"

"Actually, he's good. He's substitute teaching. He likes it. He has some pretty awful days, but I think he'll be okay."

Mimi's drink arrived, and they ordered. Harold yanked at his tie a couple of times and cleared his throat.

"Mimi, there are some things I have to talk to you about."

"Well, yes, that's what you'd said on the phone."

"I think I'm well."

"Yes, it looks that way."

"I want to start over."

Mimi looked away. "Harold, I don't ... "

"No, Mimi, not us. We can't. We shouldn't have been together in the first place."

She looked at him a long while.

"You're going away again."

"I am."

"With Leda."

"Yes."

"She doesn't just take care of you, then."

"She did. But this time, when she came to Chicago . . . "

"Yes, well, she's very beautiful."

"You're beautiful."

"I'm forty-one."

"You're not being replaced."

Mimi had an urge to slap him, to shake him by the shoulders, but she saw Myrtle from the corner of her eye, bringing their food. Myrtle refused to look at Harold.

"Anything else, honey?"

"Nothing, Myrtle, thank you."

Mimi looked blankly at her food.

"You'll be having babies, then." She put a fork to her fettuccini and moved the noodles in circles around her plate.

"Look, it doesn't matter does it? The point is we didn't make each other happy and can't. Isn't that it?"

She dropped her fork on the plate with a clatter.

"I couldn't give you a child."

"This isn't about that, Mimi. I'm not looking for a baby machine."

"Look at me. Just look at me and tell me that you'd leave if we had a child."

Harold could not meet her gaze.

"This is craziness, Mimi. We don't have a child. Yes, I would try hard to keep a family together. I would have to think of our child. But it's too late for all that anyway."

"Too late?" Mimi spoke so loudly that the couple in the next booth rose in one motion, water glasses and napkins in hand, and hurried to a table far across the room. Harold tried to take her hands in his, but she pulled them away.

"For what? A baby? It's not too late. Don't say that. There are ways—there are all sorts of medical breakthroughs. Women my age are having babies all the time, every day—every day, without husbands."

"I didn't know you still felt this way. I didn't know."

"Didn't know?" Mimi could taste rage on her tongue.

"Didn't know? Now, how could you know? How could you know anything? Guru-chasing in India and picking up young girls in ashrams and hiding out in your boyhood fantasy life, playing dead to your wife. Coming home to mommy when it looked like your nymph-nurse was going to shuffle back to her rich daddy. Now, how could you know anything? You didn't know me when you were with me. How could you know me now . . . ?"

"Mimi!"

She was on her feet.

"Why?" She was glaring down at him through her tears. "Why did I try to find you? You are boring and heartless and selfish and childish. Start over Harold. Ruin another woman's life."

Mimi turned on her heels, then turned back, grabbed her purse and coat, spun around and ran from the Sea Horse.

*   *   *   *

Mimi allowed the car to drive her, and soon Myrtle Hill appeared in the darkness. Slowing down, she found a parking space at its base and slid in. She exited the car, sat down on the sidewalk, and pulled off her high heels.

"Damn, stupid contraptions," she yelled, rising and pitching her shoes into the rear seat. "See if I ever wear them again, for anybody!"

She charged up the hill, hitching up her skirts and tucking them into her waistband. The grass was frosted. The moon was a cucumber slice, cold and crisp. Despite herself, when she got to the top and took in the moonlight on the surging creek below, the newly gentled branches of trees, the houselights blinking in the distance, her heart soared. Mimi threw open her arms to the wind, then took off her blazer and opened the buttons of her blouse. The wind whipped, frozen and delicious, ruffling her hair, playing with her blouse, finding the scoops of her armpits. She released her skirts from her waistband and twirled round and round. The doors had opened. The truth had been told. The doors had closed.

Mimi lay down on her back; she could feel blades of frozen grass on her skin. She made her hands into a circle that seemed to hold the moon and she shouted, "You, moon, you will be my only lover."

*   *   *   *

March, April, and May were to be the craziest period of her life. Harold left, quietly, with Leda early one morning. He'd thought they'd have clear weather all the way to Idaho. He'd knocked on her door the afternoon before, holding two dozen white roses and a card she could not bring herself to open. Alice had given Leda and Harold a good-bye dinner. Ben's mother was diagnosed with uterine cancer; he had gone to Washington D.C. to nurse her. An invitation arrived from Link announcing her marriage to Joey—*Mary Marsha Maculhey*, no less. Another from Jan for a shower for their friend. She'd signed Stephan up for a sculpture class Gerry Mertz had recommended. Two evenings a week, and the boy came home glowing and had begun a notebook with drawings of pieces he wanted next to do. Mimi suggested he date each drawing so that the journal became a kind of chronicle of his rapidly growing skills.

She and Stephan went out weekends searching for a new apartment, even though Mimi did not see how she could afford one. This search brought them closer than ever. One Sunday afternoon in May, when it seemed they had run out of newspaper ads and were headed home, Stephan yelled for Mimi to stop, to pull the car over. He leapt out from his side and she followed. Almost exactly where she had been able to pull over, a *For Rent* sign had been stuck at a crazy angle into the parkway between the sidewalk and the street. Surrounded by a very old, rusting cyclone fence stood a peeling baby blue clapboard house, entirely out of sync with the 1970s, redbrick ranch-style homes around it. The windows were oily. The roofline dipped. A long, narrow, front yard was rough with weeds but green. Hesitantly, Mimi opened the creaking gate; Stephan zipped by her and up to the front porch.

"Look at that, would ya, the kitchen and living room are one room!"

Mimi placed her hands on the picture window to darken the glare and, sure enough, what she saw was a large room, fireplace at one end and a single wall of kitchen at the other.

"Well, that's kind of weird, Stephan, don't you think?"

"It's cool. You could see the fire while you ate."

Mimi considered this, and her heart skipped a beat.

"Where's the rest of it, I wonder?"

But Stephan was already tearing toward the rear of the house, and she followed. A sliding door faced the back yard, but there were no steps or deck leading up to it. Stephan reached up to it, grabbed each side of the door and wiggled it. He turned to Mimi, beaming.

"I knew it! It's open!"

"But . . . "

"Mimi, make your hands go like this." He shaped his into a stirrup.

"Stephan, we could, you . . . "

He was dancing foot to foot. "Just do it, Mimi!" His voice was shrill. They stared at each other wide-eyed. Mimi looked all around, but there seemed to be no activity anywhere in the neighborhood. She bent and shaped her hands and, lightning fast, Stephan stepped up, slid open the thin glass and popped in behind a sun-bleached curtain.

"It's a bedroom! Pretty small but with another big window on the side," he called out to her. She heard him running though the house, then back to the sliding door.

"Come to the front door," Stephan ordered.

Despite herself, Mimi went to the door, which Stephan had unlocked and opened about nine inches. He pulled her inside to the large kitchen/living room, his eyes sparkling.

"I found another bedroom." He caught her hand and pulled her down the hall, which opened to the right of the kitchen. Sure enough, across the hall from the small bedroom was a generously sized room with four large paned windows. Shadows played on the walls from a budding weeping willow tree. Stephan caught his breath and pushed her through the doorway.

"Your room, Mimi," he said, pressing in to stand beside her.

He drew his arm through hers and watched her face, then leaned against her.

"Don't worry Mimi, it's what God wants."

She patted his head. "What, you little heathen?"

"Us, for this house."

*   *   *   *

To comply with the strictures of Family Services, Mimi had given Stephan her bedroom. After reading *The Hobbit* much too late into the evening, she had finally gotten him settled and ready for sleep. She then gathered the Sunday papers, made up the sofa into her bed, closed curtains and finally gathered all the week's mail and sorted through it. A plain white envelope was in the pile, and she remembered—Harold's good-bye card. She picked it up, but just as she meant to break the seal, Stephan called to her.

Her exhaustion made her patience short.

"Can it wait, Stephan?"

"No."

She tossed the bills and the card into her mail basket and went to him.

"I think you should call about that house."

"Stephan, we can talk about the house tomorrow and you know, we can't afford much more than what we have—a whole house! Good Lord!"

"But Mimi, remember after what happened to my mom, you said I could talk to God—it didn't have to be a real prayer?"

"Yes, but if I recall correctly, you said that you did not believe in God."

"Well, I thought I'd try it out again."

Mimi sighed deeply. "When did you start?"

"Just now."

"Oh. How'd it feel?"

Stephan sat up. He did not look at all sleepy.

"Good. I already got an answer."

"Pretty speedy. Was it the one you wanted?"

"You bet!"

"Okay, good night!"

"So, are you gonna call?"

"Call?"

"About the house."

"But . . . "

"Please, Mimi!"

"It's nine o'clock!"

"Please!"

Stephan perched on the kitchen stool as Mimi dialed the number. A very old man answered.

"Kirby Smith, here," he offered faintly.

"I'm Mimi Malone and . . . "

"What's that?"

She spoke loudly. "I'm Mimi Malone and I'm calling about the house you have for rent in Elmwood."

"The house?"

"Yes, the one you are renting."

"Mine's not for rent."

"But . . . "

There was a tussle then on Mr. Smith's end of the line and the receiver was dropped onto a plastic or wooden table. She could hear some sounds of protest from the old man. A woman barked into Mimi's ear.

"Are you calling about the house for rent?"

"Yes, the one in Elmwood."

"We only have one house—it was my father's. Well, now we're thinking of selling the house."

"Oh!"

"Well, frankly, neither my father nor I can do the work to rent it. We just have to unload it."

"Oh."

"Say, who am I talking with?"

"Mimi Malone."

"Are you married?"

"Ah, well, no I am not."

"Um hum, because there's not much room."

"Yes, I realize . . . but, I don't have the money to buy a house."

"What do you do?"

"Do?"

"To feed yourself, Miss Malone."

"I make jewelry."

"Nice room there for you with the windows."

"Perfect."

*   *   *   *

Now, eleven o'clock, Mimi sat with her tea on her couch, pressing the warm cup rim against her chin while she thought. She rose suddenly, plucked the flashlight from the floor by the couch, went into Stephan's room and pulled open the top drawer of her dresser. She could hear the boy's breathing and she turned to look at him. He was blue silver in the moonlight. He had thrown one pale arm up on the pillow. The window was open a crack to the spring night, and the white Priscilla curtains blew softly over him.

"Oh, God let me keep him forever!" she whispered. *That's wrong,* she thought, a wrong prayer. His mother should have him. She turned back to the dresser, flipped on the flashlight, pulled Pete's purple velvet box from the drawer and returned to her place on the couch. She switched on the lamp, opened the box and looked at the ring carefully. *About five carats of good, clear, deep sapphire surrounded by small diamonds set in platinum. You don't know much about fine jewelry.*

"But if I had to guess," she thought aloud, "I'd say the ring is worth about ten thousand dollars, which is a lot for a ring but nothing for a house."

Mimi realized she would not be able to fall asleep for a while. She went to her room and replaced the ring box in her drawer, closed the window and returned to the living room where she picked up the mail, dug for a pen in the basket and retrieved her checkbook from her purse.

In the kitchen, she poured another cup of tea and began to write checks for her bills. When she was finished, she sat holding Harold's card in her hands. "Well now's as good a time as any," she said, and slipped open the card. A slip of paper fell out of the card and into the palm of her left hand. She read the note.

Mimi, it turns out my dad did leave some money for me. I'm giving half of it to you for loving me more than I deserved, for all the years you gave me, and for all the pain my abandonment caused you. I will always be there for you. Call me night or day. Love, Harold

She unfolded the note and a check fell down onto the table. "One hundred thousand dollars," she read aloud. "And no cents! No cents!"

THIRTY FOUR

THE STARS THAT ARE LOANED TO US

By June first, they were moved, if not unpacked. Mickey and Teddy shocked her by offering their help; they and her father did everything—the entire move. She and her mother and Jan scrubbed the old wooden kitchen cabinets and lined them with fresh paper. Mary Beth and Link had borrowed her spare key from Mrs. Horowitz, a nice if nosey neighbor, and hand washed and waxed the old cherry floors. They placed a remnant of eggplant-colored office carpeting down on the wildly ugly old linoleum in the kitchen area. Even Suzy sent a rubber tree plant for the living room. After everyone had gone and it was very late, Stephan emerged from the bathroom in his camouflage pajamas.

"Come outside, Mimi."

"Stephan, it's very late and you have school tomorrow."

"This is the first night, Mimi!"

"And so it is, you wise old man." She held out her hand. "Lead me."

They went out the front door, over the old cracked cement walkway, and around to the back yard. There was an apple tree— half living, half dead—at the end of the lot. Stephan leaped into it and swung from a branch. Mimi watched him; at the same time she saw herself watching him. She saw her back, the strength of running and her life in it. She saw the house behind her, the rubber tree by the fireplace, the loose boards of front porch. Herself getting meals in the kitchen, making school lunches for

Stephan. The Christmas tree in between the front windows. The two of them seated on the sofa, Matilda in her lap, Opal cuddled into Stephan's. She saw them painting the walls all this summer, buttermilk dripping from their brushes.

"I can hang upside-down."

Mimi heard herself say, "You, you can do just about anything, you Stephan-wonder, you."

"No." He sat up on the branch adjusting his pajamas and then abruptly jumped down.

"You shouldn't jump that far in your bare feet, you could crack a bone." She mussed his hair, and they each threw one arm about the other.

"So, what's the one thing you can't do?"

"Find my dad. Get him to be my dad."

"That's two things, and one you can do."

"Find him?"

"Yes."

"Are you sure?"

"No. Not at all, but people do every day."

Mimi could see his eyes, serious, in the evening light.

"But, could he take me away from you?"

"Yes, I think he could."

"So, that's why God told me that!"

"Been talking to Him again, huh?"

"Yeah. I asked Him if I should try to find my father."

"And He said?"

"Don't."

Sharp tears stung her eyes. She patted him softly on the back.

"First night or no first night, a young man's teeth must be brushed. Off with you. Call me when you've finished, and we'll shut our house down for the night."

Stephan frowned, but went in.

Then Mimi spoke to no one or to herself. "I have a house, dear God, a house, and it's on a street named Sky. Sky!"

She sat in the grass and then lay down and smelled the earth, scratching it with her nails, sniffing and scratching.

" 'Tomatoes,' the dirt says. And 'green beans' it says, and maybe some 'Concord grapes drowning out the cyclone fence' says the fence." She looked at the fence, but now fat lime-colored leaves flew up and down in the night breeze. *Life is a miracle that keeps happening. This dirt is miraculous as those stars.* She turned over and looked at them. *And the dirt and all that sits on it and in it is mine, while the stars belong to God and are only lent to us the way we are lent to each other.* So brief is each evening of our lives, she thought. And our lives.

"Mimi." Stephan chirped from the house.

Oh God, was his voice starting to change? She had never heard quite that sound.

"I'm ready."

She saw him then, poking himself in front of the curtain at the sliding door, back lit by his lamp that was set on the floor—no table for it yet.

"Why are you lying in the dirt, Mimi Malone?"

"Because you are here, and we are in our house, and it is almost summer, and God has loaned us the stars again, and because I know I will never be happier than I am this very minute."

But Stephan only chirped in response, "Happy or not happy, a woman's teeth must be brushed."

Mimi rose up, went to the apple tree, grabbed onto the branch and swung back and forth a few times. She saw herself swing and drop, and then she watched as she strode around the house and into her front door.

The End

AUTHOR'S NOTES

JCWatson has been writing from the age of twelve; her youthful success spurred her on to write poetry, short fiction, and novels. She self-published her first volume of poetry, *Argument for Mercy* in 2000. In 2005 she published a novel, *Current Wisdom*, by LBF Press and in that same year, two short fictions, *Reckless* and *The Flying Horse*. In 2012, a poetry chapbook, *The Journey of Lost Things*, was published by Finishing Line Press. In 2013, *A Lake in Heaven*, was published by Violetclaire Press, and is a fictionalized memoir and her first novella.

She is currently working on a Chapbook, *The King of Bees* and has a full length Poetry Manuscript, *The God of Pittsburgh*, out for publication. Currently, she is completing a collection of short stories, *Marcocito is Almost Dead*.

She was born in Pittsburgh, Pennsylvania, the third of seven children under a double yoke of hard scrabble poverty and a fierce Roman Catholicism.

She has been a behavioral therapist for autistic children, an English Tutor, a classroom teacher for first generation Americans, taught for Stanford University. She has also been a retailer, teachers' aide, nursery school teacher. And while attending Carnegie Mellon University, a cashier with the University's financial department.